LANCE STAR
Sky Ranger
Volume II

AIRSHIP 27 PRODUCTIONS

Airship 27 Presents
LANCE STAR: Sky Ranger Volume 2

Editor: Ron Fortier
Associate Editor: John C. Bruening
Production and design by Rob Davis

Airship 27 Productions

ISBN-13: 978-0615864877
ISBN-10: 0615864872

Printed in the United States of America

10 9 8 7 6 5 4 3 2 1

CONTENTS

╋ *Lance Star* ╋

"Homefront"

by
Bobby Nash

One

This is too easy.

That was the first thought the intruder had after piercing the perimeter. With the dignitaries expected to be in attendance the next few days, he had expected a heightened state of security and had planned accordingly. Surprisingly, there had been no resistance up to this point.

Too easy, his mind screamed, waiting for an alarm to sound. When none was heard he moved on, fearing that each step could be the one where he got caught. Perhaps the reputation of the compound's proprietor had been grossly exaggerated, he wondered.

After a quick look to confirm that he was alone on the field, the uninvited guest sprinted from a hiding place behind a fuel dump depot toward the nearest hangar. For a moment, the intruder wondered if the pack he wore on his back would give away his presence. In the silence of the night, every noise sounded as loudly to the man's ears as if it had been broadcast over the public address system.

His heart thundered in his ears as he came to rest on the far side of the hangar. His back to the wall, the intruder took a moment to slow his breathing. The last thing he needed was to hyperventilate. That would put an end to the plan before it even began.

Once he was certain no one had seen his mad dash across the darkened field, the intruder eased out into the light and jimmied the locked door. It was not the first lock he had ever picked. In his line of work such illicit skills were almost a prerequisite. Much to his surprise, it was nothing more than a simple lock. The going was easy as the U-shaped bar popped loose from the clasp.

He hurried inside and closed the door behind him.

He was so close to his goal he could taste it.

The hangar was filled to capacity, which came as no surprise to the intruder. He knew that every hangar on the field was similarly stocked in preparation for the next day's festivities. Once a year the owner of the field sponsored an air show to raise money for charity. And each year the show seemed to top the previous year's event as more and more celebrities, politicians, and the like came out in droves to support such a worthy cause.

Several corporations had even gotten into the act, the intruder noticed as he ran a finger along the sleek lines of General Motors Corporation's prototype of the car they hoped would be all the rage of the following year, the 1942 Buick. The intruder smiled as he took in the car's attributes. *It's a beauty*, he thought while making mental note of his next car purchase. With those sleek airfoil fenders sweeping the entire length of the automobile's frame, it truly fit in with the aerodynamic air vehicles stored in the hangar. The powder blue paint job was the same shade one might see when staring into a crisp blue, cloudless sky.

It was a thing of beauty, no doubt.

Unfortunately, he did not have the time to indulge his passion for the automobile since there were far more pressing matters taking precedence. Forcing himself to look away from the new model, the intruder turned his attention once more to the reason for his clandestine visit.

After a five-minute search, he found what he was looking for.

The airplane was covered with a tarp, keeping any dust off of its freshly polished exterior. Careful not to damage the finish, the intruder slipped beneath the draping and slid under the plane. Pulling a flashlight from his pack, he searched the underbelly of the plane until at last he found the hatch he had been looking for. *Bingo!*

Lying on his back on the cool concrete floor, the intruder carefully removed the four screws that held the hatch plate in place with a screwdriver produced from the backpack. The hatch came away easily and noiselessly. Clutching the screwdriver in his teeth, he reached inside the plane's underbelly, his fingers feeling along the inside of the hidden compartment for something, anything, to grab hold of. His elusive prize was supposed to be there.

Finally, he found it.

Success!

His fingers wrapped tightly around the waiting package and with a slight tug it pulled free of its hiding place.

"Right where he said it would be," the intruder whispered. He smiled as he looked at the small bundle in the beam of the flashlight. It was wrapped in burlap and secured with an old, well-worn rope. He unwrapped his prize with the zeal of a kid at Christmas opening that first present from Santa.

The files that made up the bundle were wrapped tightly, its contents highly valuable to the future. Several men and women had risked much to smuggle the bundle into the United States. Some had given their life to protect the valuable information he now held in his hands.

The intruder read quickly under the beam of the flashlight, skimming through the documents for certain words and obvious phrases. He found several that screamed out at him from the parchment.

What he read made his blood run cold.

The United States of America had been targeted.

The war that seemed so far away just this morning now seemed a whole lot closer.

War was coming.

And it was coming here.

He knew he had to warn someone. He had to warn everyone. And he had to do so quickly. He could not delay, could not wait until his scheduled rendezvous at sunrise. He had to make contact now. The information in his possession was too important not to risk exposing himself before his extraction. He needed a plan, but even more importantly, he needed to get the hell out of the cramped hangar before he was found out. He knew that he was not safe there. The last thing he needed was one of the airfield's security guards, all former military from the look of them, to catch him sneaking around the hangar after hours. Especially considering the valuables locked inside tonight.

He knew he had already tarried far longer than was sensible. Although getting in had been far easier than he had expected, the intruder had a sneaking suspicion his luck was going to run out sooner or later.

Extinguishing the light, the intruder rolled from beneath the metal flying machine after reattaching the hatch plate and leaving the plane in the same condition he had found it, if not a few pounds lighter. Stealthily, he made his way back toward the entrance, more focused than he had been before. Even the smooth lines of the new Buick no longer swayed his thoughts the way they had before.

Waiting in a crouch beside the silver plane nearest the hangar door, which he had been told was the main attraction of the air show, he listened for anything out of the ordinary. No guard could be heard. No one coming. No one knew he was there. He was going to make it.

He let out a sigh of relief.

He thought he was safe.

He did not see the attack coming.

A large wrench came down swiftly, catching the intruder on the back of the head. The impact pitched him forward, smashing him face first into the silver plane he had crouched beside. Blood splattered from the impact, dripping atop the freshly scrubbed concrete floor of the hangar. Dazed by the first blow, the intruder dropped the bundle. In the darkness of the hangar, he did not see it slide beneath the rolling toolkit near the silver plane's wheel housing.

Thankfully, neither had the person who attacked him.

The second blow was all it took for the intruder's world to go dark and silent.

He would not see another sunrise.

Two

Lance Star rose early.

Though finding the pilot *up and about at the crack of dawn,* as Red would say, was nothing unusual. This was a special day. It was the day before the biggest air show to hit Long Island, New York since... well, since the last air show Star Field produced was scheduled to begin.

As the morning sun sleepily peeked over the horizon, Lance went for a morning run around the perimeter of Star Field. As was his custom, Lance ran the field each morning. Not only did it help get him started on his day, it was also the only time of the workday that he would have any time alone with his thoughts.

Lance was a people person most of the time. He had a great camaraderie with his pilots and staff that he would not trade for the world. Still, there were moments when even the most gregarious person needed a little time to himself.

For Lance Star, that time was early morning, before the hustle and bustle began.

Though he was not what one would refer to as a "morning person," the celebrity air ace had managed to force himself into a tight schedule. His morning run helped him wake up and prepare to face the day.

Star Field was quite large for an independent airfield. By the time Lance circumvented its diameter, he was drenched with sweat. The morning sun having brightened considerably, the temperature began climbing. This was not unusual for July on the Eastern Seaboard. It had been a hot summer and there did not appear to be an end in sight.

As he did every morning, Buck Tellonger was waiting for his friend at the end of the run. Leaning against a fifty-five gallon drum, Buck sipped at his morning coffee–black with three sugars–between puffs from the cheap cigar firmly clenched between his teeth. Even when the weather was warm, as it was this July morning, the World War I flying ace could not begin his day without a spot of coffee and one of those cheap, smelly cigars he so loved. Lance thought they smelled worse than the inside of a footlocker, but his friend seemed to love them.

Buck held out a towel as his employer came to a rest, bent over with his hands on his knees, giving his heart a chance to slow to something resembling a normal rate. Once his breathing was back to normal, Lance took the offered towel with a breathless "thank you."

"You're slowing down, Boss," Buck said, forming a big smile around the stogie clenched tightly between coffee stained teeth. "Must be getting old, eh?"

Lance toweled off his face. "I didn't realize it was a race, Buck."

"Sure you didn't."

"It relaxes me."

"Uh huh. You don't look relaxed to me, Boss."

"Trust me, Chief. I am relaxed," Lance barked.

Buck was unconvinced. "You're just cranky because you're slowing down in your old age. It's understandable."

"I am not getting…" Lance started, but stopped at the sight of his friend's crooked grin. If there was one thing that Buck Tellonger excelled at more than flying, it was his uncanny ability to get under someone's skin. Plus, he took a sort of perverse pleasure in telling those far younger than he, such as Lance in this case, that they were getting old. "Not a spring chicken" was another favorite little saying he enjoyed tossing around.

Lance snapped Buck with the towel when he saw his friend's grin.

"Touchy subject, huh?" Buck snorted.

"It's not about speed or how quickly I can run it, Buck. I enjoy it."
He noticed his friend's skeptical expression.

"Really," he emphasized. "Not only does it help me stay in shape,
it gives me time to think."

"And what do you think about, exactly?"

"Well, for starters," Lance said as he took a swig from the canteen
of water his chief of staff had brought him. "I think I may have
solved that stabilizer problem we were having on the new Ranger."

"Well that's something. Damned thing's been giving McDouglas
headaches for the last couple weeks. He'll sure be happy to get
around this little stumbling block."

"No doubt," Lance said as he wiped the sweat from his face again.
"But he'll have to wait until after tomorrow. Right now the air show
is our top priority. I don't want him to even think about rolling that
plane out of Hangar Eight until after the festivities. You got it?"

"Of course."

"I guess all that running must do some good after all," Buck
suggested.

"You're always welcome to join me."

"Thanks for the offer, Lance, but I think I'll pass. It's just not
normal for a youngster like me to get up before the crows."

"Your loss."

"I'm sure," Buck guffawed.

"Are we all set for the practice runs today?"

"Ready as we'll ever be," Buck said as he fell into step with his
boss as they headed toward Lance's quarters. One of the advantages
of owning the field was being able to live close to his work. Lance
had a small house for himself away from the hangars and the day-
to-day life of the airfield. He had picked the space for his quarters
so as to have a nice view of the lake. It was a short walk from his
hammock to the pier.

"That's what I like to hear, Chief," Lance said as he clapped his
mentor on the shoulder. "I knew there was a reason I hired you."

"And here I thought it was my good looks and charming
personality," the short, bulldog of a man joked as he stroked his

handlebar mustache and lifted his eyebrows.

Lance could not help but laugh. These two men had been through a lot together in the few years that they had known one another. Lance's late father, who was also an exceptional pilot, had introduced them. Lance was glad his friend had agreed to come on as his chief of staff when he started Star Field. It was a partnership that had yielded great gains for both of them, personally and professionally.

"Well, maybe I'm just immune to your charms, sir," Lance joked. He pulled at the sweaty undershirt that was sticking to him in the rising temperature. "Looks like it's going to be a hot one, Buck."

"Yep."

"I think a shower is in order."

Buck pinched his nose closed with two fingers. "Well, I wasn't going to say anything, but..."

Lance cut him off mid joke. "Why don't you rally the troops for a staff meeting in, say, twenty minutes. I'm sure Walt has everything under control, but it can't hurt to go over everything one last time before everyone shows up for practice."

"Sounds like a plan to me, Boss," Buck said as he made a crisp, military about face and marched off toward the main hangar where he knew the pilots would be gathering any time now. "See you in twenty."

Although they were not required to live on the premises, Lance had small apartments available for each member of his team. With all of the long nights they put in when designing a new bird, Lance felt it was necessary that each man had a place to go to that was all his own. Lately, they had spent many a long night working on the Ranger, a personal project Lance and his team were developing. The unique nature of the plane's design had caused a few unexpected issues that they were still working through, one of which looked to be solved during Lance's run.

Many of his pilots kept homes off base, some had families, but a few had moved in permanently.

As he stepped onto the front porch of his small home, Lance took a moment and stared out at the dream he had built. Star Field was his legacy. He hoped that this place would outlast him, that someday he would have a son to carry on the family business. But those were thoughts for another time.

Tomorrow was a big day.

Lance would get to spend the day doing what he loved to do while surrounded by those closest to him. He could think of no better way than to end his special day than standing in the middle of Star Field under a starry night sky and holding hands with his girl as they watched the Fourth of July fireworks explode overhead.

It was quite possibly the closest thing to perfection that Lance could imagine.

He looked up at the Stars and Bars flapping overhead on the morning breeze and smiled. "Happy Birthday, Old Glory" he said before heading inside. There was still a lot of work to be done before tomorrow and he had to get started.

Tomorrow was going to be a big day.

Three

"**G**ood morning, gentlemen."

Walt Anderson stood at the front of the pilot's briefing room. As he did on most occasions when they were all gathered together, Walt ran the briefing. As the operations manager for Star Field, the day-to-day tasks involved with running Lance Star Incorporated fell to him.

Walt had Lance's full confidence, and the pilots' as well. After all, Walt wasn't just some paper pusher in a suit Lance had brought in to manage the countless behind the scenes odds and ends required when running a business. Walt was one of them, a decorated Sky Ranger. He was a pilot first and foremost, so he understood the work of pilots, designers, engineers, and field hands better than any outsider ever could. It was a tricky job, balancing the needs of Lance and his crew with the financial responsibilities of running an operation such as Lance Star Incorporated and Star Field.

Yet somehow Walt Anderson made it all work.

Lance was a hands-on kind of employer. He was not afraid to get his hands dirty right next to the guys building the planes. In fact, he preferred it that way. He was more at home in the cockpit of a plane than he would ever be sitting behind a corporate desk.

You could put good money on it that no plane left Star Field without having been flown by Lance Star personally. Nothing left Star Field without the noted air ace's personal seal of approval. It was that attention to detail that continued bringing clients to their door.

For the past several years, Star Field held an annual Air Ace Show to raise money for the local hospital. Lance had recruited some of the top pilots from around the country to perform at the show. Every year seemed to outshine the previous year, which thrilled the hospital's board of directors and the head of the charity committee, Lance's girlfriend, Betty Terrell.

Once upon a time, Betty's younger brother, Skip Terrell, had been part of the Star Field Team. The boy was a breath of fresh air. His enthusiasm and youthful exuberance seemed to keep the older pilots young at heart. His excitement was certainly contagious. Lance and the pilots instantly took a liking to the lad.

Skip was like the little brother Lance never had.

Sadly, Skip lost his life at the hands of a vile madman, the Austrian aristocrat Baron Otto Von Blood. Though the murdering bastard had not been caught, Lance and the other pilots in his charge knew that they would cross paths with the Baron again. And when they did, Lance had vowed that their fallen comrade would have justice.

It was during the group's next encounter with the Blood Baron that Walt took shrapnel to the leg. The injury very nearly cost him his life. Were it not for the meticulous skills of a group of surgeons stationed at a temporary Army surgical hospital outside of Belingrad, the pilot would certainly have lost his leg, or even perished.

Obviously, Walt survived, but his days inside a cockpit were over. He had long since managed to lose the cane he had been forced to carry those first months of his recovery, though he still walked with a pronounced limp. Running was out of the question entirely.

Thankfully, Lance Star was a loyal man. He had told the wounded pilot that there would always be a place for him at Star Field. And he had been true to his word. As operations manager, Walt took on many of the duties that had long overwhelmed Buck Tellonger, Star Field's chief of staff. With Walt's help, the chief was able to go off with Lance on any of his grand adventures with confidence that someone would be at home minding the store. Essentially, Walt became third in command of Star Field after Lance and Buck, respectively.

Walt missed flying. Sure, he went up on occasion with some of the other pilots, but it wasn't the same as holding the stick yourself.

There were many reasons to hate Otto Von Blood. This was Walt's. He owed the Baron for permanently taking him out of the cockpit. His only hope was that on the day Lance caught up with the bastard, he'd be there to see it.

At last word, Von Blood had been reported in Germany, working for the growing Nazi Third Reich. With Germany's war machine rolling across Eastern Europe and the Axis conquering many of their neighboring countries, Lance and his men knew that it would only be a matter of time before they met up with their friend's killer again.

But those thoughts were for another day.

Today, they would celebrate Skip Terrell's life, not his death.

When Betty had first approached Lance about setting up a charity benefit, he had agreed on the condition that he could name the charity. Thus was born the Skip Terrell Foundation. The charity raised money for the hospital's children's ward as well as made preparations for the pilots to give tours and special flights for those children fit enough to come to Star Field. For those who were unable to leave the hospital, the pilots went to them and told them stories, played games, and generally tried to brighten their day. Sometimes Betty wondered who got more out of the visits, the kids or the pilots themselves.

The Skip Terrell Foundation was a roaring success, and the air show was the highlight of the year.

"If you'll take a look at the schedules Buck is passing, out you'll see that I've juggled things around a bit from last year," Walt said as Buck Tellonger passed out a small folder to each of the pilots and staff. "After last year's show, I took a look at how we had been working and made some modifications. I've opened things up so that each of you can have a small break to get out and enjoy the festivities."

That brought a round of applause from the assembled team, many of whom never got a chance to enjoy the air show they worked so hard to run.

"Will we be able to cover everything while these bums are out bird dogging the rich single women in attendance?" Lance asked as he entered. He dropped a dollar bill into the large glass pickle jar near the door as he stepped inside the crowded room. The briefing had begun without him. Walt was a stickler for starting on time. With Lance's permission, he had started the rule that anyone late to the morning briefing was required to drop a dollar into the pickle jar. The money from the jar would go into a separate fund to be donated to the Skip Terrell Foundation once a year.

No one was immune from this rule. Not even the boss. Although Walt often wondered if Lance wasn't late on occasion just so he could add a little more money to the pot. Not that Walt would ever pose the question out loud, of course. "I think we'll be able to manage, Lance," he said with a smile.

"Good. I think it'll be good for these guys to rub elbows with the rich and famous for a bit," Lance said as he mussed Red Davis' mop of bright red hair as he passed the pilot's chair. "Might class them up a bit."

Another round of laughter filled the room. Red's cheeks brightened to just a shade lighter than his brightly hued mane.

"What about you, Boss?" James Nolan asked between puffs from the tiny French cigarette he smoked. The smell of the cigarettes made for a truly noxious odor when combined with Buck's stodgy nickel cheroots.

"Oh, you know how it is, Jim," Lance said as he cleared the smoke from his face with a wave of his hand. "I've got class running out my ears."

The comment brought another roar of laughter from around the table.

"Walt's got me on a tight schedule. I have to do the usual song and dance for the folks with the money. It'll be a lot of handshaking and listening to boring stories. Hell, I might even kiss a baby or two if given the opportunity," Lance joked. "But it'll all be worth it if it gets them to open up their wallets and purses."

"Sounds like a tough assignment, Boss" Cy Hawkins said with a smirk.

"Absolutely terrifying," Lance joked.

"Wanna trade?" Buck asked.

"In a heartbeat," Lance agreed. "Except Betty would kill me."

Buck grunted a laugh. "Then I inherit Star Field and we all get promoted," he said calmly. "I don't see a downside, Boss."

"You wouldn't," Lance grinned.

Five minutes later the laughter died down enough for Walt Anderson to continue the briefing.

Four

Practice flights had been running most of the morning without incident.

Lance was impressed by the flyers he had seen so far. Obviously, no one wanted an accident, but they always planned for the worst as a precaution while hoping for the best. Such precautions kept his pilots safe. And no matter who was holding the stick, if you taxied the runway at Star Field, especially during the air show, then Lance Star considered you one of *his* pilots. That's why only the best were invited to participate.

"Looks like it's going to be a great show this year, Walt," Lance said to his operations manager who stood beside him. "Mr. Calvin up there has come up with quite a few good maneuvers." Lance popped a piece of chewing gum in his mouth, a habit he had developed after long years of friendship with Red Davis, who had introduced him to the sugary concoction.

"That double barrel roll was very impressive," Walt agreed.

"What's up?"

"Oh," Walt said absently, turning his attention away from the planes to the stack of papers under his arm. "A couple cancellations, I'm afraid."

"Oh?"

"Work commitments," Walt said as he flipped through the pad in his hand. "Mr. Barnes had an unscheduled trip to the South America pop up. He sends his regrets."

Lance nodded.

"Okay. Who else?"

Walt hesitated.

"Well?"

"Niles Isburgh."

"Ice?"

"Yes. He said that the Navy cannot allow him time away from salvage operations to make the trip for just an air show."

"*Just an air show...*" Lance mimicked with a grin. "It's okay, Walt. We've still got plenty to keep the crowds enthralled."

"True."

Lance turned to look at his friend when he fell into silence.

"Something else?"

"I'm curious about something, Lance."

"What's on your mind, Walt?"

"It's about Niles Isburgh," he started uncomfortably.

"You want to know why I invited him?"

Walt felt his cheeks flush. "Actually, yes. While it cannot be argued that he is a competent pilot, he does not strike me as the sort of person who would even want to do an air show, much less one run by you."

"Ice and I have an... understanding," Lance said, choosing his words carefully. "It's complicated."

"With you two it usually is," Walt said as he turned and walked away from his smiling employer.

Lance brought the wireless radio close to his mouth and clicked the talk button. "Who's up next, Tom?"

"Dalton's bird is airborne and holding at the outer marker on your signal," Tom Vincente answered from the tower. "And I've got Colonel Ryan's Patriot I on the runway ready for take off once Dalton starts his run. After that we've got Jim and the other Brits' planes being wheeled from the main hangar as we speak. We're planning a break for lunch after Santini's run."

"Sounds good, Tom. Is the Colonel set up to test the drop as well? I'm still iffy on that one."

"Yes, sir. Kevin verified that the bomb bay door is operational.

The Colonel's men placed the payload last night and checked on it this morning. I don't know who's more nervous, the Colonel's flight crew or Mr. McDouglas."

"Alright, Tom. Keep to the schedule and remind Kevin to breathe," Lance said as he sidled into the off-road vehicle that Buck had brought from the motor pool. The off-roadster was the first non-flying vehicle designed and built by Star Field, although they did receive some help from the Chrysler Corporation.

"Buck and I are going to move out for a better look at the Colonel's demonstration," Lance informed Tom. "If he can't pull it off in practice, we'll abort the drop and stick to the fancy flying."

"He won't like that," the superintendent of communications said.

"That's his problem," Lance said before tossing the radio into the space between the seats. He held on as Buck floored it and sent the off-roadster bouncing across the grassy field for a better vantage point to watch the drop.

"You think he can pull this off?" Lance asked his mentor even as he gripped the dashboard for stability.

"We'll know in a few minutes," Buck said around his cigar.

"That's not very reassuring."

Buck Tellonger laughed as the off-road vehicle went airborne over a small raised patch of earth, leaving a plume of dust in its wake.

"Are you aiming for those things on purpose?" Lance shouted.

"Who? Me?" Buck asked mischievously as he brought the all terrain vehicle to a stop near the drop coordinates. "Now why would I do that?"

"I wonder," Lance said as he used his hands to shade against the midmorning sun. "Looks like Colonel Ryan is taking wing."

"Yep," Buck agreed as he watched the antique bomber roll across the tarmac before angling up into the wild blue yonder. From their vantage point on the hill at the far end of Star Field, Buck and Lance had a clear view of the entirety of airfield. They could even see New York City on the horizon.

"The fireworks are going to look great from here," Lance said, and Buck agreed. "I've already got a nice little spot picked out for Betty and me," Lance said, pointing a little farther up the rise. "Right over there."

Where they were standing at the moment was going to be open to the public for the air show and fireworks, but Lance had reserved a small section for Star Field personnel. They worked so hard to make sure the event ran smoothly that they missed a good deal of it. The least they could do was have the chance to enjoy the fireworks.

"Sounds mighty romantic, Boss."

"Yeah," he blushed. "I hope she likes it."

"I'm sure she will. You planning to make an honest woman out of her, Lance?"

The air ace almost swallowed his gum. "I beg your pardon?" he asked around a choked cough.

"You heard me," Buck said, matter of fact. "When are you planning to marry that girl?"

"Well, I..." Lance stammered, clearly caught off guard.

"You know I don't mean to pry, but..."

"Uh-huh. Right," Lance interrupted.

The bomber that had been named Patriot I completed its turn and made its first pass over the field, straight toward Lance and Buck's position.

Buck continued as if his friend had not spoken. "So what are you waiting for, huh? She clearly loves you, and even a blind man could see the way you feel about her. So what's the problem?"

"It's... complicated."

Buck *harrumphed.* "With you two it usually is," Buck said just as Patriot I flew low overhead. The bomber was low enough that the two land-based pilots could feel the ground vibrate beneath them as the powerful plane flew past.

"What was that?" Lance asked. Buck's last comment had been drowned out by Colonel Ryan's flyby.

"Nothing," Buck said slyly even though his friend clearly wasn't buying it.

"That's what I thought you said," Lance muttered.

"The bomber...made its first pass over the field..."

Five

Colonel Wesley Ryan came around for another pass.

A veteran of the United States Army Air Corps, he had been flying planes longer than some of the crew at Star Field had been alive. He loved doing these air shows. It gave him a chance to really enjoy himself while doing the thing he loved most in life–flying. Like most pilots, the colonel was never as much at home as he was when he was in the cockpit.

A decorated World War I flying ace, Colonel Ryan had convinced the Air Corps to reclassify the bomber he was flying for just this sort of activity. The plane he had dubbed Patriot I after laying eyes on the plane's beautiful new paint job had flown several missions during the Big War.

A few of them under the command of Wesley Ryan.

Even though hostilities on the other side of the world once more threatened to engulf the planet in yet another World War, Ryan wanted to use one of the planes, an instrument of death oftentimes in war, as an instrument in the pursuit of peace. Everything on Patriot I shone brightly. On the ground, it was a rolling museum dedicated to the men who had fought for the country's freedom–both for those who died as well as those who survived.

In the air, the brightly painted bomber was unmistakably American. The nose of the plane was blue and dotted with large white stars. Red and white wavy bars flowed along the side of the plane where they slowly changed into a beautifully painted flying eagle with a magnificent wingspan. It was truly a remarkable paint job that some of the Air Corps' top designers had worked on for months.

Instinctively, Ryan nudged the stick and lined up with his target as Patriot I began its run.

The plan was to come in low, then pull up and open the bomb bay doors. Packed tightly inside were hundreds of red, white and blue streamers. When released from the planes they would unfurl and float toward the ground, and the waiting crowds below–souvenirs they could take home, compliments of the United States Army Air Corps.

At least that was the theory.

Ryan understood his host's skepticism concerning the stunt. The spectators on hand were his responsibility. He had to put their safety above all else. Colonel Ryan respected that. So far he had been very impressed with everything about the man's operation. Lance Star ran a first class operation.

The pilot pulled back slightly on the yoke and felt his back push into the seat as the nose lifted heavenward. This was the part he liked the most. There was no way you could experience the exhilaration of pulling against G Forces on the ground. This was something you could only experience in the air.

"You ready?" he called to his gunner.

"On your order, Colonel," came the reply from below.

"On my mark," Ryan said. "Now!"

The gunner opened the bomb bay door and the streamers flew off the spool exactly as planned. Colonel Ryan watched enthusiastically as the weeks of planning came to fruition. "It worked!" he shouted excitedly. "It worked!"

That's when he saw something else fall away from the bomber.

Something that was definitely not supposed to be there.

Lance was impressed.

Colonel Ryan's skills as a pilot were widely known. When the Colonel and Lance's own chief mechanic came to him a few weeks back with their proposal for the streamer drop, Lance was dubious. However, the combined enthusiasm of the men convinced him to grudgingly to allow it. Provided there was a successful test run.

So far, Lance liked what he saw.

"Nice, huh?" he asked Buck, who was also slightly slack-jawed as the streamers unfurled exactly as planned. A rain of red, white, and blue fell upon Star Field.

"Incredible is more like it."

"You sound like you didn't expect it to work."

"I didn't," Buck said matter-of-factly. "Damn. Now I owe Kevin ten dollars."

"You bet against Kevin on this?" Lance could scarcely believe his ears.

Buck smiled sheepishly. "Well… Let's just call it extra motivation to make sure it worked."

"Uh-huh. If that's your story."

"It's the one I'm stickin' to, Boss."

"Gotcha."

"What's that?"

"What?" Lance asked, suddenly all business.

Buck pointed as a large object fell from the bomber, trailing streamers in its wake. "There!" he shouted.

"I see it!"

"Did the spool release break loose?" Buck wondered allowed.

"Beats me," Lance said as the dark object hit the ground with a loud *THUNK!* at the bottom of the hill, near the end of the main runway.

"Is that the spool release mechanism?" Buck asked, trying to shield his eyes from the sun to get a better look.

Lance hopped in the vehicle.

"Only one way to find out!" he shouted. "Come on!"

Six

Lance and Buck were the first to arrive.

They slowed before getting too close and walked toward the heap lying in the dirt at the end of the runway. It had missed the concrete by less than ten feet. Instead it hit the soft sand at the end of the runway. The sand was a precautionary measure in case any planes came in too hot and could not stop in time. No matter how fast a plane was rolling on concrete, nothing rolled very well through loose, shifting sand.

"What is that?" Buck asked as they moved closer.

Lance knelt next to the unknown object covered in streamers. "It's not the spool release mechanism, that's for sure."

"Then what is it?"

"That's a very good question," Lance said as he reached out for it. "It's not hot. Looks like something has been wrapped in a tarp. Here, help me get this thing unwrapped, Buck."

The chief of staff produced a knife and passed it handle-first to Lance.

"Thanks," the pilot said as he used the knife to cut away the thick streamers that had managed to wrap tightly around the object before impact.

"Here comes the colonel and our boys," Buck said, motioning toward Patriot I as it rolled slowly toward them on the runway. Star Field's ground crew were hot on his tail in trucks and off-roadsters.

Lance cut the final streamer loose and pulled at the heavy cloth tarpaulin. It came open easily. The air ace stared at the figure for a long moment, unsure what he could say that would explain what he saw.

"Buck," he finally said. "Give me a ten foot perimeter around this spot. Keep the colonel and the field crew out. The only people I want around this are you, me and Doc Potter. Everybody else stays out until we can get the police out here."

"The police? Why would we need…"

A serious look from Lance told him that this was not the time for discussion.

"What is it, Boss?" Buck asked.

Lance carefully peeled the tarp back far enough for his inquisitive chief of staff to see clearly.

"Who is he?" Buck asked once he got over his initial shock.

"I don't know, Buck," Lance said as he recovered the body. "But I intend to find out."

Buck whistled sharply.

"But first, I need that perimeter."

"I'm on it, Boss."

As Buck moved to intercept the approaching crews Lance pulled the wireless radio from the vehicle.

"Tom, this is Lance. I need a secure channel."

"Go for it," came the swift reply. In an emergency situation the laid back manor at Star Field quickly took on a serious, almost militaristic feel. As many of the pilots on hand were former military men, it was an easy transition.

"I need the police out here A.S.A.P. We're going to need a bus as well."

"One of ours?"

"Negative," Lance said. "ID unknown at this time. Ask for Detective Bishop, homicide. Tell him it's a personal request from me. Have Walt meet the police at the gate, Tom. He can escort them to my position at the end of the main runway."

"What about the air show?"

"As of right now, nothing has changed," Lance decided. "We'll see what Bishop has to say before we make any determination about tomorrow, okay?"

"Understood."

"Ground the rest of the flights and get them back in the hangars. We'll resume practice as soon as possible. I want this end of the field restricted to Star Field and police personnel only until further notice. We're in lockdown until further notice. No one in or out without my direct say so."

"I'm on it, Boss. Vincente out."

The radio went dead. Lance knew Tom was already on his first call to the police while getting men to the runway to help secure the scene. Lance watched as Buck took charge of the approaching men on the runway.

Lance tossed the radio into the seat and blew out an exasperated breath.

"Hell of a way to start the air show," he whispered.

Homicide Detective Barney Bishop arrived at the airfield quickly.

The detective was quite familiar with Star Field as this was not his first visit to Lance Star's famous address. It was one of the first places he visited upon moving back to New York two years earlier. He had come in for a flight lesson on a lark, more for the privilege of taking lessons from the world famous air ace than any other reason. He had only planned to take one lesson just to say that he had done it, but found that himself enjoying it far more than he expected.

He had been flying ever since.

He had also struck up a friendship with Lance and had gotten to know some of the men who worked at the airfield and had an open invitation to the weekly Saturday night poker game in the squad room. Cy Hawkins, Star Field's resident card sharp, had gone home with the detective's money on more than one occasion.

Unfortunately, this was Bishop's first visit to Star Field in an official capacity.

A New Yorker by birth, Barney Bishop had spent his formative years in California, where he had the distinction of being the youngest police officer in the Hollywood PD to make homicide detective.

When the opportunity to transfer to his hometown arose, he jumped at the chance. California was nice, but there was nothing like coming home. And New York would always be his home.

Walt Anderson, the major domo of Star Field met him at the gate in an all terrain vehicle.

"Thank you for coming, Detective," Walt said as he shook his visitor's hand.

"I got here as quick as I could, Walt. Where's Lance?"

"He and Buck are out on the field. I've been asked to escort you out there. If you'll hop in," Walt said as he motioned toward the vehicle.

Together they rode out to the crime scene.

"How bad is it?" Bishop asked the unusually quiet operations manager.

"Bad enough. If we have to cancel the show tomorrow, then it'll quickly elevate to disastrous."

"In other words…"

"Solve this thing quickly. Yes."

Despite the seriousness of the situation, Detective Bishop smiled as they bounced across the uneven terrain.

"I'll do what I can."

Seven

"I need some good news, Barney."

Lance Star was not, by nature, patient man. It was one of those little personal failings that he tried hard to change, but thus far with little success. He promised to work harder at it. Starting tomorrow.

"Not sure how good this is," Detective Bishop said as he knelt beside the body, chewing as he usually did on a wad of bubble gum. "But he was dead before he hit the ground."

"And just how the heck can you figure that?" Buck Tellonger asked.

"Lack of blood and bruising from the impact. Looks like the body is already rigid. Had the impact been fatal…"

"Had it been…" Buck started, but a curt look from Lance, who was in no mood for levity, cut him short.

Detective Bishop continued as if Buck had not interrupted. "Had the impact been fatal, there would be a lot more blood splattered around. More bruising from impact too. Granted, this is all just my best guess, but it's probably a good guess."

"Well, you're the expert," Lance said.

"We'll know more once the coroner does his thing. Cause of death isn't really our biggest concern, though. There is a bigger question we need to answer."

"And that is?"

"How did the body get inside the plane?"

"Yeah. That is a stumper," Buck said.

Lance turned to look at Patriot I and her crew. "I can think of a good place to start."

Bishop smiled and clapped Lance on the shoulder. "Not bad," he said. "We'll make a detective out of you yet."

Buck *harrumphed* loudly, but quickly fell into step with the two men as they walked over to Colonel Ryan and his crew.

"Hey, guys," Lance called to the pilots. "Got a second?"

"Of course," Ryan said. He had been expecting questions from police, so both he and his copilot had decided to stick around.

Lance made the introductions. "Colonel Wesley Ryan, U. S. Army Air Corps, and Doug Myers, his gunner. This is Detective Bishop of the NYPD. He has…"

"A few questions," Colonel Ryan said as they shook hands. "I thought you might. Of course we'll be happy to help out in any way we can, Detective."

"I appreciate that, gentlemen," Bishop said as he popped another piece of gum into his mouth. "I think it's safe to assume neither of you put the dead body in your plane."

Ryan did not so much as blink at the question. "No," he answered simply.

"I didn't think so," Bishop said with a boyish grin. "But I had to ask."

"Understood."

"Any idea how the stiff ended up inside your plane?"

"No idea whatsoever, Detective. We first became aware of the body when it dislodged from the plane. Do you know who it is?"

"Not yet," Lance said.

"When was the last time you checked your plane?"

"Yesterday as we rolled her into the hangar. There were several members of Mr. Star's staff on hand at the time. The hangar was locked after we finished up inside."

"I'll want to take a look at that hangar," Barney said to Lance.

"No problem."

Doug Myers stepped forward. "Before we started our practice run I made a checklist run-through. I did not visually inspect the ejection pod, however."

"Why not?"

"We'd gone over it with a fine-toothed comb last night. I made sure the bay door was secure, which it was. There was no sign that anyone had tampered with the lock, so I assumed it was in the same condition it had been the night before. The plane was in a locked, secure hangar so there was no reason to think that anyone had gone near it."

Bishop shook their hands. "I appreciate your time, gentlemen. I may have more questions so I would appreciate it if you both stayed on the premises for the time being."

"That is not a problem, Detective," Colonel Ryan said. "We'll be here if you need us."

Lance turned to his operations manager. "Walt, why don't you set up some temporary quarters for the colonel and Mr. Myers."

"Of course," Walt Anderson said, motioning toward the vehicle. "If you gentlemen will follow me."

"Make yourselves at home, guys," Lance said. "If you need anything, just contact Mr. Anderson or myself."

"Thank you," Ryan said. He motioned toward his plane. "What about my bird?"

"I'll need to impound it for inspection," Detective Bishop said.

"I'll have it towed to the hangar and secured," Lance added. He offered a sincere, but sad smile. "Don't worry. I'll take good care of her."

"Thank you, Mr. Star," Ryan said. "I appreciate that."

"I'll check in with you later," Lance said as the colonel climbed into the passenger seat of the all terrain vehicle. Lance slapped an open palm against the hood before Walt and his passengers rode off toward the horizon.

"Well?" Barney asked once they were out of earshot.

"Well what?" the air ace answered, not certain of the question.

"You think either of them did it?"

Neither Lance nor Buck could believe their ears. "Absolutely not," Lance said.

"Ryan is many things, Detective," Buck started loudly, but

composed himself. "But he is no murderer. I'd stake my reputation on that."

"How well do you know him, Mr. Tellonger?"

"Well enough," Buck said, his cheeks reddening. "That man saved my life during the big war. You don't go through something like that and not get to know someone. That man is a patriot, son. There's no way he is involved!"

"Stand down, Buck," Lance told his mentor. "He's just doing his job. So, do you think the colonel had something to do with this man's death, Barney?"

Bishop shook his head. "Not really. Still, everyone involved is a suspect until you rule them out."

"Even us?"

"Even you."

"Now wait just a damned minute!" Buck started, but once again Lance stopped him with a gesture.

"Easy, Buck. Easy. I think Detective Bishop is just trying to get you riled up, right?"

"Maybe." The detective smiled. "Did either of you kill this man?"

"No." both pilots answered in unison.

"Then I guess I can cross you off the list of suspects."

"That's mighty generous of you," Buck muttered, his anger subsiding. Being accused, even in jest, had wounded Buck's pride. Lance gave his friend a look that spoke volumes, but said nothing.

"Come on," Barney finally said. "Let's go take a look at that hangar."

Eight

Betty Terrell was excited.

She looked forward to the annual July Fourth Air Show at Star Field with a mix of trepidation and fondness. As one of the proprietors of the Skip Terrell Foundation, Betty was all too happy to meet the visitors, arrange tours with Walt Anderson, and to smile for the newspaper photographers. All of these things were necessary for raising the much-needed money for area hospitals.

Money that Betty and her staff would put to good use.

That made her happy.

The Fourth of July also reminded her of her baby brother. Skip had been her world since the untimely death of their parents years earlier, which had led to her becoming his official guardian. It was her devotion to Skip that had introduced her to Lance Star.

She had wanted her brother to be happy. He was a bright kid and he wanted nothing more than to learn to fly. Saving up enough money for a lesson, Betty had surprised the enthusiastic boy with a trip to Star Field.

Lance Star was already something of a celebrity by this time. Betty had seen his photograph on the cover of *Time* Magazine as well as in a few newsreels playing at the movie theater a few blocks from her modest apartment. The photos did not do the man justice. He strode into the hangar as one of the pilots was instructing her and Skip on pitch and yaw.

At which point Betty Terrell suddenly developed a real interest in flying.

She had never been one to believe in love at first sight, but the moment she first laid eyes on Lance Star, Betty Terrell's heart had skipped a beat. By the time he shook her hand and introduced himself to her she was deeply, madly in love with the man.

It took a few more trips to Star Field for lessons before he had asked her out, but it had been worth the wait. She readily accepted and they had been together since. Unfortunately, they were each so busy with their respective lives that they did not spend as much time together as either of them would like.

Betty spent her days at medical college, working toward becoming a doctor while her nights were spent working at a hospital. And Lance was always off on some grand adventure, traveling to far off locales and facing great dangers.

Her heart sank every time he told her he was going away. She wondered silently if it would be the last time she would see him. Then he would return, hail and hearty and all would be right with the world again.

Except for when he came home with news of her brother's death.

Skip had died a hero's death. That was what Lance had told her, and she believed him. It made her feel somewhat better to know that her brother had been a hero. He was a man she was proud to have known.

The one downside to being in love with Lance Star was that he never seemed to want to move on to the next level in their relationship. Once she thought he was ready to propose to her. He had taken her out to the grassy knoll at the farthest tip of Star Field. He had brought a picnic basket with food and drink. They had sat on a blanket and ate, laughed, and drank. Once the sun had set they stared at the stars and the jewel that was New York City at night off in the distance.

She really thought he was going to pop the question.

But he hesitated.

A week later Skip had been killed, and everything changed. Lance retreated into himself for weeks. He spoke to no one, cancelled all of his appointments and locked himself away in his office. He did not bathe or shave. He ate sparingly and slept even less.

Eventually he came out of it, and life at Star Field slowly returned to normal. Lance and Betty's relationship, however, would never again be the same. Oh, she certainly still loved him and he loved her, but every time they were together now there was a giant elephant sitting in the room between them.

Over the course of the years since Skip's death, the couple had gone through their ups and downs, including separating for a time. Now, she was happy for what time she could spend with him. If that was all he had to give her, so be it.

She would take it.

"Betty."

"Hmmm…" she said as she returned to the present. "Sorry, Cally," she said embarrassed. "What were you saying?"

"Are you okay?" Cally Thomas asked.

"Just lost in thought. It's okay. What's up?"

Cally handed over a stack of papers. "Latest VIP list for tomorrow. We should have everyone here in time for the pitch. Once Dr. Benedikt finishes his speech, we can start shuttling them over to the airfield."

"Sounds good," Betty said as she took the offered papers. Thumbing through the list she saw several notables as well as a few surprises. "Ferris Air? I was under the impression they weren't coming."

"They have a new plane scheduled to roll out next year. Where better to introduce it to potential buyers?"

"Then Carol will be happy to make a nice donation so her customers will see her generosity. Let's make sure we approach her when she's in a crowd."

"Good plan."

"Also, your friend Ellen has arrived," Cally said, holding out a folded piece of black paper. "Wayne is getting her settled into her hotel. She wanted me to give you this."

Betty took the paper and opened it. Even if Cally had not told her who it was from, she would not have had to ask. Only one person she knew wrote with white ink on black paper. "Ellen," she said as she read the note. "She wants to get together tonight for dinner and drinks. Tell her I'll be happy to, Cally. Tell her I'll meet her at the hotel around eight."

"Will do."

"Anyone else?"

"Just the usual suspects. I've already assigned people to attend to each of them. All of our bases are covered."

"Baseball, Cally? You've been spending too much time with Mr. Red Davis."

Cally's cheeks reddened slightly. Betty had introduced the two of them a few months ago and they seemed to be hitting it off. Betty respected her friend's privacy and did not want to pry, but curiosity threatened to get the best of her. Her friend's blushing cheeks were enough to sate that curiosity. For the time being at any rate. She would make it a point to broach the subject again after the air show.

"I'll have Lance ready for the meet and greet."

"I bet he's looking forward to that," Cally said sarcastically.

"Don't let him fool you," Betty said, smiling. "He loves this stuff."

Nine

"**B**oss, you've got visitors!"

Lance Star and Detective Barney Bishop were inside the main hangar at the south end of the airfield. Patriot I had been secured in the hangar the day before, along with four other planes and a brand new car, fresh off the showroom floor.

"I'm a little busy at the moment, Red," Lance said with a hint of annoyance.

Red shuffled his feet. "I know that, but I think you'll want to talk to these guys."

"Who are they?"

"They say they're from the government."

Lance and Barney gave one another a look.

"Suddenly, this just got a lot more interesting," Barney said.

"Show them in, Red."

"You got it."

"And Red?"

"Yeah, Boss?"

"Sorry about before. I shouldn't have…"

"Don't sweat it. It's okay."

Red went back to the hangar door and opened it. He signaled for the visitors to step inside. "This way, folks," he said with his usual calm demeanor. Nothing ever seemed to faze Red. At least to those who did not know him as well as Lance.

Two men accepted the invitation and entered the hangar. In stark contrast to Red's down-to-earth manner, these two were refined, each step perfectly manicured. Had Lance not already known that his visitors were with the government, he would have pegged them as G-men. They had that look about them with their dark tailored suits.

"What can I do for you, gentlemen?"

"Are you Lance Star?"

"Yes," Lance said, extending a hand. The lead agent accepted it and shook. "And you are...?"

"Oberman. Department of Justice. This is Lanning."

"Mind if I ask what you're doing here, fellas?"

"I'm sorry, sir," Oberman said. "You are?"

"Barney Bishop. Detective. NYPD Homicide Division."

The answer caught Lanning off guard. He recovered quickly, but not before Lance noticed. "I think I have a strange notion of why you gentlemen are here," Lance said as he motioned toward a table surrounded by several folding chairs. "Why don't we step over here and have a little chat in private. Red, can you watch the door?"

"You got it, Boss."

The men took seats around the table. Once Red was at the door, Lance spun a chair around and sat, his arms resting on the back. "What's his name?"

"I'm sorry?"

"Look, Mr. Oberman, I have no time for games, alright? I've got several thousand people coming here tomorrow expecting an air show. I've got a few hundred things that need to be done before then. The last thing I have time to do is sit here and do this little cat and mouse dance with you two."

"I'm sure you're here for the same reason I am," Bishop added.

"I seriously doubt that, Detective."

"Can you I.D. the body, yes or no?"

"I..." Oberman started, then stopped. He seemed to deflate. "We think so."

"Good. Now we're getting somewhere," Lance said. "Start talking."

"They had that look about them with their dark suits."

Oberman leaned forward and put his elbows on the table. "This is strictly off the record, of course."

"Of course."

"For almost a year now, someone has been feeding us information on the growing Axis powers. As you have no doubt heard, the Axis are running rampant through northern Europe. Just last month the Germans launched an attack on the Soviet Union. Our mole found out about the attack and warned us that it was going to happen. Unfortunately, we received the information too late to be of any good use. When our informant contacted us last week he told us that he had uncovered something major."

"How major?"

"We don't know," Oberman admitted. "The information packet was going to be dead dropped to avoid potential delays like we had last time. Time is of the essence, we were told."

"Where was this dead drop?" Lance asked, although he feared the answer he would receive.

Lanning continued the story. "One of our operatives was slated to recover the information from the drop. The informant hid the information inside the secret compartment of an airplane being flown into the United States from London."

"That does not narrow our odds as much as you might hope," Lance said. "There are several British planes here at the moment. Several of my staff flew with the Brits during the War. They are set up to do some aerial stunts and a recreation of one of their campaigns in the show tomorrow."

Bishop pushed back from the table. "As fascinating as this is, why don't we verify that the body we have is your missing operative before we go jumping the gun? These could very well be two separate incidents."

The government agents nodded in agreement. "A sensible precaution, Detective."

As they walked toward the hangar exit, Lance turned to his friend. "Do you really believe these two events aren't related?"

"No," Bishop said uncomfortably. "But it never hurts to know for sure."

"This is bad."

"Yeah. It is. And I'm afraid it's going to get a lot worse before it gets better."

Ten

"That's him. That's Williams."

Agent Oberman knelt next to the body, now known to be Agent Williams. To keep the knowledge of his death secret from the air show attendees–and more importantly, the press–the body had since been covered by Lance's people with a hastily constructed tent. They wanted to preserve the scene as well as keep onlookers from seeing the body. There was nothing like a corpse on the runway to spoil a good air show.

"Would you care to explain why one of your dead agents is lying on my tarmac, Agent Oberman?"

"It's... complicated."

Lance took a step closer to the G-man and pulled himself up to his full height. "Simplify it for me." The air ace was by no means a menacing guy outside the cockpit, but he his reputation preceded him. And he had heard enough. He wanted answers.

"Williams was the one with connections to the informant. As a matter of security, the identity of said informant was kept secret. Aside from Williams, only the director of intelligence knows his or her identity."

"That seems rather foolish," Lance said.

"Not really. If there were any complications, the United States would have plausible deniability. It also protects other assets from being discovered by the enemy."

"The enemy? And who exactly would that be, if I might ask?"

"Come now, Mr. Star," Oberman said, his tone indicating that he could not believe that anyone who had seen as much action as Lance had could still be so naive. "You of all people know that the world is full of over eager zealots ready to kill untold innocents to get their way. That idiot over there in Germany is a prime example. Do you honestly think he'll stop with Europe, Mr. Star? Will he stop with the Soviets? If I recall my geography lessons, Mother Russia is right next door."

"You don't have to remind me," Lance said, the image of Lord Baron Otto Von Blood flashing across his mind's eye. "I have a very good memory."

"Plus, the odds of something drastic happening to both the informant and the courier are astronomical," Lanning interjected.

"So your informant has contacted you?" Bishop asked.

"Not exactly."

"Not exactly," the detective repeated. "What exactly does *not exactly* mean?"

"It means they don't know who their man's contact is, how to get in touch with him, or what information was smuggled into the country," Lance answered before either man could speak up. "That about cover it?"

"Yes," Oberman said quietly, clearly unhappy with his predicament. "That about covers it."

Despite the seriousness of the situation, Detective Bishop could not keep a smirk from his face. "Sounds pretty drastic to me," he said. "How about you?"

"Astronomical," Lance agreed.

Lance was exhausted.

Since there was a timetable in place - *"the air show will start on time,"* he had told them - Lance and Barney Bishop came up with a game plan. Lance and his senior staff broke into small groups and began a systematic search of the airfield, the hangars, and the administration building. While the pilots and Star Field personnel would conduct their search, Detective Bishop, Agent Oberman and Agent Lanning began interviewing all of the pilots and civilians currently on site.

Agents Oberman and Lanning had agreed to the plan.

Reluctantly.

Lance dropped to the concrete floor and leaned against the front wheel housing of the Skybolt II. The Skybolt was Lance's pride and joy. Especially when she sparkled as she did at that moment. Kevin's team had done an outstanding job of making the sesquiplane sparkle in preparation for the air show. The Skybolt was traditionally the final act of every air show at Star Field. When he was behind the Skybolt's stick, there was nothing he couldn't do. In the cockpit there were very few men who could stand toe to toe with Lance Star.

Of those few who might possibly match Lance's prowess in the cockpit, most were on site for the air show. With only a few exceptions.

Lance could easily sit and stare at his beauty for hours on end. In fact, he often ventured out to the hangar and spent time leaning against the Skybolt's wheel. He found it soothing. Unfortunately, he did not have time to enjoy his moment. There was too much at stake for more than a five minute rest break. "Anything?" he asked as Cy Hawkins eased himself to the floor beside him.

"Sorry, Boss."

"It's okay, Cy. I'm beginning to think this is turning out to be one giant wild goose chase."

Cy smiled. "Could be. It certainly would not be our first one of those, would it?"

"No," Lance said with a smile. "I guess it wouldn't. Is your team finished?"

The pilot nodded his shaggy head. Hangars one, two, four and this one are finished. I was about to seal it up for the night when I saw you sitting here."

"You know, it never occurred to me."

"What's that, Boss?"

"Security. I mean, sure, we lock up the hangars at night and we close the entrance gate. That's just good common sense with all of the expensive equipment we keep here. But I never really expected anything like this to happen here. I couldn't tell you how many nights I've crashed in my quarters and left the door and windows open so I could enjoy the night air."

"Growing up on the farm was the same way for me," Cy said, his mind's eye drifting back across the years and the continent back to his family's Midwest farm. "Our closest neighbor was five miles away. Who would have thought anyone might try to break in? It was unheard of."

"World's changing, Cy," Lance admitted with a sigh. "And I'm not so sure it's for the better."

Cy started to reply, but Lance stopped him.

"Don't mind me. I'm just tired. You know how cranky I get when I'm tired. Buck's right. I must be getting old."

The World War I Flying Ace smiled at that since he, like Buck Tellonger, had a few years on the man. "I've seen hell, Lance," Cy told him. "Over France. During the War. America, the entire world for the matter, might be going through some changes right now, but I think the ol' girl's still got quite a few good years left in her."

"I hope you're right," Lance said as he got to his feet and offered the older pilot a hand. "But sometimes I..." Lance fell silent and whipped his head around quickly, his eyes scanning the room. "Did you hear that?"

"What?"

"There's someone here."

"Are you sure?"

Lance brought a finger to his lips, silencing his pilot. He motioned with his hand toward the door where the junction box that controlled the lights hung from the wall.

Cy Hawkins nodded his understanding. Someone was hiding in the darkness. All he had to do was take away the darkness and the intruder would be revealed.

As Cy moved off in one direction, his employer went the opposite. Crouched low, he stayed close to the Skybolt II. There was a tool cart against the wall at the tail of the plane. The pilot hoped there would be something there that might prove useful in a tight situation. If worse came to worst, there was a sidearm secured inside the Skybolt's cockpit. He kept it there just in case of an emergency.

Getting to it without being spotted wouldn't be easy though.

Lance ducked under the wing and duck walked, keeping his back to the Skybolt's silver hull. If someone came at him, he wanted to see them coming. With the plane at his back, he knew no one could sneak up on him.

On the tool cart laid a large hammer with a rubber face, a large wrench, several smaller wrenches, and a half-empty can of thick, gooey grease. It wasn't much, but it was better than nothing, he supposed.

Lance reached out for the cart.

At that moment a shot rang out from the darkness.

Seconds later, Lance Star was face down on the hard concrete.

Eleven

Lance Star hit the ground hard.

The instant he heard the crack of the blasting cap, saw the muzzle flash from the darkness, the ace pilot's instincts took over and he dove for cover, throwing himself to the cold concrete of the hangar floor. The bullet ricocheted off of the silver hull of the Skybolt II where Lance's head had been only seconds before.

Lance scurried across the floor, covering the distance to the tool cart quickly. He rolled the last few inches, coming to rest with his back against the far wall of the hangar. He took a quick scan of the room, but could see nothing in the darkness.

A second shot rang out and he flinched out of reflex.

This time Lance was not the intended target.

Sparks flew from the damaged junction box that controlled the lights of hangar three. Lance saw brilliant blobs of light flash across his vision, making it even harder to see. He had to blink away the residual flashes going off behind his eyes.

Though it would easily let the shooter know his position, Lance had to know what happened to his friend. "Cy!" he shouted.

No answer returned from his pilot.

The shooter, however, answered with another bullet in Lance's direction.

The bullet smacked the concrete near the tool cart, throwing tiny rock fragments into the air. Lance did not move, did not speak. He needed a weapon. But what? He needed something that could work in his favor against a gun in the hand of someone who obviously knew how to use it.

Lance eased into a crouch and chanced a peek from behind his cover. He still could not see Cy anywhere in the darkness, punctuated only by small areas of moonlight filtering through the skylights. No reply from his pilot did not necessarily mean the worst. Cy was a seasoned warrior, a veteran of several campaigns during the War. He knew as well as Lance to take cover and not give away his position.

Lance grit his teeth. *Where are ya, Buck?* he wondered. Surely someone had to have heard the gunshots and raised an alarm.

He could not count on anyone coming to his rescue, though. The search of the airfield had his men scattered all across the place. It was entirely possible no one had heard the shots and he and Cy were on their own. He would have to proceed accordingly, based on that assumption.

In a crouch, Lance began rolling the tool cart away from the wall. The wheels creaked as it moved. Normally, this was a minor annoyance. Tonight, however, the sound was louder than anything he had ever heard.

Apparently, it was loud enough for the gunman to hear it as well. Another crack and Lance felt the bullet impact the opposite side of the tool cart, tipping it over toward him. He only had a split second to get out of the way before the heavy steel tool cart fell on him.

Lance rolled.

The tool cart landed flat against the concrete, accompanied by a resounding *thud*, quickly followed by the loud clanging of tools bouncing across the floor.

Lance made a break for it.

He knew he would never make it into the cockpit of the Skybolt before the gunman got the drop on him, so he quickly abandoned the idea. Instead, he made a break for the row of planes covered in tarps and sheets in preparation for the morning's show.

He knew he only had seconds before he was discovered. Luckily, he made it under the cover of a sheet covered bi-plane without more bullets being fired his way. He knew the bi-plane's owner. Howard

M. Murdock was a madman inside a plane, but there was no one who had more control over a plane. Lance had once deduced that if he strapped a pair of wings to a brick, H. M. would be able to fly it. With his partner, John, they performed a magnificent barnstormer act that never failed to wow the crowds.

Unfortunately, there wasn't much there that helped Lance. He doubted there were any weapons aboard. Ducking beneath the biplane, he eased out from beneath the sheet into darkness. He could not see the man with the gun, but he assumed he was still out there.

Lance got to his feet and slowly walked around the plane. There was a wall mounted wooden ladder that led up to a series of small catwalks that criss-crossed the hangar. His people used these catwalks when working on large aircraft. That meant they were maneuverable and could be raised and lowered by rope.

Lance slowly removed his shoes. With one last look over his shoulder, Lance padded up the ladder quickly, his socked feet making barely a sound as he climbed.

Once on the catwalk, Lance stepped carefully. The catwalk swayed slightly and in the darkness it was a disturbing feeling. The pilot scanned the room for movement. Then he saw it.

Someone was near the Skybolt, where Lance had taken cover. The darkness did a magnificent job of masking the person's identity, but Lance could tell that the intruder was searching for something.

Was the package the G-men been after still in the hangar? Lance wondered. If so, that meant that Agent Williams' killer was still on the grounds. The realization hit him like the proverbial ton of bricks. That meant that the killer, the spy, the traitor was part of the air show.

There was a killer at Star Field.

And Lance Star had invited him there.

Buck Tellonger was exhausted.

His team had been searching Star Field for the last five hours with no success. Not only were they unsure of exactly what they were looking for, but there was still the matter of finding Agent Williams' killer. Buck was not sure what he expected to find by searching the grounds out beyond the runways, but there he was nonetheless.

"There's nothing out of the ordinary out here, Buck," Red Davis announced for the fourth time. "I think we should head back in."

Buck smiled tiredly. "Okay, you've convinced me." He whistled a shrill, sharp note that got everyone's attention. "Alright, you yahoos, lets pack it in and get back to base. I'm about ready to call it a night."

A chorus of consenting comments filled the night.

"Besides, we've all got a big day tomorrow. I'd hate to have one of you boys falling asleep on the job."

"Since when are you the only one allowed to do that?" Red joked.

Buck winked. "Sometimes being chief of staff has its privileges, carrot top."

The men all laughed along as they began walking back toward the main building. Thankfully, the weather forecast remained positive. Though it was a little warm, it was rather unseasonably cool for July Fourth weekend.

"Not a cloud in the sky," Red murmured.

"Yeah," Buck agreed. "Perfect weather for flying."

"And just our luck, that's what we'll be doing tomorrow."

"What a remarkable coincidence," Buck said. "It's almost as if…" he stopped short, his head whipping from side to side.

"What is it?" Red asked.

"You didn't hear that?"

"Hear what?"

Buck listened intently, silencing his men with a wave of his hand.

"Buck?" Red Davis prodded.

"I could swear I heard gunfire."

"Gunfire? You sure?"

Buck shot his friend a look. "Kid, I've been shot at more times than I care to get into at the moment. Trust me when I tell you I heard gunfire."

"Okay," Red said. "From where?"

"I'm not sure," Buck said, listening for anything out of the ordinary. "Tell you what, let's get back to base and make sure everything's okay."

"Good idea."

Buck broke out into a run toward the buildings of Star Field. "Let's go!" he shouted as his search team fell into step behind him. "Double time!"

Twelve

Lance Star gave the rope a hearty tug.

Standing high above the floor of Star Field's main hangar, the beloved air ace put his plan into action. In reality, it was less plan and more desperate maneuver. Someone had taken a shot at him in his own hangar. For all he knew, the gunman had killed Cy Hawkins, one of his pilots.

The intruder was kneeling next to the Skybolt, where Lance had been before. Was Lance the sole target of the attack, or had he simply been too close in his investigation into the government agent's death? Lance had no answers, but he knew who did.

The man with the gun.

Bracing himself, Lance tugged once more on the thick rope, releasing the catch that held the catwalk immobilized high above the floor. The catwalk dropped. Or more accurately, one end of the catwalk dropped toward the floor. Lance held onto the rope and the catwalk handles as it crashed toward the floor.

The edge of the catwalk splintered into tiny fragments as the wooden planks hit the cold hard concrete of the hangar floor.

Lance kicked off from the free falling walkway seconds before it hit the floor. Using the rope, the pilot pulled himself through the air as if he were Ki-Gor the Jungle Lord, one of Lance's favorite pulp heroes.

Hearing the crash, the intruder spun and fired in the direction the noise originated from.

But his target was not there.

Lance swung forward on the rope, letting go at just the right angle to throw himself toward his attacker. Lance hit the gunman in a flying tackle, both men hit the hard deck in a tangle of arms and legs. The intruder's gun flew from his hand and went sliding across the floor.

Lance pressed the attack, putting a knee to the man's gut. In the darkness he could not clearly see his attacker. He was dressed all in black, including a solid black face mask that covered everything but his eyes and mouth. That's when Lance noticed a familiar scent. He also saw the small burlap bundle squeezed tightly in the man's fist. Unfortunately, he only got a brief glimpse before that same fist connected with his jaw. He knew that this was the information that Agent Williams had died to retrieve.

Lance fell backward and the intruder pressed the attack. An uppercut threw Lance backward, his head impacting the Skybolt's silver hull.

The air ace saw stars.

Lance lost his balance and dropped to the floor. The intruder had him, but then a new sound assaulted his ears. The sound of wood scraping wood filled the darkness as the hangar door slid open. He could hear Buck's voice. His chief of staff was shouting orders, though Lance could only make out bits and pieces over the ringing in his ears.

Secure the area!

No one in or out!

Close the gate!

Find Bishop!

Lance pulled himself to his feet just as Cy Hawkins reached his side. Through his distorted vision, Lance could tell that the big guy was injured. Blood covered the left side of Cy's face and continued oozing from several small cuts on his forehead and face. Despite the blood, the man appeared to be otherwise hale and hearty.

"Where'd he go?" Lance asked.

"Lance pressed the attack, putting a knee in the man's gut."

"Just take it easy, Boss," he heard Hawkins reply.

"Where'd he go? Lance demanded.

L ance ran outside.

Cy Hawkins and Red Davis were immediately at his side. Red and Cy were now armed, just in case they caught up with the man who had taken potshots at the two pilots. They each scanned the area, looking into the night.

"Where are my lights?"

"Any second now, Boss!" Buck said as he ran over to them. "Tom and Kevin are on it."

As if on cue, every light in Star Field ignited as one, burning away the dark shadows as if they were only so much smoke.

"See anything?"

"No."

"Dammit!" Lance shouted.

"Easy, Lance."

"Don't," Lance told Red before he could try to calm his friend. "Get Cy over to the infirmary and get his head stitched up."

"You got it," Red agreed. "Come on, Hawk."

"What about me?" Buck asked.

"You're with me."

"Where are we going?"

"To talk to Bishop," Lance said. He was angrier than Buck could remember seeing him in a long time. Not since Skip's death had Lance snapped at his people the way he had at Red Davis just seconds before. When this was all said and done, Buck knew he and Lance would have to have a nice long chat.

But that was another day. Right now there were bigger fish to fry.

"I need you to find Jim Nolan and bring him to me. I've got a couple questions I'm hoping he can clear up for me."

"What questions? I'm not sure I understand, Lance."

"Just find him, okay, Buck? Just find him."

"Okay."

Lance made a beeline for the administration building with Buck, as ever, at his side.

"This ends tonight," Lance decreed.

Thirteen

"**W**elcome to Star Field."

Lance Star was wearing what he referred to as his "public flight suit." The suit was cleaned and pressed, with nary a wrinkle or stain on it. It was a total reversal of the flight deck coveralls he normally wore during his workday. He kept this one pair cleaned and pressed for occasions such as these.

"A pleasure to meet you," he said to the umpteenth politician who had arrived for the air show. There had been so many to arrive that he'd lost count. He knew that all of the fat cats in attendance were the ones who made major donations to the hospital and the charity fund. That did not mean he had to like hanging out and making small talk with them.

No, the people that Lance enjoyed meeting were those who lined the makeshift bleachers or were sitting on blankets on the hill. They were the ones who were there for more for the show than for the opportunity to get their picture in the paper.

Lance would make it a point to go out and greet that crowd a little later.

But for now, he, and the other pilots headlining the air show were required to get out and *press the flesh*, as it were. The big money donators wanted to meet these amazing pilots, and they paid good money for the privilege of shaking their hands and grabbing a few minutes of conversation. It was Lance's least favorite part of the charity event, but it was a necessary evil. Sometimes he wished he could...

"Lance?"

Hearing Betty call his name brought him out of his wandering thoughts. "I'm sorry," he stammered. "What?"

"You okay?" she asked, concern tinting her voice.

He smiled at her. There was something about her beauty queen smile that was infectious. Seeing Betty Terrell always made him feel better.

"Yeah. Just tired," he admitted. "Had a late night."

She gave him a look that spoke volumes. "Oh?" was all she voiced.

"It takes a lot to get these things running smoothly, you know. We had a few bugs to iron out. Nothing too serious," he lied. Telling his girlfriend that there was a killer on the loose at Star Field was not the best way to start off the festivities. Despite his own proclamation to the contrary, they had not found the intruder or the mysterious package that had been smuggled into the country. All they knew for certain was that no one had left Star Field since the attack. That meant that whoever the bad guy was in this instance, he was still inside Star Field.

That meant there was still a chance to catch him.

"Well, we'll get you out of here in a little while so you can get some rest before your flight," Betty said.

"Thanks."

"But first, I'd like to introduce you to an old friend of mine." Betty motioned a petite blond to come over. "Lance Star," Betty said by way of introduction. "I would like to introduce Ellen Patrick. Ellen took the train from California for the show."

Ellen extended a hand and Lance shook it then lightly kissed her white-gloved knuckle. "A pleasure, Mr. Star" she cooed.

"Ellen has been a long-time supporter of the Foundation."

"We appreciate your contribution, Miss Patrick."

"Ellen, please. And this is a great cause you are raising money for. I'm happy to help. I am just sorry I have not had the chance to come out for the past few years. I've met quite a few dashing pilots in my day," she said with a knowing smile. "And a few of them are flying here this weekend so I just could not resist a trip to New York. It has been too long since I've visited The Big Apple."

"Well, I certainly hope you enjoy the show," Lance said. "Perhaps Betty can bring you by afterward and we'll give you the personal tour."

"Oh, that would be wonderful," Ellen said playfully.

"Hi."

"Ah, I was wondering where you got to," Lance said as he greeted the newcomer. He made the necessary introductions. "Betty Terrell, Ellen Patrick, allow me to introduce Barney Bishop."

"A pleasure," Betty said.

Ellen's eyes were big as saucers. "Why, Barney Bishop," she exclaimed. "It has been a long time. Your former lieutenant mentioned you had returned to New York, but this is the last place I expected to run into you."

Lance thought the detective's chin was going to hit the floor when he saw Miss Patrick.

Bishop quickly recovered and took her outstretched hand and kissed her knuckles. "Let's just chalk this up to my good fortune," he said. "And a happy coincidence."

"Indeed," Ellen cooed while Betty suddenly became very interested in a nearby potted plant.

"Ladies," Bishop replied with more charm than Lance thought him possible of showing. "Do you mind if I borrow our host for a few minutes?"

"Not at all, Mr. Bishop," Betty said as she motioned Ellen toward the buffet.

"Mr. Star. Detective Bishop," Ellen said as she followed Betty. She stopped and regarded Bishop. "Oh, Detective. We'll simply have to catch up while I'm in town. Perhaps we could meet later for drinks."

"Sounds like a fabulous idea," he replied, all smiles.

Lance and Barney exchanged a look once the ladies had gone.

"I'm guessing you two know each other," Lance said.

"Whatever gave you that idea?" Bishop grinned.

Lance rolled his eyes and sighed.

Barney's smile remained in place. "We've met," he said softly, but did not elaborate even as his mind traveled back a few years and a few thousand miles.

"So," Lance said, steering the subject back toward business. "What did you find out?"

"Nothing."

"Damn."

"What now?"

"Let's step outside for a minute," Lance said as he motioned to Betty that he would return shortly.

Betty quickly tapped one of the other visiting pilots and asked him to greet incoming guests until Lance made his way back. Smiling, the pilot took over without question.

Walt Anderson casually sidled up next to Betty. "Where's he going?" he whispered in her ear.

"I'm not sure," Betty whispered. "But he's been preoccupied all morning. Is there something going on I should know about?"

"I don't know what you mean."

"Walt," Betty whispered. "I've known you guys long enough to know when there is a problem. What is going on?"

Walt blanched.

"It's... complicated," he said.

"With you guys it usually is," Betty said coldly.

Big Jim Nolan was waiting outside.

"Lance," he called as Lance and Detective Bishop approached.

"Jim. What have you got?"

"Not much. I went over the records of everyone flying today who could have possibly had any ties to the Nazis. So far there's nothing."

Lance chewed his lower lip.

"How well do you know the British pilots who are performing today?"

"I know some of them, but not all. Buck and I flew with a few of them. I believe Cy did as well. Why? Do you think one of them could be involved in what happened yesterday?"

"I don't know. It's possible. The guy that took a shot at me last night had a familiar scent to him. It took me awhile to place it, but it reminded me of those high-dollar foreign cigarettes you fancy, Jim."

"These things aren't easy to come by, Lance. I have a friend in the Air Corps who special orders them for me. We served together. He kind of owes me one."

"Does he bring them in for anyone else?" Bishop asked.

"I don't know. I could find out."

"Please do."

"No problem, but if these guys flew in from Britain then they could have easily brought their own brand with them.

"True enough," Bishop said.

"I've been working the room, but haven't caught so much as a whiff. Then again, between the food, the various cigars and cigarettes, and some questionable perfumes, it's hard to determine any particular smell."

"Then let's check their planes."

"Somehow I doubt these guys smoked during the flight, Jim."

"No, but those planes are not designed to make the flight without refueling. They had to make stops along the way," Jim explained. "Even if they did not stand next to their planes and light up, then their clothes still had the smell of smoke on them when they got back into the cockpit."

Lance perked up.

"Apparently, I've missed something," Detective Bishop said.

"The smell of the cigarette would have clung to them and from them to the cockpit. All we have to do is check out their planes. Hopefully, we can narrow our list of suspects from everyone down to a handful."

"That's brilliant," Bishop declared.

"We have our moments," Lance said with a shrug. "Come on, let's go check out those planes."

As the three men moved off toward the main hangar, none of them knew that they had caught someone's interest. From the reception hall window, angry eyes watched them walk away. The assassin watched them go, hate burning behind his eyes.

Lance Star was becoming a problem.

A problem it was past time to be rid of.

Fourteen

"**B**uck, secure this door!"

"You got it, Boss," the chief of staff said.

"No one in but us!"

"You heard the man," Buck told the two armed guards he placed at the door. The guards were Star Field personnel. Although they were more grease monkeys than guards these days, the men had seen their fair share of combat. And then some. Buck knew they could handle the assignment.

Lance led the way into the hangar, followed closely by Detective Bishop, and Jim Nolan. Kevin McDouglas was already inside with Agent Lanning in tow. Agent Oberman had chosen to go to the reception and keep an eye on things there.

"Kevin, lets get these birds uncovered," Lance said as he pointed to the British pilot's planes.

"Aye," Star Field's chief mechanic replied with his usual Scottish brogue. "Would ye care ta let me in on what we're looking for, Boss?"

"We'll know it when we smell it."

Kevin and Buck began pulling the cloth covers from the planes in the hangar and letting them fall to the floor.

Lance popped the canopy on the first bird and opened the cockpit. The usual smells associated with the cockpit came rushing out at him. Scents that normally soothed him were suddenly an unwanted distraction. Nothing appeared out of the ordinary, which was not surprising.

And there was no trace of the specific fragrance Lance sought. "It's clean!" he shouted to the others, who were searching planes themselves.

There were twelve planes belonging to the group from England. They had searched half that number before they caught their first whiff of evidence. "Got one!" Jim Nolan shouted.

"Name?" Detective Bishop asked.

"Darren Everett."

"You know him?" Lance asked the pilot.

"No," Jim answered. "I met him for the first time when they touched down for the air show."

Lance looked at Agent Lanning. "He on any of your watch lists?"

"No," the G-man said as he flipped through a stack of file folders laid out on the folding card table. As a precaution, they had pulled as much information on the pilots in attendance as possible. Lanning skimmed the file. "Darren Everett. Age twenty-eight. He's only been with the air group for six months. Born in Glasgow, England, 1913. Other than that he's a clean slate. There's not much else in his file. Not even so much as a flight history."

"How'd we miss this guy?" Buck asked.

"British Air Group filed their pilots' applications as a group," Lance said. "All of their passports were up to date and no red flags were raised when we submitted their names to the Federal Air Marshals."

"How about the other planes?" Bishop asked.

"All clean," Jim said. "I just checked the last one."

"What do ye want ta do, Lance?" Kevin asked. "We've got birds wheels up in less than an hour."

"Find him," Lance said, pointing at Bishop and Lanning. "He should be at the reception. Jim, you go with them."

"On it, Boss."

"Kevin, get the Skybolt ready for her show run. I don't want anything getting in the way of the air show."

"Where are you going?" Agent Lanning asked.

Lance looked at him as if that were the dumbest thing he had ever heard. "I'm going to change," he said.

Agent Oberman knew something was wrong. When Lanning and Bishop returned to the reception he made a beeline for them, meeting them near the entrance.

"What?" he asked.

"Darren Everett," Lanning said.

"Who's that?"

"He's a pilot with the British Air Group."

"Any idea where they are?" Bishop asked.

"Over there," Jim Nolan said as he pointed to a small group huddled together in the corner. Without waiting for the others he moved through the crowd until he reached a man who smiled as he approached.

"James!" the older man said with hearty laugh. "I was beginning to think you weren't going to make it. Thought maybe you had learned the American art of sleeping in."

"It's good to see you, Rupert," James said, offering a halfhearted smile. "I need to talk to one of your pilots."

"Oh? Is something the matter?"

"Darren Everett. I need to talk to him."

Rupert took a step away from the crowd and Jim followed. The older pilot lowered his voice. "Has something happened?"

"I just…" Nolan started, but his voice caught. He had known Rupert Moore for too many years to lie to him. "How well do you know him?" he asked instead.

"Not very well. He was pushed off on us about six months back when Daniel Hogg caught pneumonia. I had never flown with him before then. What's your interest?"

"There was a man killed here the other night. He was a government courier sent to intercept a packet of vital information that was smuggled into the country."

"And you suspect Everett?"

"We just need to ask him a few questions, Rupert. It's important."

"Come on, let's go find him."

Together they made their way through the crowd. Unfortunately, there was no sign of Everett.

"Anything?" Bishop asked.

"Nothing yet," Jim said as they met near the entrance. "I think he's slipped out."

"Where do you think he…"

Detective Bishop's words were drowned out by the booming voice of Tom Vincente over the P.A. system. "All pilots to the flight line, please! All pilots to the flight line! We've got a great crowd out here today, folks. Have fun and be safe."

"Damn," Jim muttered. "Finding this guy just got a whole lot harder. Come on!"

Swept along with the crowd, they moved toward the flight line out on the field. The air show would commence with the introduction of the pilots and a short welcome speech by Betty's boss at the hospital followed by a word from Betty to get the festivities kicked off.

"He's not on the line," Rupert said.

Jim clenched his teeth. "You should take your position, Rup," he said as he clapped his friend on the shoulder. "We'll find him."

"What next?" Oberman asked.

"I think he knows we're onto him," Jim admitted.

"Then he's running."

"Yes, Detective, I believe he is."

"We've got the exits covered," Lanning said. "Nobody gets out without being questioned."

"Are there any other ways off this base?" Bishop asked.

Jim looked at the pilots as they dispersed from the line and headed for their planes. "Well," he said dejectedly. "There are a whole lotta planes about to take off out there."

"And Everett could be in any one of them."

Fifteen

"**A**nd we have liftoff!"

The crowd went wild as a convoy of planes taxied down the runway to a prearranged staging area just off the tarmac. Each plane would be manned and ready when it was their turn to take off.

The Skybolt II, the pride of Star Field, and the finale of the air show, was not yet on the field. Lance preferred to keep his silver bullet inside the hangar until the proper moment.

Jim Nolan and Barney Bishop reached the main hangar at a run while the agents headed out to search the crowd of spectators. They met Lance at the door. He was in his flight gear and ready to go.

"Bad news, Boss."

"We lost him," Bishop admitted as they stepped inside the hangar.

"We're pretty sure he can't get off the base though."

"Find him," Lance said. "Before—"

They all heard the sound at once. A soft moan. Running toward the sound they quickly discovered its origin.

"Colonel Ryan!" Lance shouted as he untied the pilot. Ryan's wrists and ankles had been bound and a cloth was tied around his mouth. A rather large red and purple lump was growing on his forehead. Someone had hit him hard.

With a gun, from the looks of it, Lance thought.

"Colonel! Are you alright, sir?"

Still woozy, Ryan got to his feet with the aid of Lance and Jim.

"I... I'll survive," he said weakly. "Something... some*one* conked me good."

Bishop scratched at the stubble on his chin. "Wait, if you're in here," he started, "then who is out there flying your plane?"

The pilots looked at one another and answered as one.

"Everett!"

Lance bolted for the Skybolt II, shouting orders as he ran.

"Jim, get that door open and clear all traffic. Tell Tony I need immediate clearance. Tell him to hold all traffic at their designated hold zones."

Lance dropped into the main cockpit.

"Tell him to keep that plane on the ground!" he said as he pulled on his helmet.

As Jim ran off to take care of his assignment, Detective Bishop helped Colonel Ryan to a chair.

Once strapped in and with the Skybolt's powerful engine thrumming beneath him, Lance toggled the Skybolt's mic. "Tower, this is LS01. Requesting emergency clearance on runway one-one-alpha!"

"Lance?" Tony Vincente's surprised voice filtered back. "What's going on, Boss? Jim said—"

"No time to explain, Tony," Lance interrupted. "Just clear the road for me!"

"It's clear, Boss! Holding all planes at their markers."

"Good. Where's Patriot I?"

"Lance," Tom shouted. "Patriot I refuses to acknowledge hold signal and is moving onto runway one-one-alpha."

"Dammit! He's onto us!" Lance shouted as he thumbed the frequency to a broader signal band. "Everett! Darren Everett! This is Lance Star! You are ordered to power down your engines and return to the hangar A.S.A.P."

Static was his only reply.

"If that plane leaves the runway, I will be forced to take you down!"

More static.

"It's over, Everett! Let's call it a day before anyone else gets hurt!"

"He's not going for it, Boss," Tom said, breaking the static. "He's picking up speed."

"I'm on him," Lance said as he lined the Skybolt up on the runway. "There you are," he said as he pushed forward on the yoke and sent the silver bullet plane rocketing down the tarmac at top speed.

The crowd went wild. They assumed it was all part of the show.

Patriot I was airborne seconds ahead of the Skybolt. The pilot, Darren Everett, tucked to the right, banking the plane around in a wide arc.

The Skybolt took to the sky. Lance, a noted air ace, easily copied the maneuver. "You're not getting the drop on me that easily," Lance said.

Lance nudged the stick and looped the Skybolt into position. "Nowhere to go, Everett," he called into the mic. "That plane you've stolen stands out. There's nowhere you can set down that you won't be found. Stand down now or I will be forced to"

That's when Patriot I opened fire on the Skybolt.

Sixteen

Lance jerked the Skybolt into a roll as a hail of gunfire narrowly missed him.

"Dammit!" he shouted to no one in particular. "None of these planes are supposed to be carrying live ammo!" He took the plane into a defensive dive. "Then again, there aren't supposed to be any traitors in these planes either," he muttered.

The traitor opened fire again.

His shot went wide and Lance avoided it easily. "What I wouldn't give for a good .50 cal right about now," he said as he sidestepped another barrage.

The bomber fell in line behind the Skybolt as the pilot squeezed off another barrage of gunfire.

Lance took the Skybolt into a dive.

The ground was coming up fast, but the ace pilot showed no intention of veering from his course. At the last possible second, Lance pulled back on the yoke and the Skybolt was airborne once more, barely missing impact with the ground by anything more than inches.

Lance's opponent was more cautious. He pulled up earlier. Unfortunately for him, the bomber was more bulky than the sleeker silver sesquiplane. The underside of Patriot I would require a new paint job from the scraps along the barren fields just outside of Star Field.

The crowds continued to cheer even as the planes flew farther into the distance.

Patriot I miraculously stayed on the Skybolt's six. Everett unleashed another volley of fire.

"This is getting ridiculous," Lance said as he performed evasive maneuvers. "Okay, you son of a buck, let's try this."

Lance veered hard to the right, putting the Skybolt's wing perpendicular to the ground. "Catch me if you can!"

The stolen bomber copied all of Lance's moves, though with less proficiency. "Oh, you are good," Lance muttered as a strategy came to mind. "But I'm better."

He took the Skybolt into a dive again, this time at Sperling Ravine, a deep-rooted riverbed with more twists and turns than a rollercoaster. You could run out of room real quick in there. The ravine was named after the fabled moonshiner who had originally owned the property. Legend had it that Old Man Sperling, as the locals called him, had so many stills hidden in various nooks and crannies along the river that you could get tipsy just by walking along the ridgeline.

Lance wondered how exaggerated those stories were. Not that it mattered. It was a good story. Today, however, the ravine served another purpose.

Lance angled the Skybolt down toward the river, tree limbs smacking the underbelly of the Skybolt as it passed. Suddenly, he found himself surrounded by trees, dirt, and rocks. It was a tight squeeze, but he knew the Skybolt would make it.

"Come on, baby," he whispered.

Darren Everett dropped his stolen bomber into the ravine, hot on Lance's rear. A kick from his mounted canons sent debris crashing toward the riverbed.

"Come on!" Lance shouted as his grip tightened. "Come on!"

The Skybolt navigated a bend in the river. Familiar with the area, Lance knew what was coming up next.

His adversary did not.

Lance jerked back on the yoke and pulled the Skybolt into a steep climb. He felt a tightening in his chest as he was pushed back into the seat. Teeth gritted, he held fast to the yoke as it jerked and bounced in his hand.

The Skybolt blasted out of Sperling Ravine, scrapping treetops as it did.

Patriot I was not so lucky.

Caught off guard by the rapidly approaching incline, Everett had no time to pull up, alter course, or bail out. Only one out of a hundred pilots could have performed that maneuver. Darren Everett was not the one.

Patriot I crumpled in on itself as it slammed into the hill.

Seconds later, a massive fireball erupted from within the ravine. The smoke trail could be seen from as far away as Star Field, where the crowds cheered.

Lance circled the crash site. He was not surprised to find no evidence of a survivor. The murderer, thief, and traitor was gone. Unfortunately, so was the information that he had killed Agent Williams to keep out of American hands. Lance regretted that he had been unable to recover the information that Lanning and Oberman had convinced him was of vital national security.

Unable to do anything from the air, Lance set course for Star Field and returned home.

Flaming debris drifted down into the waters of McCarty River, which flowed through the center of Sperling Ravine.

By the time fire units reached the area, most of the fire would be extinguished and some of the wreckage downstream, carried off by the current. The cleanup of the crash of the Army Air Corps' bomber, Patriot I would not be an easy task.

Had anyone reached the scene sooner, they might have noticed the singed burlap bundle that floated downstream.

Had anyone noticed this bundle, perhaps they would have picked it up and read the official communiqué from Japan's Admiral Yamamoto to his superiors, dated January 7, 1941. The translation would further outline the admiral's suggestion to attack the United

States naval base at Pearl Harbor, Hawaii. A credible threat to the United States might have been averted had anyone noticed the burlap bundle.

But no one did.

Unfortunately, by the time anyone reached the wreckage, the bundle and its contents would be long gone.

Its secrets lost in the wilderness.

Seventeen

Fireworks exploded in the night sky.

The remainder of the air show had gone off without a hitch. The charity had raised a record-breaking amount and everyone had gone home happy. Oberman and Lanning were not happy that whatever information had been smuggled into the country had been lost. Lance had to admit that it bothered him as well, but there was really nothing he could do about it.

Fire and rescue had found no trace of the burlap bundle Lance had seen in the hangar. It had probably been consumed by the fire.

Barney Bishop considered the case closed on the murder of Agent Williams. He would continue investigating Everett as a precaution, but somehow Lance doubted he would receive much cooperation from either Washington or London.

The last Lance had seen of his friend, he was walking hand in hand with Ellen Patrick. They were off to find "*a perfect spot to snuggle up and watch the fireworks.*"

Lance decided to follow their example.

All he wanted to do was enjoy the moment. He stood upon the hill at the far end of Star Field, holding the hand of the most beautiful woman he had ever met. As the fireworks popped overhead, he squeezed Betty's hand tight. He enjoyed the few precious moments they had together. Of late, moments such as these had become few and far between. Lance knew that it was his own damned fault and vowed to spend more time with his girl than he had been.

He leaned over and kissed Betty on the cheek.

"What was that for?" she asked.

"Do I have to have a reason?"

"Not really."

She smiled and Lance's heart soared higher than any plane could take him.

"Good," he said and kissed her again. "Happy Fourth of July, honey."

"So, uh…" Betty prompted. "You planning to tell me what happened today?"

Lance smiled. "It's…"

"Complicated," she said, speaking over the word as it left Lance's mouth.

They laughed. It felt good to laugh. Lance had not been doing too much of that lately. His life had become too… he laughed at what he was thinking. …complicated.

Perhaps it's time to simplify things, Lance thought.

"Complicated," he whispered.

"With you," Betty joked. "It usually is."

Never The End...

HOME IS WHERE...
By Bobby Nash

My first introduction to Lance Star was in early 2006, when our esteemed editor, Ron Fortier, tapped me (along with three other fantastic authors) to chronicle the adventures of this new pulp hero. Okay, so Lance Star isn't as popular as The Shadow or Doc Savage, but then again, who is? In fact, I was perfectly happy with the fact that Lance Star was not a household name. That meant there was plenty of room to play around with.

Off topic a moment (or as we like to call it in my family: *Left Turn*). I'll admit that I have a particular fondness for the lesser used and/or second tier characters. For example, my favorite character in the Star Wars universe is Wedge Antillies. Not Han. Not Luke. Not even Chewie. Wedge. Go figure.

Not that I think Lance Star is a second rate character. Quite the contrary, in fact.

Okay, back on track. In my first Lance Star outing, I had our hero travel to Hawaii in January, 1941 to help out an old Navy pilot buddy who had gotten himself into a jam. It was pure pulp excitement from the opening sentence right up to the blazing dogfight over Pearl Harbor. Even more fun for me was inhabiting the world of pilots, if only for a brief time.

I told Ron that, if the opportunity to revisit Star Field arose that I would very much like to visit again.

Airship 27's first new pulp anthology, *Lance Star: Sky Ranger,* debuted in 2006 to very favorable reviews and quite a bit of excitement among pulp fans eager for new tales. The re-release in 2008 proved every bit as exciting. Like everyone else, I devoured the tales of Lance and his team of heroes as they embarked on perilous missions. The Sky Ranger team of writers took Lance and company to fabled lost cities, pit him against old enemies, and introduced him to fantastical creatures and vile villains.

I reiterated to Ron my desire, if the opportunity arose, to revisit Star Field.

Well, our esteemed editor must have decided a return trip was indeed in order, because here we are. Or he just wanted to shut me up. One can never be certain, but the end result is the same. I was on my way back to Star Field, Long Island, once more.

I began working through scenarios for Lance's next big adventure while working on my Domino Lady story (which appeared in an anthology published by Moonstone Books in March 2009) when it finally hit me. I had mentioned my desire to return to Star Field, home base for Lance Star and his companions. That's when I realized that we had spent very little time at Star Field in our first anthology. We had Lance running all over the world from one grand adventure to another. Not wanting to rehash what I had done before, but instead build on it, I knew it would have to take place after "Where The Sea Meets The Sky" from Lance's first anthology.

The idea hit me as I typed a line of my Domino Lady story that mentioned a charity air show that our heroine donated some of her ill-gotten gains to. The pieces sort of fell into place after that. In fact, since she helped form the idea, I invited Ellen Patrick along for the ride. In fact, not only does the Domino Lady herself follow us to Star Field, but another member of her supporting cast refused to stay behind and joined the fun.

"Home Front" shows us the world of Lance Star on and around July 4, 1941. War is raging half a world away, but getting closer every day. Lance and his team are focused on a charity event close to their hearts, but one that brings back bitter memories of a fallen friend.

"Home Front" also gives us a glimpse into life at Star Field. We get to see Lance and his Sky Rangers as they are between saving the world. Not that this story is without action, adventure, and intrigue or anything. Oh, no. As was recently pointed out to me, I cannot seem to write anything without at least one dead body showing up. "Home Front" is no exception.

There's some great pulp sauce packed between these two covers. Ron Fortier has really assembled a great group of writers for this book and I'm honored to work with them. And what can I say about Rob Davis' art besides "WOW!" And let's not forget that Rob also puts these volumes together with great pulp affection. And also a big thank you to Michael Poll at Cornerstone Books for getting these books out to the masses. Lance Star could not ask for a better flight crew.

One bit of huckstering before I sign off. If you enjoyed the tales in this book, please check out our first anthology book, *Lance Star: Sky Ranger Vol. 1.* It's available on-line and at your favorite pulp bookseller. I guarantee you will not be disappointed.

As I've rambled on long enough–also not unusual in these essays–I see that our pilot has turned on the "Fasten Safety Belt" sign. Star Field is just over the horizon and we're ready to land.

Until next time.

The checker's green. Call the ball.*

Bobby Nash
Bethlehem, GA

*Yeah, I stole that last line from *Battlestar Galactica.* But if you're going to swipe, swipe from the best, I always say.

Author Bio:

Bobby Nash is the writer/artist of the comic strip *Life In The Faster Lane*. Comics written by Bobby include *Fuzzy Bunnies From Hell* (FYI Comics); *Bubba The Redneck Werewolf* (Brass Ball Comics); *Demonslayer, Threshold, and Jungle Fantasy* (Avatar Press); and *Yin Yang: Bounty Hunters* graphic novel (Arcana Comics).

Bobby's prose work includes his 2005 debut novel, *Evil Ways* (Publish America) and the 2006 novel *Fantastix* (Optic Studios/ FYI Comics). Bobby's pulp anthology work includes *Lance Star: Sky Ranger* (Cornerstone Books); *Startling Stories Magazine #3* (featuring Samaritan - Wild Cat Books); *Sentinels Widescreen Special Edition* (short story - White Rocket Books); *Real Magicalism* (Demon Press - August 2008); *Domino Lady* (Moonstone Books); *Full Throttle Space Tales Vol. 2: Space Sirens* (Flying Pen Press); and *Sentinels: Alternate Visions* (White Rocket Books - coming late 2009).

For more information on Bobby Nash, including past, present, and future projects, please visit him on the web.
www.myspace.com/bobbynash
www.comicspace.com/bobbynash
www.fasterlane.blogspot.com
www.bobbynash.com

Bobby lives in Bethlehem, Georgia.

THE THREE MOSQUITOS

"The Flying Shadow of Death"

by
Aaron Smith

Major Ronald Green loved flying. To him, there was no greater feeling than that of soaring through the clouds, looking down at the world below and, when necessary, raining fire and lead down upon the enemies he faced in aerial combat. It brought him joy!

Major Green was fifty years old, much older than most flying aces of the time. Military aviation was still a new game, and most pilots were not much more than boys, freshly commissioned officers with the daring and recklessness that usually faded away with the passage from youth into middle age. But Ronald Green was different. He had been a soldier for his entire adult life, and he had always been willing to take the next step, to learn a new skill to use in service to his country. He was proud to be an American soldier, and he would do whatever he could to do his duty.

He had begun his career in the cavalry, racing across the plains of the Dakotas as a young lieutenant, chasing down Indians and stagecoach robbers. Now, decades later, he flew, battling Germans in the skies over Europe, happy to be taking part in the greatest war that the world had ever seen.

On this particular day—a bright clear early morning—Major Green was high above the French countryside scouting for German troop activity in the area. So far, he had seen no sign of anything worrisome, but he was enjoying the flight too much to turn back to base now. He had taken off from the Chaumont Air Base alone and gone on his scouting run. Green was not part of any of the squadrons headquartered at Chaumont. He held a special position as a pilot who often worked alone, or attached himself to any squadron that needed to borrow his expertise and vast experience for a mission.

He flew a SPAD S.XIII, one of the most effective fighter planes in use by the Allied air forces. The Spad was 20 feet 6 inches long, had a wingspan of 27 feet, had a maximum speed of 135 miles per hour, and was equipped with 2 7.7 mm Vickers machine guns. Major Green's personal plane was painted green—of course—and, unlike the planes of many of the younger, more flamboyant pilots, was not adorned with any bright images or attention-grabbing decoration.

Green was a bit disappointed at finding no signs of enemy activity on his morning scouting flight. He had been hoping for a little action, or at least some hint of German presence to report. Having found nothing, he was about to turn around in mid-air and head back to base for an early cocktail and perhaps read whatever newspaper he could get his hands on, having recently become more proficient in his ability to read French. Just about to begin his maneuvering to reverse course…he saw it!

At first, Green was unsure of exactly what he had spotted. Down below, just above the surface of the countryside, he saw something dark, like a large shadow, but could not see what might have been casting it. He kept his eyes on the growing blob of darkness, watching with curiosity as it began to rise. Whatever it was, he noticed, it was quite large…and getting bigger with every passing second. Up, up it rose, coming closer and closer. The speed of the shadow increased as it approached his altitude.

Suddenly, with incredible swiftness, the great shadow was on an even level with the major's Spad! Darkness surrounded him! He reached up to straighten his flight goggles, but it was a futile gesture. In an instant, it had gone from being a clear, bright morning to a state of utter darkness! Major Green could not see a thing. He felt a sudden collision; his plane hitting something! He lost control! He struggled to steady his plane and his nerves, but it was useless! Rat-tat-tat! His machine guns sputtered and spit hot lead straight ahead! The firing of his guns, instinctive and desperate, would be the last sound that Ronald Green would hear. The plane went into a sudden, irreversible nosedive! The pilot never saw the ground rushing up at him. The Spad hit the solidity of the earth. *Boom!* The fuel in its tank went up in an inferno of destruction! The long, successful career of Major Green was at an end, as was his life. Within seconds, all that remained was a smoldering wreck on a little grassy plain in a continent far from where he had come of age in the cavalry. Major Green would not return to base that day.

Lieutenant Travis leaned against the wooden outer wall of the barracks where he slept and lit his first cigarette of the morning. The sun was just beginning to rise on the horizon as the night's darkness began to part. Travis took a deep drag and savored the taste of the smoke. He was beginning to like France, and was starting to daydream frequently about the day when the war would finally end and he could see the parts of this foreign land that he really wanted to see; the museums of Paris, the Eiffel Tower, and the Seine. Travis had seen much of the world in his time and he wanted to add Paris to the list. A college professor before going off to serve his country in battle, Travis spoke multiple languages and was among the best educated and most well read officers in the United States Army air service. His early morning dreams and the wonderful taste of the tobacco smoke were suddenly interrupted as a running man, a young corporal, raced up to Travis.

The young soldier snapped a quick salute and began to speak through breath that he was trying to catch.

"Lieutenant Travis?"

The tall, lanky lieutenant nodded.

"Lieutenant Travis, Sir," said the corporal, "Good morning. The general wants to see you right away, Sir— you and the other two 'skeeters!' It's important. You've got to come right away!"

Travis sighed. Such urgency could not be a good sign. "Hey, Shorty, wake up!" he called into the still open door of the barracks.

"Get out here!"

Moments later, Lt. "Shorty" Carn, another member of the elite trio of pilots known as the Three Mosquitos, came out of the building, still in the process of pulling up his uniform trousers.

Ten minutes later, Lieutenants Travis and Carn stood in the office of their commanding officer, Brigadier General Saunders. The stern-faced general did not look happy.

"Where is Captain Kirby?" he demanded, obviously unsatisfied to see only two of the Three Mosquitos standing before him.

Travis nervously answered the general's question, not wanting to anger the senior officer. "Umm…sir, umm…Captain Kirby never reported back to the barracks last night. He went out for awhile and didn't come back. He wasn't in his bunk this morning."

"Dammit, Travis," bellowed the red-faced general, "Where the hell is he? Why I ever promoted that reckless fool to his current rank is something I ask myself every day! Well, no sense in wasting time waiting for him. Here's the situation, lieutenants! I regret to inform you both that Major Ronald Green was killed yesterday."

Travis and Carn lowered their eyes and shook their heads in sad disbelief. Major Green had been a mentor to them both and all three "Mosquitos" had looked up to him as inspiration.

"Those lousy Germans," Travis exclaimed in his Southern drawl, slamming his fist down on the general's desk, forgetting for a moment that he was in the presence of his commanding officer. "Sorry, sir, I wasn't aware of any action yesterday. If there was a dogfight, why weren't we called in?"

General Saunders began to explain. "It wasn't a regular engagement, Lieutenant. I sent Green out on a scouting flight. He was to look for ground movements, nothing more. We still don't know exactly what happened to him. The wreckage of his plane was found by a foot patrol yesterday afternoon. It was a hard impact, debris scattered over a large area. The major must have been killed instantly. But… there was no sign of any other fighting. Now I think you'll both agree when I say that Green was too fine a pilot to have crashed like that from any mechanical failure. No, gentlemen, something else happened out there…but I don't know what that was. I want you two—and I wish that damned Kirby was here too—to take a ride out to the crash location and see if you can figure out what happened. The soldiers who found the wreckage were not pilots, just infantry. You boys might see something that they missed, some clue as to what really brought Green down. I want you to head out there at once. Corporal Edwards will drive you in one of the company cars. That's all, lieutenants. Report back to me when you return. And tell Kirby I want to see him!"

T ravis and Carn checked the barracks one more time, but there was still no sign of Captain Kirby. They were soon in a car driven by Corporal Edwards, zooming along the barely paved roads of the French countryside. An hour after beginning the trek, they came to the edge of the wide zone of scattered wreckage. Both Carn and Travis were experienced flying men, and both had seen many crash sites before, but this one was noticeably different. They could tell immediately that Green had completely lost control while still in the air and his dive and subsequent impact had been a random, ugly, deadly one. They got out of the car to look around.

"Holy cow!" said Shorty Carn. "The debris went everywhere." He glanced around at the metal, wood and glass that had been reduced to fragments, pieces littering the green, grassy plain. Then he saw something that startled him, made his jaw drop open in shock. "Travis...what the hell is with all these feathers? Look at them all, some of them charred; some just laying around like they fluttered down from some mid-air explosion of pigeon parts! Where'd all this mashed bird come from?"

Travis took note of the feathers at the crash site at the same time Carn did. He was just as surprised. "When I saw a few feathers stuck to the underside of one of these pieces of wreckage, I didn't think much of it. A random bird or two get caught all the time when a plane goes down...but then I saw more and more feathers. Something's very wrong with this picture, Shorty. A pilot with the skill and experience, never mind the guts, of Ronald Green just doesn't collide with a flock of birds. That's something that might happen to an amateur...not to Major Green!"

The two lieutenants spent an hour walking about the field of debris, stopping occasionally to give closer examination to one piece or another of the fallen plane. They did notice that almost every piece of the downed Spad had some bit of gore, some fragment of a bird—a feather, a spot of blood, a severed talon or beak—either on or under it. They both scratched their heads at this strange fact. Corporal Edwards, knowing little to nothing of aviation, sat by the car smoking cigarettes while he waited for the officers to finish.

"Travis, come over here," called out Lt. Carn, waving his hand to signal his friend over. When Travis came over he found Carn holding what was the biggest fragment of the plane that could be found; one of the side wall panels of the green Spad.

"Look, Travis," said Carn. "If Green really had gone down in a fight, chances are this panel would have at least a few bullet marks in it, but there's nothing. I can see scrapes and burns…but no holes. I don't think it was a German ace that brought him down. Either something went wrong with the engine…or something else happened. I don't know what, but it's got to have something to do with all those birds going down at the same time."

"Well, Shorty," said Travis in agreement, "it seems we have a little mystery on our hands."

Captain Kirby woke up with an aching head. He groaned and opened his eyes. The sunlight, streaming in through the window, stung his head even more. He knew a bad hangover when he felt one, and this was one of the worst he had ever had. He slowly, painfully sat up in bed. He looked around, trying to remember exactly where he was. It certainly wasn't the barracks at Chaumont! He took in a deep breath and a smile crossed his face. He smelled the inviting aroma of something cooking! He inhaled again, trying to place the smells he had detected. Bacon! Eggs! Freshly brewed coffee! His stomach grumbled and he forgot all about his hangover as the knowledge of where he was came rushing back to him.

It had been a long night, but a damn good one! He had left the base to go out for a drink and had wound up in one of the little taverns that dotted the area. He had intended to stop in for a quick drink and then get back to his usual quarters for the night…but things got complicated.

Kirby had had his drink…and then another, and then a third. Then he had spotted the dainty little French girl across the crowded tavern, and he just couldn't help himself. He walked on over to her and, though she didn't speak a word of English, flashed his best flying ace smile and sweet talked her in his clumsy French. The next thing he knew it was day again, and he was waking up in her small apartment not far from the tavern!

He got out of bed and found his clothes. He put on his wrinkled uniform and walked into the kitchen.

"Morning, Yvette," he muttered, managing to remember the girl's name. She smiled at him, standing there in very little clothing, with a spatula in one hand and a cup of coffee in the other. Kirby glanced at the clock on the wall.

"It's almost noon!" he shouted, followed by a swift curse in English. "General Saunders will have my head!" He gave Yvette a quick kiss and bolted out the door. Running at full speed down the little dirt road that led from the tavern to the Chaumont base, Kirby hoped and prayed that his absence had not been noticed by the base's commander.

Miles away from the Chaumont air base, a small cave lay hidden in the side of a hill at the edge of a heavily forested part of the French countryside. From the edge of the tree line walked a uniformed German soldier. He was an officer, the captain of a squad of soldiers who had been making camp there among the trees where they could easily hide from the American flying scouts. For over a week they had been camped out in those woods, their purpose being twofold. First, they awaited reinforcements so that they might launch a ground assault on the Americans. Second, they were there to ensure that an experiment would be carried out, an experiment that could, if successful, prove to be of great help in defeating the American air forces that fought to prevent the German advance.

The captain strode out of the woods and into the cave. He squinted to see through the shadowy darkness until his eyes began to adjust to the dimness. Deeper into the cavern he walked, until he finally saw the glow of a small fire within. As he approached the flaming light, he could see the figure of a single man, old and slightly hunchbacked, boiling water for tea over the fire.

"Good morning, Herr Whistler," said the German captain.

"Hello, my friend," was the old man's reply. "Have you brought my prize along with you?"

The German took a wad of money from his pocket and handed it to Whistler, who counted it greedily. As the old man counted, the captain glanced around the cave. His eyes paused as he looked at a large blanket that covered some form, some heap of objects.

"You have done well, Herr Whistler. Your apparatus performed most admirably. Your first strike against the American flyers was a swift and deadly one. Not only did you strike down one of their most experienced pilots…but you have caused confusion for them as well. So far, it has been a double-edged victory!"

The captain and Whistler spoke for a few minutes more. Plans were made. Once Whistler's water had boiled, he began to brew his tea and ushered the German officer out of his cave, assuring him that he understood the latest part of their plans. The captain returned to the woods, and to his men.

Lieutenants Travis and Carn sat on their bunks in the barracks at Chaumont. Carn, as usual when not flying his Spad into battle, had his nose buried in a book. In this case, it was a history of the French Revolution, as Carn was a firm believer in reading the right book in the right place. Travis was deep in thought, puffing on a cigarette and contemplating the scattered remains of Major Green's doomed plane, trying to think of what sort of scenario might have led to the great pilot's death.

"Afternoon, gents," said Captain Kirby as he entered the barracks. Carn and Travis looked up simultaneously. Travis spoke first. "You'd better go see the general, Kirby. And be warned…it won't be pretty."

Kirby laughed. "I've already been. It wasn't so bad...once he was out of breath from letting me have it! Anyway, he'll forgive me. After the scolding, he gave me the news about Ron Green; that's a damn shame. Green was a good man, a great flyer. I learned a lot from him. I'll tell you what, Mosquitos; I'm not letting him go unavenged. I know it didn't look like a regular fight was what killed him; I read your report to Saunders, Shorty. I don't know what the story was with all those feathers, but it can't be birds that caused Green to crash; it just can't! He was too good a pilot for that. I don't care how many damn feathers you both saw, the whole affair stinks of German involvement and I swear I'll get to the bottom of it. You boys saw the wreckage from ground level, but I think we ought to scope it out from above. What do you say?"

"Sounds good to me, Captain," said Travis.

"Great," answered Carn. "I've been itching to get off the ground."

Kirby smiled. He was always ready to lead his small squad into flight, no matter what the mission was. "All right, Mosquitos...let's go!"

The three American aviators grabbed their flight goggles and literally ran to the runway. Within minutes, each man was seated in his Spad. The engines were started, the blocks removed from the wheels, and the Three Mosquitos took flight. The trio of khaki colored Spads, each with a black mosquito painted on its nose, soared high above the Chaumont airfield. The ground crew looked up and watched them fly off, knowing that those three young men were quite probably the best there were at what they did in that great war.

The Three Mosquitos flew over the French plains and hills in their usual formation, a V-shape, with Captain Kirby in the lead and Travis to one side and slightly behind, with Carn on the other side, also slightly behind. They were used to flying together and had no need to communicate with words. Simply watching the captain's actions and following his lead was usually sufficient to indicate to the lieutenants what they should do. On some occasions, they made use of a series of hand gestures they had worked out to facilitate airborne communication. It was a system that Shorty Carn had devised, based in part on the signs used in baseball for coaches to tell players whether to bunt, or swing away, or steal a base, or whatever the case may have been.

The trio of khaki Spads raced through the air and soon found themselves above the field of wreckage and debris that had once been the plane and, sadly, the body of Major Ronald Green. Each of the three pilots looked down at the wreckage as they flew overhead, each trying to find some sign or clue or piece of vital evidence that may not have been visible on ground level. They passed over the sight and then deftly went into maneuvers to reverse course and take a second look from the opposite direction. They also each took a turn flying in low so that they could inspect the scene from several different altitudes. An experienced fighter pilot could tell much from such a scene, including the angle at which the doomed plane had plummeted to the ground, the speed at which it had descended, exactly what damage had occurred, and how large of an explosion, if any, had resulted from the crash. Considering the terrible degree of damage, the near obliteration that had been done to Major Green's now demolished Spad, all three of the observing flyers judged it to be one of the worst crash sites they had ever seen.

Once they had made a series of passes over the site, Captain Kirby, still in the lead, raised his left hand to make the signal for them to begin the flight back to Chaumont. He began to turn into a course reversal when something caught his eye. He raised one hand to shield his eyes from some of the sunlight and looked ahead and down below. *What is that,* he asked himself? He could have sworn that he saw something move–something big and dark, a large, lingering shadow of some object. He blinked twice and then looked again. *There was something there,* he thought. Yes, he told himself, *the ground looks darker than it should!*

alf a mile from the site of Green's wreckage, a pair of eyes peered out from under a large boulder that sat in an otherwise empty field. Anyone in the area might see the rock, but would have no idea that it was actually the entrance to a long tunnel that connected to a network of caves underneath the fields and hills of this part of France.

Whistler squinted as he looked up into the bright sky, his eyes still adjusting to daylight after hours alone in the caves. His left hand rested upon the equipment he had brought with him through the tunnels. He felt a sense of twisted satisfaction as he touched the machinery. He was proud of his invention. He had taken a phonograph player and made some adjustments to it, some innovations. It was this creation which had led the German officer for whom he worked to call him "Whistler."

The phonograph machine was portable, running on a special battery that Whistler had devised. This enabled him to take it with him to any part of his subterranean labyrinth. The portability, however, was not the most interesting thing about Whistler's invention. The machine was, in fact, a terrible new weapon to be used against the flying aces of the French, Americans, and British!

Whistler turned a knob on the phonograph machine. The record disc attached to the device began to spin. A needle made contact with the grooves in the disc. A strange whistling sound began to emerge from the machine. He turned another knob, causing the eerie sound to grow louder and louder. The frequency increased, the sound became weirder, almost other-worldly. The pitch grew more and more intense. Whistler's own ears began to ache...and the noise suddenly ceased, or at least seemed to stop! Whistler, being the creator of the device, knew better; the sound had not stopped, but had become something inaudible to human hearing! The strange sound now continued outside the range of normal human ears! It did not, however, go unnoticed by certain other creatures in the immediate vicinity of Whistler and his malicious equipment.

On the field surrounding the boulder under which Whistler hid, the sound was heard and heeded by thousands and thousands of birds! The small beaked inhabitants of the French countryside were mesmerized by the sounds coming from Whistler's phonographic weapon. As the man altered the tone of the sound that only the birds could hear, they began to respond to the signals sent out by the needle riding the grooves of the disc. The wings of the birds began to flutter, all at once, in perfect synchronicity.

Kirby looked down in disbelief and confusion as the shadow on the ground began to move, to rise, to hover above the ground and to come closer to his altitude! Suddenly, with incredible speed, so fast that even his great airspeed could not outrun it, the rising shadow was at his height. His plane was surrounded, whatever had risen from the ground now blocking out all daylight! Kirby may as well have been blind, for all the good his eyes were doing him at that moment! His finger twitched on the trigger of his Spad's mighty Vickers guns…but he hesitated, stopped himself from firing into the strange darkness. Travis and Carn were near, he knew, and he could not risk his barrage of bullets striking them or their planes. He had to remain calm, he told himself, and figure out what was happening.

Travis and Carn had seen the weird sight of the giant shadow rushing up to surround their captain's plane and they had flown off to a further distance on either side of him. Both rising up to an altitude of about fifty feet above the mass of flying blackness, the two remaining Mosquitos met in the sky above the blackness that contained Kirby. They each stared down at the dark shape, amazed by what they were witnessing. Birds; thousands of birds! Perhaps a hundred-thousand winged creatures, all working together, forming a great blockade around the plane of Captain Kirby! Their eyes met in the air, looking to each other from their separate planes. Travis shrugged; Carn pointed downward and made a sweeping gesture with his hand. Travis immediately understood what his comrade was suggesting. He nodded in agreement.

Carn and Travis parted, each flying off to one side of the huge mass of birds. Then, both pilots moving at precisely the same speed, keeping pace with the flying shadow and hoping that Kirby was able to keep his wits about him on the inside of the crowd of birds, they began to inch towards each other, literally squeezing the flying army

**They each stared down at the dark shape...
Birds; thousands of birds!**

of birds with their planes!

As if they thought and moved with one single group-mind, the birds resisted the approach of the planes, but Travis and Carn kept coming closer on both sides. Birds slid and stumbled against the sides of the two Spads. Travis and Carn could see feathers coming loose and drifting about in the air. A few birds thudded against the side panels of the planes hard enough to be knocked senseless or even dead and spiraled to the countryside below. Tighter and tighter the twin Spads moved in, gradually scattering the edges of the mass, then working in towards the center.

Captain Kirby was fighting off panic. He was not a man who frightened easily, but this weird event had happened so quickly, the day turning so abruptly to night, that he had been pushed over the edge into the abyss of shock and terror! Still, he was alive and had managed to keep up his speed and fly straight, his battle-honed instincts guiding him when his vision had ceased to be adequate. He knew that Carn and Travis were out there, and he trusted those two men as if they were his own brothers. He knew they would come for him. They had to, or all was lost!

The minutes ticked by. Kirby had lost all sense of where he was, how high he flew, how fast he was moving! He had no idea if he were high above France...or inches away from a deadly crash like the one that had killed Major Green. Even with his iron will and great mental discipline, Kirby was moments away from losing hope. Then...as suddenly as the darkness had come upon him, a spot of light appeared to his left! He could see again! Then the darkness began to break on his right. In one sudden movement, one incredible instant of revelation and salvation, daylight flooded his vision...and the great mass of shadow, the terrible nocturnal Hell into which he had been thrust, was gone, replaced by a bright blue sky, and several hundred birds fluttering about in confusion and chaos, their synchronized aerial dance of doom interrupted!

Travis and Carn flew in close to Kirby, flanking their captain's plane, looking over to see if he was all right. What they saw was Kirby laughing, grinning, and letting out a glorious cry of joy. "Wahoo!"

Resuming their standard V formation, the Three Mosquitos headed back to base, tired, spooked by the strange event with the mass of birds, and eager to land and try to figure out just what had happened up there above the world.

"**A**nd that's the story, General," said Captain Kirby. "I know it sounds crazy, but it's all true."

General Saunders nodded. An hour earlier, the three pilots–Kirby, Carn and Travis–had come barreling into his office, each almost interrupting the other in their rush to tell the tale of the nearly deadly bird formation that had almost been the end of the Three Mosquitos. The story now told, Saunders sat there digesting it. Then he replied.

"Captain Kirby, you're a scoundrel and a consistent pain in the neck when you want to be...but you've never lied to me. I believe you, men, strange as the story seems. So that's what brought Major Green down, a flock of birds! But why...why do they fly like that? Like one mass body of feathers and beaks, coming together to take down our planes? I've never heard of anything like it before! Lieutenant Travis, you're a smart man, used to be a college professor! What do you think?"

"I don't particularly know, sir," said Travis in the slow Southern drawl that sometimes caused others, who didn't know him well, to underestimate his intelligence. "But we need to find out fast. We can't keep our planes from flying over that area for long, but until we figure this strange phenomenon out, we can't risk it either."

The general scratched his perpetually clean-shaven chin. "Carn, what do you have to say about all this?"

The shortest Mosquito spoke. Carn was a voracious reader, and this series of events had him thinking like a detective in one of the many mysteries he had read as a boy. "Well, sir, it seems to me that something must be causing this strange bird behavior, and we've got to find out what that might be. These two attacks, the one on Captain Kirby and the one on Major Green both happened while we were flying over that area, but maybe something on the ground triggered them. Maybe we ought to take a closer look at the area from down there instead of another flyover."

"Sounds about right to me, son," agreed General Saunders. "Kirby, you're the leader. I'm leaving it up to you to formulate a plan. Get going. We can't afford to waste any time. If the Germans notice we've stopped flying over that zone, they might start moving their ground troops around and get too close to Chaumont for us to stay comfortable here."

The meeting with Saunders having reached its logical conclusion, the Three Mosquitos stood, saluted, and left the room.

An hour later, every pilot the Mosquitos could round up on short notice had been gathered on the Chaumont runway. Forty men stood waiting for whatever Captain Kirby was about to say. In the background, the ground crews prepared forty Spads for the forty airmen.

"Men, we have a job to do," said Kirby as he stood on a large packing crate and looked out at the assembled flyers. "This is going to sound strange, but we've got a serious bird problem on our hands. We're all going to head out and make a run over a small area over the countryside. When we get there, if things go like they did for me this afternoon, we're going to see a hell of a lot of birds come flying up. I think forty planes ought to be enough to keep those feathered freaks scattered. Now, we'll need to be careful out there. There's something mighty strange about those birds and the way they behave, but we can best deal with them by keeping in motion and not letting them surround or confuse any of us. Is all that understood?"

"Yes, sir!" came the loud, unanimous response.

"Good," said Kirby. "While we fly over the sector, my friends Lieutenants Travis and Carn will be on the ground below, trying to spot whatever might be causing these birds to attack our planes. They got a good head start by motorcar, so we should head out now and try to get there around the same time as they do. Let's go!"

With that, forty officers of the United States Army air services raced to their Spads and took to the skies.

The small car sped towards the flat plain that contained the wreckage of Ron Green's ill-fated Spad—the same stretch of land below the day's earlier incident involving birds and Captain Kirby. Lieutenant Travis was behind the wheel; his passenger was Lieutenant Carn.

"We're almost there," said Shorty as the twisted remnants of Green's plane came into his view. The little car went a bit further and then stopped. The two lieutenants got out and scanned the area.

"Nothing much that I wouldn't expect to see here," said Travis. "Other than an unusual number of birds, things seem pretty normal." There were an awful lot of birds in the region, but they seemed to be behaving quite sanely this time, simply pecking around the ground in search of worms or other morsels of sustenance, or flitting about from rock to tree to shrub and back again. There were a few small flocks skimming the air overhead, but the overall picture was one of simple, serene nature—"except of course for the shredded pieces of the downed Spad that littered the grassy fields.

As the two officers stood upon the field, a noise became apparent in the background; a steady hum, becoming louder and louder.

"Here they come!" said Travis as he pointed to the sky's horizon. Carn looked upward and outward. The large formation of forty American Spads was quickly approaching the area.

"Now's the time," said Carn. "If something is going to get these birds going, it should happen soon."

As if on cue, a sudden whistling sound came from somewhere in the vicinity of where the two grounded pilots waited. Travis and Carn watched in amazement as the birds in the area all began to flock together. A few of the feathered animals buzzed by their heads, causing Travis to curse and Carn to duck! The birds amassed on the grassy plain—an astounding sight, as if every small winged beast in all creation had come together in the same time and place, merging together into one immense being with many wings and one mind!

"That whistle we just heard—it must be what set them off like that! It was some sort of signal," said Travis as the great flock began to rise. "But where did it come from? Look around, Carn. We have to find the source!"

In the skies above, Captain Kirby saw the now familiar sight of the rising mass of tightly woven birds approaching his altitude. He flew in the lead of the large squadron of planes that had arrived on the scene. Up came the birds and all Hell broke loose! The planes broke formation and flew in strange, looping patterns, being careful to avoid hitting each other, but doing their best to keep the birds from remaining assembled in one flying mob of death! Kirby's plan began to work. Against the single plane of Major Green or even against the three Spads of the Mosquitos, the great grouping of avian predators had been a formidable force, but against the onslaught of forty planes the feathered beasts were helpless. Despite the signals being transmitted in an inaudible frequency from below, the birds just could not stay grouped together to surround so many planes. They simply flew around in a chaotic tangle of confusion and dismay. The planes maneuvered about...and the birds scattered!

"Over there!" shouted Shorty Carn. "That rock! Something moved underneath it!"

Travis turned in the direction indicated by his partner. When they had arrived on the scene, Travis had thought the large boulder had looked out of place in the otherwise flat and empty field, but had simply chalked it up to the random ways of nature. Now he took another look. There, under the great stone, was some sort of opening and from within stared a pair of eyes, startling white against the shadowy black! Travis drew his pistol and Carn did the same. They began to rush towards the boulder.

Under the rock, in the small cavern at the end of the tunnels, Whistler and the German captain watched the chaos in the skies. Whistler was furious that the Americans had overwhelmed his pets with the sheer number of their planes. The captain was furious at Whistler, for this time his machine had failed to cause the birds to destroy the flying Americans. Now, on top of all that, there were two Americans on the ground nearby...and they had seen the space below the boulder. With guns drawn, they were coming!

"Take your damned machine and run, you idiot!" the German captain shouted to Whistler. The altered phonograph machine was quickly scooped up by its inventor, who carried it swiftly away down the tunnels under the plains of France. The German, meanwhile, had drawn his own gun and was taking aim at the approaching American officers.

Somehow, through some little miracle, a beam of sunlight managed to penetrate through the mass confusion of the multitudes of birds and planes overhead. The sunlight glinted, just for a second, off the raised and aimed barrel of the German officer's handgun. Shorty Carn saw the instant of glare. He knew that a loud bang, followed by a speeding bullet would come next. He leaped to the side, knocking Lieutenant Travis down, just as the sound echoed from under the boulder and the bullet whizzed by, narrowly missing them both! Knocked off his feet, but aware of what was happening, Travis took a laying down sideways aim and pulled the trigger of his own gun, hoping that his aim would be accurate enough to keep the next shot from flying from the hole in the ground!

The German captain felt Travis' bullet bite into his right shoulder! The officer screamed in agony and dropped his pistol. Travis and Carn were up off the ground and running toward the boulder. Carn, the smaller and faster of the two men, got there first, reaching into the small opening, grabbing the German by the jacket collar and wrenching him forcefully from his hiding place! The German, in pain and bleeding from his shoulder wound, cried out as he was pulled into the light. Carn decked him with a punch to the jaw, sending the German plopping down into a seated position on the grassy ground.

"How were you doing that?" Carn demanded. "What did you do to those birds?"

The German officer, knowing he was caught and helpless, let his cowardice overtake his bravery and spoke. "It wasn't me! It was him! It was the Whistler!" He pointed to the hole from which he had just emerged.

"Dammit, there's another one in there," said Carn. Travis, not wasting any time, still firmly gripping his gun, went into the opening under the boulder. Travis was a tall man, but he was lean and lanky and was able to squeeze into the narrow space.

"I'm going after the other one," said Travis from within the hole. "Stay with this German fool, Shorty."

Up above the boulder and the cave, the birds were beginning to disperse. With the inaudible signals from Whistler's device stopped, there was no longer any man-made rhyme or reason to the birds' movements and the presence of so many Spads was enough to drive them away. Within minutes, the sky was clear of feathered fiends. Captain Kirby, in his khaki plane, waved his hands in a signal for his squadron of forty men to turn and head back to Chaumont. He hated to leave Travis and Carn behind, but the plan they had devised had called for them to split up, so he had to keep up his end of it and get the other planes back safely. Kirby hoped his friends were doing all right down below, and he smiled at the thought that the birds had been taken care of without one Vickers gun firing a single shot.

Lieutenant Travis ran down the tunnel. The light was barely present and he was having a hard time seeing, but he followed the sound of heavy footsteps and heavy breathing up ahead. He could tell by sound that the man he was pursuing was weighed down by the need to carry something quite heavy. He pointed his gun up ahead.

"You there! Stop and turn around! Surrender or I'll shoot!"

Travis' warning went unheeded. The grunting and running up ahead continued.

"Dammit," muttered the lieutenant, "I can't just shoot him in the back!" He kept running. Gradually, the distance between the two men decreased. Travis' long legs moved him along quite quickly, while Whistler's burden slowed him down. Travis' eyes had now adjusted to the light that was barely present. He closed the gap. With Whistler almost within arm's length, Travis pushed himself just a bit harder, made a small leap, and brought the fleeing man to the cavern floor! The phonograph machine slid across the dirt. Pieces of the equipment broke off with a sharp snapping sound. Whistler tried to break free, but Travis had him pinned down. The agent of the Germans reached down to his belt. Travis heard the sliding sound of a knife being drawn from its cover. Whistler took a swipe at Travis' face with the newly drawn dagger. The blade grazed the young aviator's cheek, drawing blood and a yelp of pain! Travis swung his arm up and knocked the dagger from Whistler's hand. The empty hand came back down and slammed into the side of Travis' head.

Despite his age and apparent frailty, Whistler was no weakling. Travis knew he had to end the fight as fast as possible. With one hand, he blocked Whistler's next blow. With the other, he groped around on the cavern floor, hoping to find something, some object with which to even the score. He did! His fingers grasped something, a small thing that felt hard and jagged. He did not know what it was, but it would have to work! He took a gamble and made his move.

Whistler groaned in pain. His eyes rolled back in his head. He slumped backwards and died there on the dirt floor of his subterranean home. The man who had made his living coercing the birds of the French countryside into aiding the war efforts of an invading nation was dead, lying in his labyrinthine grave, with a jagged shard of a phonograph record wedged in the space between his ribs!

The Three Mosquitos sat in their barracks. Kirby had just finished describing the aerial maneuvers he had used to disperse the great flock of birds. Carn was writing a letter to his family back in the States. Travis was smoking; he had a smile on his face, contrasting the bandage on his cheek where Whistler's knife had grazed him. He hoped it wouldn't leave much of a scar, but if it did, he figured it would make an interesting story.

"So the general says we can have a few days R&R," said Captain Kirby. "That weird machine that riled up the birds is being examined by our technical division. The Germans who were hiding in that forest have all been mopped up. The Brits were kind enough to lend us one of their infantry platoons for that job."

"Great," said Travis. "So what do we do with our time off,

Captain?"

"Well," answered Kirby, "I had the good fortune to meet this little French dame named Yvette. I've been wondering if maybe she's got a couple sisters or cousins or anything. What do you say, Mosquitos? Let's go!"

"Of War and Words"
By Aaron Smith

When Ron Fortier asked me to write a World War I aviation story, the first emotion that came into my mind was panic! I felt like kicking myself. What had I gotten myself into now?

I had just finished my latest story for Airship 27 Productions, a *Dan Fowler: G-Man* story, my second featuring that federal agent of the 1930s. That story done, I had no idea what I was going to work on next. Taking pride in my ability to write almost anything once I put my mind to it, and enjoying trying different styles of story, I wrote to Ron and asked if there was anything he needed me to write next, any book that needed a story to complete it. Ron said he needed one final aviation tale to finish the book you are currently reading. He suggested that I might be interested in spinning a yarn a trio of old pulp characters, World War I flying aces called the Three Mosquitos.

For a day or two, I thought I had bitten off more than I could chew. I found myself possessing very little confidence in my ability to write an aviation story. The reason, I suppose, was a simple one. I don't like technical stuff. I have a car and know how to drive it, but I'm not interested in the specifications of the engine or such things. I love *Star Trek*, but it is the characters who appeal to me, not the technical details of how a warp drive operates. I'm a writer who relies on situations and emotions to get a story told. I minimize my research and write quickly and instinctively. I did not want to get bogged down in having to explain the exact specifications of 1918 fighter planes and other equipment. I almost turned down the job. Still, Ron had asked me to take on the assignment, and he's been such an awesome editor–and a friend–that I felt I had to at least give it a shot.

I learned a bit about planes of the time, just enough to get the basics right without going into too much detail...and then I got to work coming up with a plot. The basic descriptions of the Three Mosquitos, their personalities and their relationship helped me out too, for Captain Kirby and Lieutenants Carn and Travis started to remind me of one of my favorite fictional trio, Kirk, Spock and McCoy!

Once I had a plot in mind, the job started to speed up and I found myself having a blast! It then occurred to me that I had two potential stories in mind. I also realized that both stories could be best told in a shorter format, so I asked Ron if I could write two short, short stories instead of one longer short story. He agreed, and the Three Mosquitos were ready to take flight again.

I had started the job with a head full of doubt, and it turned out to be not only a lot of fun, but possibly the quickest writing job I've ever done, due to the fact that I was having so much fun that I didn't want to stop until both stories were finished!

Ron Fortier is now under strict orders to hit me in the head with a frying pan if I ever express doubt about my ability to write in a certain genre!

The first of the two stories, "The Flying Shadow of Death," was inspired in part by a recent real-life event. In the skies over New York City, several months ago, a passenger plane struck a flock of birds and nearly crashed. The pilot, Chesley "Sully" Sullenberger, a true modern day hero, "landed" the plane on the Hudson River! He saved every single one of the 155 passengers aboard the aircraft!!

The second story, "Two Outs, Bottom of the Ninth," concerns one of my favorite pastimes, baseball. One thing that has always intrigued me is the early history of baseball. In those days, before the coming of the great juggernaut, Babe Ruth, the game was populated by players who have been largely forgotten by today's fans. Most fans would certainly remember the name of Ty Cobb, but the other real-life player who appears in my story, Sam Crawford, has a much less recognizable name. Still, I feel that every true fan of the game should remember him, for he was one of the best ever.

Crawford played in the Major Leagues from 1899 to 1917. He was elected to the Hall of Fame in 1957. He had a career average of .309, 2961 hits, and 1525 runs batted in. He was the first player to ever lead both the National League and the American League in home runs and, perhaps most impressively, still holds a record that will probably never be surpassed, with 309 triples! Sam Crawford was inarguably one of the best to ever play the game, and I'd bet that at least seven out of ten of today's fans would not know who he was!

Writing a baseball-related war story also made me recall how many ballplayers had to put their careers on hold to serve their country in various wars. Ted Williams certainly comes to mind, having flown combat missions in not one, but two wars (World War II and Korea)! But there were many others. The one I think of the most is Joe DiMaggio. You see, when my grandfather was drafted into the Army during World War II, he was sent to Atlantic City, New Jersey, where he served under Sergeant DiMaggio for a time.

The baseball aspect of the story, combined with the war aspect, which naturally brought to mind my family connection with DiMaggio, came full circle in my mind due to an event that occurred while I was writing these Three Mosquitos stories.

On May 29, my grandmother died. It was not a tragic event, not a reason for sadness. After all, she lived to be 87 years old, had a long, full, happy life, and enjoyed good health up until that final week of her life. She did well!

I got through the funeral and the related events with no great emotions at all. A week after her death, the family began to go through the contents of her house. That, for me, was more emotional. It was not her death that affected me then, but a death that had occurred almost twenty years earlier.

When I was thirteen, my grandfather died. I did not cry at the time, for it was a relief. He had been sick for two years at that point, and what he had once been was gone, never to return. I saw death as a merciful thing then, and I still do as it relates to him. But, going through the things in my grandmother's house, I missed him again.

I found a few things in that house that I now have in my possession. I found a small book he had bought during the war, in which he recorded his travels through the United States and Europe, as well as the names of his buddies who had been killed in action. I found a photograph of him in uniform in France, looking so young and dashing, like Bogart with a hint of Errol Flynn. I found a swastika armband, with a bullet hole going right through, that he had taken off a dead Nazi. Lastly, I found his dog tags. I am proud to now have those tags, as I know that he wore them all throughout the greatest conflict this world has ever known!

As a writer of heroic fiction, I often think of my influences. It's easy to point out writers, or films, or historical events as having influenced one's work, but sometimes there are other things too. Looking back on my life, I now realize that my grandfather was one of the strongest inspirations for my love of stories of heroism.

I think that, in my earliest childhood, when my imagination was just beginning to form and fill up with what might be called "archetypes," my grandfather instilled in me the idea of what a man is. That might sound strange to someone else. It really can't be adequately explained, but that's how I feel. He was a strong man, a powerful man, a tough man, but it was more than that; more than the sun-bronzed skin of a lifelong construction worker and carpenter, more than the great physical strength that he possessed even into his sixties, more than the way he could shrug off pain when he hurt himself on the job.

It was the way he acted, the way he carried himself. If I had to choose one word to describe his personality, it would have to be "solid." He knew who he was, and he never deviated from it. He was honest, brutally so at times. He never wavered from what he felt was right. I didn't always agree with his opinions or his actions, but I never, ever, felt anything but respect for him. He had the bearing of a man who could, and would, act when necessary, no matter the danger, no matter the risk. Although I knew him late in his life, it was not hard to imagine him showing great bravery in war. I don't really know how much action he saw in Europe, since men like him do not talk often of such things, but I have full faith in the idea that he acted when he had to. I even had one demonstration of it in my own life.

I was at the small cabin that my grandparents used on weekends in upstate New York. My grandfather and I were working near the tool shed one summer afternoon. I must have been about nine. I pulled the shed's door open and inadvertently disturbed a hornets' nest. Those nasty little kamikazes came buzzing out ready to sting the hell out of me! Grandpa shoved me aside and started to yell at me. For a second I thought he was scolding me, and then I realized he was telling me to run. He wouldn't let those angry insects go after me. He took the full attack for me…and he was covered in stings when it was all over. My grandmother gave him some cold rags and ice to put on the painful stings, and then he acted like nothing had happened at all; not one groan of misery, not one complaint. Solid!

A few years later, he was waging a war against cancer, a war he was destined to lose. He was home, but we all knew he'd be back in the hospital before too long. He was smaller, having lost the muscular build he had had for so long. He could barely stand, let alone do much else. Still, he would not let Grandma help him with "personal" matters. He would not subject her to that. He had spent the forty-five years since the war building things. He could make anything. Most of the furniture in their house was handmade, but you'd never know it by sight! Even in his weakened, dying state, he tried to live up to what he had always been. One afternoon, he forced himself up from the bed, took the long walk into the bathroom, refusing help as always. He came out a few minutes later. In his hands was a small block of wood that had been in the bathroom for the purpose of holding the window open. My grandmother asked what he was doing with it. Without hesitation, as if just for a moment he was his old, strong self again, he replied, "I want to make something for you." Solid!

Any time any of you readers read one of my pulp stories, every time you find me writing about some hero, some tough private eye, or war hero, or federal agent, the kinds who just won't quit no matter what, you can be sure I put a little of my grandfather into that character, even though I might not have realized it at the time.

It wasn't only him. He was one of many, many men who went off to fight that war, and other wars, and came back "solid." But he was the one I knew, the one who showed me how to be a man. When I was a kid, he was my best friend. Now that I'm older and he's no longer here, he's one of my heroes. He was the one who encouraged my creativity the most when I was small. He grew up wanting to be a cartoonist. The war took away that opportunity, for he had to find work when he came back home; no time for drawing pictures anymore! But he never complained about opportunities lost; not once.

I'm glad I didn't turn down Ron Fortier's request for these stories. My grandfather wouldn't have wanted me to.

So, I took the job that Ron gave me, and I wrote my aviation stories. I think they turned out all right. As my first real war stories, I'd like to dedicate them to two groups of men. First, the ball players who left behind their fame and fortune and put their careers on hold to do their duty to their country; and second, to the men who never knew fame or fortune, but also went and did what they had to do. Those were the men who went off and fought for us all and, if they were lucky enough to survive the experience, came home and worked to bring up the next generation of Americans. They didn't talk too much about what they did or what they saw over there, but we knew they had done their jobs, for we could look at them and see men who were solid. Corporal Ross R. Muse (1921-1990) was the one who meant so much to me personally; he is still the finest man I have ever known, but they were all heroes.

"Conspiracy of Terror"

by
Van Allen Plexico

Like some monstrous, malformed bat, the jet-black seaplane swooped in low over the nighttime waters off the eastern shore of Long Island. Its twin Pratt and Whitney radials purred as it hugged the choppy surface, racing for land. Moonlight peeked through the heavy cloud cover and dappled over its hull, revealing the ungainly yet somehow elegant shape of a Sikorsky 1-S38—a flying boat.

"There," came the harsh, barking tone of a shadowy figure seated directly behind the pilot. A gloved hand snapped out, motioning at the murky vista barely visible through the cabin windows. "You see, ja? Just ahead."

The pilot frowned, lines creasing his rough-hewn visage. He peered into the dim distance, then saw where the other was pointing and nodded. Throttling back, he settled the big ship gently onto the top of a roller, and sent it gliding inland, toward the now-visible mouth of a hidden cove.

Within moments, the flying boat had coasted across the relatively gentle waters of the cove. As it bumped softly against the end of a pier, the four passengers stood, anxious to move. The co-pilot clambered out first and secured the Sikorsky, and then the door swung open and the four men emerged: four bizarre figures, standing stock-still in the eerie moonlight. The co-pilot glanced at them, then looked nervously away—though not before seeing that three of them carried odd, spherical objects in their hands.

The newcomers all paused there for a moment, standing rigidly, the air of military men about them. They took in their surroundings, gazing up from the dock area to the sloping, grassy hillside beyond, and finally to the ancient gothic mansion that loomed high above them, lights dancing in its windows.

"We have drilled carefully," their leader hissed, turning to face one of them after the other. "You all know what to do. Do not fail me!"

With that, three of the men lifted over their heads the spherical objects they carried—strange, glassy helmets—and brought them down, latching them in place. Brandishing rifles and pistols of an unorthodox, futuristic design, they trudged up the hillside toward the mansion.

The leader watched them go for a few seconds, then brushed off the tuxedo he wore and turned to the co-pilot, who was anxiously crouching next to the Sikorsky.

"Wait here. Be ready."

The co-pilot looked up at the awful countenance that faced him, swallowed nervously, and nodded.

"Ja, it will be as you say, Herr Terror."

At that, the leader smiled grimly and turned to walk toward the boat house. Before he reached it, he paused and gazed briefly out to sea, his eyes seeking the U-boat he knew would be there, somewhere.

Then, nodding to himself in satisfaction, he sank into the shadowy recesses of the boat house. But before the door closed behind him, the dim moonlight once more pierced the clouds and revealed his face—the leering grin of a hideous skull!

....the dim moonlight...revealed ...the leering face of a hideous skull!

Your luck has deserted you well and good this fine evenin', me boyo," Paddy O'Brien chuckled, raking in a pile of chips from the center of the table.

"I'm just gettin' started," the Irishman across from him retorted good naturedly, cracking his thick knuckles and hunkering over the table. "Deal the cards."

It was an hour earlier, and Barney O'Dare sat in a local dive he frequented along the waterfront. The joint's owner, his occasional poker buddy, Paddy O'Brien, sat grinning just across from him. Two other locals sat on either side of him, neither of them any happier than Barney with Paddy's lucky streak.

He glanced at his watch and saw that he still had a little more time before he was due to pick up his employer, the noted ballistics expert, Kerry Keen. Keen was currently dining with some acquaintances at the finest hotel in the area, and was then expected to attend another function—some kind of high-falutin' shindig, as Barney had put it—later that evening at Darkenmoor Manor. That wasn't for a while yet, though, so Keen had graciously allowed Barney to drop him off and then go tend to his own business. That business, of course, had led Barney straight to Paddy's.

After picking up Keen and delivering him to the shindig, Barney planned to head back to Keen's estate, Graylands, and the secret aircraft hangar located there. Then he could spend a leisurely couple of hours poring over the 2000-h.p. Pratt and Whitney Double Wasp engine of the new Black Bullet—the aircraft belonging to the mysterious Griffon! And, on the way, maybe he'd pick up a few extra bottles of his beloved O'Doul's Dew, too, since he recalled now that his supply was dwindling. As long, that was, as he didn't lose his shirt in this game.

Paddy dealt out the next hand, a big pile of chips in front of him, as Barney reached for his ever-present bottle of that self-same O'Doul's Dew. Taking a snort of it, he coughed, then sighed contentedly. "Ah, that's the stuff," he muttered.

"Still drinkin' that rot, are ye, Barney?" Paddy teased him.

"Arrrr-rh! Ye can't beat this sweet nectar, Paddy. O'Doul's Dew fer fightin' men!" He grinned at his old friend. "Now I feel a bit of luck comin' on."

Paddy rolled his eyes theatrically and started to reply. Just then the door flew open and two men entered. Barney glanced up at them and frowned, not recognizing them. But Paddy grinned and nodded.

"Come on over, fellas," he told them. "Grab some chairs." And then, as a soft aside to Barney, "These two have been comin' by for the better part of the last two weeks. Good fellas, but not great conversationalists." He snickered. "But their money spends as well as yours does!"

At that, Barney gave his friend a sour look, then glanced sideways over at the two new arrivals, taking their measure.

Big, strapping fellows with close-cropped blond hair, wearing black jumpsuits, they walked over and seated themselves. Paddy dealt them in. One set a nearly-empty bottle of whiskey on the table. They greeted Paddy with accents that, despite being slurred, Barney easily identified as German.

Time passed swiftly, Barney made something of a comeback, and several rounds of O'Doul's Dew and other beverages of questionable quality and vintage were consumed. The two new arrivals warmed up and exchanged a bit of banter with the regulars. Then, even as Barney prepared to make his excuses and head for home, he suddenly found himself listening to the story one of the new guys was telling. Quickly he settled back into his seat, his ears perking up.

"The operation is tonight, at Darkenmoor Manor," the man was saying. "Herr Vogler's terror weapon will strike fear into the hearts of anyone who opposes the—"

A fist smashed down on the table, startling everyone present. Barney blinked, looked up, and saw that it belonged to the other German, who now leaned across the table and glared angrily at his companion.

"Silence! No more!"

The other, chastened, nodded and sat back. Both of the men were clearly sober now.

Barney took all of this in, the gears in his mind turning. Then, swallowing another slug of O'Doul's, he summoned up his best poker face, sat there impassively through two more hands—he couldn't remember later whether he won or lost them—and then made his excuses and left. Climbing into the long, black Dusenberg he had parked there earlier, he revved the powerful motor and tore out of the parking lot, racing for the hotel where his boss, Kerry Keen, was dining.

Behind him, in the parking lot of the bar, a shadowy figure watched him go. A second later, the man climbed into his own deep blue DKW F5 Meisterklasse sedan, started up the engine, and pulled out on the trail of the Dusenberg.

"My dear, I can assure you the study of ballistics is neither stuffy nor tedious."

Kerry Keen, dressed in an elegant tuxedo and with an ingratiating smile spreading across his face, leaned closer toward the high society blonde seated across from him. All around in the hotel's grand dining room, the buzz of gossip and the dull roar of monotonous conversations among monarchs of industry and sons of fabulous wealth assaulted him—yet he scarcely allowed his discomfort to show.

The sounds Keen truly longed to hear, however, were the buzz and the roar of the 2000-h.p. Pratt and Whitney he had improbably installed in his new, heavily modified Yakovlev monoplane chassis. While he occasionally found himself missing the old, water-cooled, Czechoslovakian-manufactured Avia W-44 engine that had driven his previous craft, the sheer speed and raw power of his new Black Bullet more than compensated for the loss of the old amphibian. And indeed he and his able assistant, Barney O' Dare, had agreed to put in some work on that self-same engine later that evening.

Trapped at this dinner party for the moment, though, and with no action to distract him as of yet, he had decided to make the best of things.

Thus he was quite startled when, just as he had his lovely companion's full attention and had nearly convinced her of the many joys and excitements of the world of ballistics study, none other than

Barney himself sidled up to him, leaning close.

"Time to go, boss," the little Irishman muttered into his ear.

Keen glanced at Barney, frowning. The little man wore his full chauffeur's uniform, cap in hand.

"You're early."

"Something's come up. Something I think you'll be wantin' to hear about."

Keen looked at his friend intently, the playboy expression he affected so easily now banished. He started to nod, and then caught the eye of the blonde across from him. She could tell something was up, and she appeared distressed. Smoothly, the easy smile returning to his face, Keen moved around O'Dare and leaned in toward the lady.

"I'm afraid duty calls, my dear. But I do hope to see you again, sometime soon."

The blonde blushed and returned his smile.

"Certainly, Mr. Keen. Do call on me when you have the chance."

With another smile and a slight bow, Keen turned and followed the very obviously upset Barney out of the hall and down the steps to the front door of the hotel.

"See here," Keen said tensely to O'Dare when they'd gotten down the stairs and away from the crowd. "What's gotten into you?"

Barney didn't bother to look back at him. Instead he pushed past the startled butler at the door and led Keen out into the crisp evening air, heading him toward the sleek, black Dusenberg that sat parked near the exit of the circular driveway.

Trusting his redheaded assistant implicitly, but still insatiably curious, Keen seated himself in the back of the long automobile and waited as Barney turned the engine over and guided the big car out onto the main road.

"Now will you tell me just what has you so distraught?" Keen demanded.

"O'course I will," Barney replied, glancing back at his boss nervously. "I was down at Paddy O'Brien's, and, well…"

Barney laid out the gist of what he'd heard, even as he steered seventeen thousand dollars' worth of mechanical precision and automotive luxury out onto a narrow highway running along the edge of the sea. Moonlight dappled down on the waves lapping at the cliff face, far below.

Keen listened closely to what little his friend could tell him. Upon mention of the name "Herr Vogler" he perked up.

"Vogler, eh? Yes, I know that name. A noted weapons innovator in Germany. I've heard rumors recently that he had fled the Nazi regime and might be coming to the States, but—"

"There's more, boss," Barney said. He described the rest of the brief conversation.

"A terror weapon. Well." Keen shook his head. "War has never been a pretty thing, Barney, but I fear this new, modern age we live in, will usher in horrors beyond all comprehension." He gazed out the window at the moon racing alongside. "The days when men settled disputes with their hard-won skills, on the field of honor, are probably gone forever."

O'Dare could only nod his agreement. Then, "So, whaddya think he means? At Darkenmoor Manor?"

"I don't know," Keen replied. "But we had best be on our guard. I—"

At that moment, headlights shone through the back window of the car, nearly blinding Barney as he attempted to navigate along the winding road.

"Ahh!"

Cursing, Barney raised a hand to shield his eyes, as the car drew closer—dangerously closer—its bright lights flooding their own car.

"What're ya doin' back there?"

Moments later, the other vehicle had caught up behind them, almost to the point of banging bumpers together. Another moment, and that's exactly what happened.

"Fer cryin' out loud, what's this lunatic doin'?" Barney cried, struggling to keep the Dusenberg on the narrow strip of highway.

Kerry Keen knew from hard experience exactly what the driver of the other vehicle was doing—trying to kill them! Leaning over and reaching under the seat, he sought the Colt .45 he kept hidden there for just such emergencies.

Before his anxious fingers could close over the weapon's handle, a hail of gunfire smashed through the back window, shattering it into a thousand flying shards. Crying out, Barney slung the big car to the left side of the road—and then the right rear window exploded as well!

Keen peeked over the now-open side window space, wind gusting in his face, and saw a deep blue DKW F5 Meisterklasse sedan coming right at him. He lurched to his left just as the German car smashed into the right side of his Dusenberg.

"You okay up there?" he called to O'Dare.

"Oh, sure, I'm right as rain," Barney hollered back, his every muscle and nerve locked in a struggle with the big car's steering wheel and pedals. "I'd be a lot better, though, if this maniac weren't tryin' to murder us!"

Just then, amid another hail of bullets, the cars banged violently together again, and Keen dove to the floorboards. His hand shot out, grasped the handle of the Colt in its hidden compartment, pulled it free, and raised it to point through the empty window frame.

"Let's see if I can do something about that, then," he called to his chauffeur.

The .45 spat round after round of deadly lead at the DKW. The first two shots missed entirely, but the third struck the windshield just ahead of the driver's door, creating a mad spider's web pattern across the glass. The fourth smashed the front side window to pieces. Keen ducked back down and reloaded as Barney fought the wheel.

The DKW swerved back and forth, nearly out of control. Then it straightened its path and veered closer, its engine roaring in competition with that of the Dusenberg. A hand reached out the back window, a pistol clutched in the fingers. Keen raised his Colt again and unloaded at the driver, firing shot after shot, emptying the big gun into the space where the front window had once been, as well as the door and the rest of the car. The already-cracked front windshield disintegrated as hands flailed out through the now-open windows.

The DKW shuddered, careening back and forth. Keen had an

instant's glimpse of the driver, now slumped forward over the wheel. Then the German car skidded to one side and shot out over the cliff's edge.

"Barney! Stop the car!"

As O'Dare brought the charging Dusenberg to an abrupt halt and pulled it onto the highway's shoulder, Keen looked back over his shoulder and watched in fascinated horror as the other automobile tumbled down, down through the darkness. Flames blossomed from its sides an instant before it plunged into the cold, unforgiving embrace of the choppy waters of the Atlantic.

Moments later, Keen and O'Dare stood at the cliff's edge, staring down at the dark sea. No signs of the events of moments earlier remained. It was as if nothing had happened here at all.

Keen frowned, thinking.

Barney, still nervous, scratched at his chin. "Who could that've been? Why'd they want to kill us?"

Kerry Keen shook his head in frustration.

"No way to know now."

"I guess not."

"Or rather," Keen added, in afterthought, "nothing to be learned here."

With that, he turned and strode back toward the Dusenberg.

Barney watched him go for a couple of seconds, puzzled. Then, with one last look down at the black waters, he sighed and followed Keen back to the car.

Half an hour later, Barney parked the somewhat worse-for-wear Dusenberg outside Darkenmoor Manor while Keen strode through the front door. He wore an opera hat perched on his head at a slight angle and his long, black cloak flared behind him. Despite the outward appearance of indifference, however, Keen was on his guard, his mind working over the meager set of clues he had accumulated so far.

Entering the grand ballroom, he nodded to a few acquaintances and looked around. A small orchestra played lilting music off to one side, while several couples danced and others milled about, deep in conversation. Waiters attired in fine tuxedos moved among them, bearing trays of expensive champagnes and hors d'oeuvres. Most of this was lost on Keen. His attention was firmly centered on searching for any signs of trouble, as his eyes flicked from one face to the next. Before he could even attempt to piece anything together, however, he was noticed by an elegant older woman in a deep blue dress, wearing diamonds and pearls. She emerged from the crowd of well-dressed attendees and approached him.

"Mr. Keen! How good of you to come."

Keen bowed and kissed the woman's hand.

"A pleasure, Lady Darkenmoor."

After a moment's small talk, the white-haired woman nodded across the wide room to where a cluster of gentlemen stood, all of them listening intently to the excited tones of the man at the center of their group.

"Have you met Herr Vogler yet, Mr. Keen?"

That got Keen's attention.

"He's fled the Nazis," she went on, "and is now helping our government."

"Why, no, Lady—I haven't met him. Would you be so kind as to introduce us?"

Lady Darkenmoor smiled and nodded, leading Keen across the room to where the tight circle of men stood. Upon seeing their hostess, they paused in their conversation and greeted her.

"Kerry Keen," the Lady Darkenmoor said, "this is Herr Ernst Vogler. Herr Vogler, I present Kerry Keen, one of our noted experts in..." The lady paused, seeking the correct word.

"Munitions, ja," Vogler finished for her, his German accent thick. "I have heard of your work, Mr. Keen. I hope we might be able to work together in the future. To accomplish something memorable."

Keen smiled and nodded, then took a glass of champagne from the tray of a passing waiter.

One of the other men leaned in toward Keen and interjected, "Vogler here says he has invented a weapon that you might be particularly interested in, Keen. One that will—how did you put it?" He smiled at Vogler. "Ah, yes—a weapon that will 'strike fear into the hearts of the enemy.'" He laughed nervously.

"Sounds like a very useful weapon to me," Keen replied. "I would like to learn more about it."

"Soon," Herr Vogler replied with a cryptic smile. "Soon, you will, Mr. Keen."

Keen nodded, sipping his drink. "Excellent."

After a few more moments of small talk, Keen excused himself and crossed the room once more, intending to ask the Lady Darkenmoor about anyone else of note in attendance. But before he could locate the high society hostess, angry and confused shouts and a woman's scream pierced the low roar of conversation. The orchestra stopped playing immediately, and the sounds of discord grew louder. Suddenly a trio of men in bizarre gray jumpsuits burst from the crowd, surrounding the group that included Herr Vogler.

Keen started forward, then hesitated, his mind working feverishly. Quickly he melted back into the crowd, but he never took his eyes from the tableau playing out in the center of the ballroom.

The three men wore outlandish, spherical helmets that distorted their faces and their voices. Each of them carried something that looked like a rifle, but included odd, seemingly futuristic accessories. Now they barked heavily-accented orders at the people around Vogler, brandishing the weapons at the high society crowd, forcing them back. One of them grasped a now-shaking Vogler by the arm and pulled him away, nearly stumbling over his own feet, toward the rear entrance of the ballroom.

"Nein—no, no! No, help me," he cried, before being dragged through the doorway, gone.

Keen watched all of this transpire with surprise and intense interest. Then, in an instant, his hand closed on the knob of a door that led into a small broom closet. Stepping quickly inside, he collapsed his opera hat, drew a scarlet mask from his pocket and pulled it down over his face, and flipped his long cloak inside out, so that its flat black exterior now bore no resemblance to the light gray cape he had worn before.

Satisfied, he stepped back outside the door, Kerry Keen no longer—now the Griffon!

He emerged just in time to see a new figure enter the ballroom from the doorway through which Vogler had been dragged, seconds earlier. As others saw this newcomer as well, a much greater hue and cry came forth, women screaming and swooning, men recoiling in fear.

The man who had just entered wore a dark gray jumpsuit, similar to the other interlopers. In place of his head, however, the hideous features of a leering skull peered out at the wealthy patrons of society.

"I am the Terror!" he cackled, his voice eerily distorted.

The people fell back, clearing out a broad circle around the man.

"Herr Vogler is now my prisoner. The ransom demands will be communicated soon. Make no effort to follow me or my men."

And before anyone could move or respond, the Terror reached up and twisted a dial centered on the chest of his jumpsuit. Instantly, the crowd wailed in fear—an overwhelming, irrational, inexplicable fear that seemed to wash over them. Not a fear coming from inside, but some strange, external force that gripped them in its awful talons and raked at their very souls.

The Griffon had started forward, only to find himself equally caught up in this terrible sensation of fear. He faltered, stumbling to one side, nearly losing his balance, as the society patrons pushed past him, fleeing. Some small part of his mind, still rational, tried to tell him there was nothing here to be afraid of—just four men in silly get-ups. But the vast majority of his mental faculties would have none of such reasoning. His mind quailed before onslaught of horror, and he went down to one knee, sweating profusely.

As he kneeled, struggling to regain his composure, he glanced around and saw the other attendees still quailing in fear, most of them trying to flee the room. All except one. Just to his right, a younger woman with blonde hair, clad in a sea-green dress, stood perfectly erect, her only expression a deeply-furrowed brow, as she gazed with uncomprehending puzzlement at the tableau unfolding around her.

And then the sensation of fear evaporated, as if it had never been—as if a switch had been thrown, Keen immediately thought. The people fighting to squeeze through the front doorway stopped in their wrestling and wrangling and gawked at one another, apparently only now aware of their actions. A general roar of questioning and apologizing swelled up, replacing the sounds of mortal terror that had filled the room only an instant earlier.

By that time, the Griffon was back on his feet, seeking signs of the four figures who had brought such discord with them. He managed three steps across the room, toward the rear exit, when someone pointed at him and cried out, "Look there!" Another followed with, "It's the Griffon!"

"Blast it!"

The Griffon looked around, seeing the people on every side recoiling in surprise and fear once more—this time a more rational fear, though; one based on a known quantity. The Griffon, for all the good work Keen had managed in that guise, remained a somewhat villainous figure in the eyes of much of the public. It was time, he knew, to take his leave.

"You there," cried a younger, tuxedo-clad man across the room, who had recovered his wits somewhat more quickly than the others and now started forward. "I say! Stop!"

Several men got up the nerve to join him and together they rushed forward. The Griffon saw them, and his first reaction was to think, "Sure—they're probably embarrassed about their actions a few moments ago, and are trying to appear brave in the eyes of their ladies now. Not that that does me any good!"

The scarlet-masked man sprinted across the ballroom, just ahead of the gang out to grab him. Leaping over a broad oaken table, his black cloak flaring behind him, he kicked the table back toward the men, who scattered as it clattered into them. Then he dashed through the same doorway the interlopers had passed through some seconds before. He emerged onto a broad, oaken deck and raced past several surprised guests.

"Stop that man!"

"It's the Griffon! He's abducted Herr Vogler!"

"Stop him!"

As the shouting pursuers emerged onto the deck, the Griffon spun one way, then the other, his cape flaring. They moved to cut off all exits, and slowly closed in on him. He did not hesitate at all. Turning, he raced towards the edge of the deck, vaulted over the railing, and plunged down into the darkness.

It was the Griffon! He's getting away!"

The pursuers rushed up to the railing and leaned out, peering down.

"Where is he?"

"He couldn't have jumped that far down!"

"Where could he have gone?"

"I don't see him!"

The men stood there a few moments longer, squinting into the dim night, their eyes moving back and forth across the broad, sloping lawn that trailed down to the boathouse and the shore beyond. There was no sign of anyone, be it the Griffon, Herr Vogler, or the man who called himself the Terror.

Finally, disappointed, they turned and hurried back into the manor house.

A few feet below, the Griffon dangled from the bottom of the deck, having swung himself back far enough that he could not be seen from above. Sensing that his pursuers had given up at last, he exhaled slowly and then swung out with aching fingers, releasing his grip in mid-arc, and dropped a dozen feet to land on a broad, horizontal support beam. His keen sense of balance saved him from a nasty plunge down to the lawn, far below. Pausing to recover for just a moment, he looked around and spotted a much smaller balcony projecting out from the mansion, off to one side and slightly below him. Quickly he grasped another beam with his tired hands and swung out again, this time dropping hard on the small deck.

"This has turned out to be a far more eventful party than the Lady Darkenmoor ever expected, I'd wager," he muttered to himself as he grasped the vertical railing beside the balcony and began to climb upwards, level by level.

Reaching the top floor, he swung back out again and landed on another small balcony that projected outside a pair of bedrooms. Perching there a moment, he pulled off the scarlet mask, flipped his cloak around again, and replaced his opera hat atop his head. Thus it was Kerry Keen and not the Griffon who walked casually through the ornate French doors and back into the manor house.

Five minutes later, after having washed his hands and brushed his clothes, he lit a cigarette and strolled casually down the grand stairway of the manor.

"Well, well, well," came an all-too-familiar voice from below. "Look who's here."

Keen sought the source of the comment, found it, and inwardly groaned.

"Ah, Inspector Lang, of the Department of Justice," he said, addressing the rumpled, unkempt figure in gray who stood below, staring hard up at him. "How...pleasant...to see you again. What brings you here, old boy?"

"You don't know?"

Keen shrugged. "I know there was some sort of trouble earlier, but not the cause of it."

Drury Lang continued to glare at him for a long moment, then rubbed his chin and looked away.

"This fellow Vogler—some kind of German scientist—has been kidnapped. It happened right here, just a little while ago. And of course here you are, Keen—as usual." Lang turned toward him again, a foul expression on his face. "But I'm sure you don't know anything about it."

"Certainly not," Keen replied with a smile. "I had stepped upstairs—to freshen up, as they say. Then I heard a commotion going on down here, and felt it advisable to stay out of the way for a bit."

Lang was nodding, as if he'd heard this same story from Keen a thousand times. In fact, he pretty much had. In the meantime, a local police operative joined them, introducing himself as Detective Monroe.

"And so," Lang went on, "unlike everyone else at this shindig, you didn't see the Griffon."

"The Griffon? He's here?" Keen looked around, his eyes wide. "Where?"

"He's long gone," Monroe replied. Meanwhile, Lang sighed, reached up and rubbed at his tired, bloodshot eyes with the heel of his left hand. "I have no doubt he's in league with this 'Terror,' though."

"Terror?"

Monroe sketched a quick recap of what had happened.

"The Griffon and the Terror," Keen said when he was done. "My, my. Well, I'm sorry I missed them." He offered the detective a cigarette from his silver case. The man politely declined.

"Yeah, yeah. Fine," Lang was muttering to no one in particular. "Just fine."

"So let me get this straight," Keen said then, replacing his case in his coat pocket. "You believe the Griffon is involved in the kidnapping of this man, Vogler? Whatever for?"

"For ransom money, of course," Lang told him.

"The demand just came in," Monroe said. "They want five million dollars!"

Keen whistled.

"Not a bad chunk of change, huh, Keen?" Lang snorted. "I doubt even you could fetch that much!" The detective was grinning; apparently the notion of someone abducting Keen had revived the inspector's spirits somewhat.

"I don't know who would be willing to pay that much for Vogler, though," Detective Monroe added. "Maybe he has some rich relatives here in the States."

"The U.S. Government will be paying, I'm certain," Keen stated flatly.

"What do you mean?"

"Vogler is rumored to have developed some sort of weapon that will strike fear, as he has put it, into the hearts of his enemies."

"That sounds a lot like what I've been hearing from the folks here tonight," Lang growled.

"Indeed," Keen said, nodding. Then he glanced over to the far side of the room and saw the blonde woman he'd noticed earlier, during the attack.

"Detective," he said, "do you know that young woman there? The one in the green dress?"

Monroe followed Keen's gaze, then smiled and nodded.

"Oh, sure. That's Helen Lilley. She's very popular around this area."

"Ah," Keen replied, nodding. "So that's Helen Lilley. I've heard of her, but have never had the pleasure."

Lang grumbled impatiently and opened his mouth to say something, but Keen cut him off.

"Just a moment," he said. "I believe she's about to leave, and I simply must speak with her for a moment." He nodded to the other man. "Excuse me, Detective, Inspector."

Monroe smiled and nodded to him as he strode away.

"Yeah, well, good luck with that," Lang called to Keen caustically, as if he knew something the other man did not.

Keen walked up behind the blonde woman and, adopting his most genteel air, said, "Pardon me, ma'am, but my name is Kerry Keen, and I would very much like to speak with you for a moment."

The woman did not move; did not even acknowledge his presence.

Keen came up short, frowning.

Clearly, she must not have heard me, he thought to himself.

He cleared his throat and tried again.

"Excuse me, Miss Lilley, but—"

The woman was walking away from him now!

Startled, Keen stood absolutely still for a long couple of seconds, out of his depths, wondering what to do. Never had a woman treated him this way before. Never! Why, she had not even bothered to—

And then an older man came up to the blonde from just ahead of her, raised his hands, and began to move them in a very deliberate fashion. The woman stopped, seemed to watch the man for a moment,

"Of course," Keen whispered to himself.

then duplicated his gestures.

"Of course," Keen whispered to himself. And then, his mind now racing, three steps ahead of anyone else in the room, "Yes. Of course."

He strode purposefully back across the room, heading for the doorway.

"Strike fear into their hearts," he muttered. "Oh, yes."

He crossed the driveway in a near-run. Motioning for Barney, he climbed into the Dusenberg, and together they raced back to Graylands.

"Whatcha workin' on there?" Barney asked, setting down a big wrench and reaching for a smaller one from his work table.

"I'm sorry—what?"

Kerry Keen frowned, then put his hands to his ears and removed a small object from each of them.

"Ah, that's better. What were you saying?"

"Nothin'," Barney replied, looking puzzled. "Just that the Bullet'll be ready in a few minutes. I just have ta replace a couple of these—" His voice trailed away as he climbed back under the engine cowling and resumed banging away at something.

"Good, good."

Keen clambered up onto one wing and looked the plane over with open admiration. A heavily modified Yakovlev monoplane prototype, he had acquired it by way of one Anthony Edwards, owner of Edwards International, a New York-based importing company. Edwards had been dealing via the black market with rogue elements from the Soviet defense establishment who were looking to make a quick American buck. Keen, in his guise as the Griffon, had busted up the black market ring, exposed several communist agents as well as Edwards's own illicit and treacherous dealings, and taken as his reward the black and silver vehicle that filled Keen's secret hangar now.

Edwards previously had made a number of modifications to the basic Yak design, and Keen and O'Dare had picked up right where he'd left off. Streamlined pontoons projected down from beneath the plane's slightly inverted gull wings, allowing the ship to land on water as well as on land, and the folding landing gear were modified to perform perfectly in either situation. A glass cowling completely covered the two cockpits, and Barney had immediately fitted Skoda sound-dampening mufflers to the engine. Six half-inch Browning machine guns resided inside the wings, three to a wing. Capping things off, the gleaming silver image of a griffon adorned the tops of those wings of the otherwise unmarked aircraft.

As much as Keen appreciated the plane's sharp lines, radical styling, and overwhelming firepower, Barney's true affection for the plane centered on the 2000-h.p. Pratt and Whitney Double Wasp engine that turned the oversized propeller. In proper form, that power plant would push the ship along at more than four hundred miles per hour.

"Nice and quick," Barney muttered to himself as he worked. "Quick to take care of business. And quicker to get me back here, to me O'Doul's Dew, too!"

"And able to execute that special barrel roll maneuver we talked about, as well," Keen added with a grin. "I'm looking forward to trying it."

"Not with me on board, you ain't," Barney shot back. "I like my lunch in my belly, where it's supposed ta be."

Keen laughed good-naturedly and went back to work on the two small objects he held in one hand.

Moments later, as Barney closed the cowling and put away his tools, Keen flipped on the radio that sat on a nearby workbench and tuned in the local station.

"She's all set," Barney reported. "Everything looks just—"

"Wait! Listen to this," Keen barked as Barney strode over.

The two men listened intently as the voice on the radio repeated an announcement: "Sources have revealed the intention of the U.S. Government to pay the ransom of five million dollars to the kidnappers of Ernst Vogler, noted German scientist and munitions expert. While the usual policy is not to give in to such demands, Vogler has been determined to be of sufficient potential value to the military that he must be returned at all costs. More on this story as it develops. In other news—"

Keen flipped off the radio, frowning deeply.

Barney whistled softly.

"Five million bucks," he whispered. "All for one guy."

But Keen was not listening. His mind worked frantically, feverishly, turning over everything he knew, sifting through it all.

"They vanished from the Darkenmoor estate with no one seeing them leave," he said softly, mostly to himself. "And they must be lurking somewhere nearby, awaiting the ransom payment."

"Stands ta reason," Barney agreed, nodding.

"Germans," Keen whispered, then repeated it: "Germans... That could mean..." His voice drifted off, his eyes narrowing.

"Mean what?" O'Dare scratched his head and gazed up at his boss, looking for all the world like some great Irish hound, fierce but deeply loyal.

Keen barked a short laugh then. He turned to O'Dare.

"The fools," he growled.

Barney nodded automatically. Then he paused, wrinkled his brow, and glanced up at his employer.

"Um—which fools would ya be referrin' to, then?"

"Both of them," Keen replied. He dashed to a nearby workbench and snatched up his flight goggles. "The so-called Terror, for failing to cover his tracks better. And the government men, for giving in so easily."

O'Dare watched Keen racing back and forth, collecting various items from around the workshop.

"But what else could they do?"

Keen's face had spread into a broad grin. He leapt up onto the Black Bullet and swung over and into the front cockpit, pulling the goggles down over his face.

"This," he called down to his assistant—and now it was the Griffon who spoke, not Kerry Keen. "This is what else they could do. Come on!"

With a deep sigh, O'Dare trundled up the side of the amphibian and seated himself in the copilot's seat. Keen closed the canopy over them and kicked the powerful engine to life.

"Oh, me heavens," Barney muttered. "I have a bad feelin' I'm gonna be doin' some repair work on this baby, before the night's done."

Moments later, the hidden doorway to the secret hangar slid soundlessly open and a sleek, black shape emerged, gliding across the waters. It sped up as it went, water splashing from underneath its fuselage. Then, mere seconds later, it reared back and leapt into the sky.

Now well past midnight, the moon's bright face had fallen closer to the horizon, its pale light dappling wildly across the waters of the Atlantic. High above, the Black Bullet raced across the nighttime skies, its Skoda mufflers engaged and keeping its powerful engine as quiet as possible.

Within a remarkably short time, the almost unrecognizably modified Yakovlev had covered the distance between Graylands and the Darkenmoor estate. As they neared the ancient manor house, the Griffon angled his aircraft out to sea, moving briskly along, high above the waves. When they were a little more than a mile offshore, he curved their flight path around into a long loop.

"Keep a sharp eye out," the Griffon called over the muffled sound of the Pratt and Whitney.

"For what?"

"For anything!"

Barney grumbled back something unintelligible but leaned out, his eyes sweeping across sea and air.

For nearly an hour they saw nothing. Barney's spirits began to flag, and even the Griffon had almost come to think he'd led them on a fool's errand. But then—

"There! That light. Do you see it?"

Barney followed the Griffon's pointing hand down, down...

"Yep! I see it. It's—it's—hey, what the devil is that?"

Far below, a mere glint against the pitch-black waters of the North Atlantic, flickered a light. It had appeared as if from nowhere, in the midst of an empty sea, and now it snapped on and off, on and off, as if passing along some coded signal.

Instantly Keen dipped the Black Bullet and sent the craft zooming down toward the waters, the Skoda mufflers doing their job.

"Ooh, we're askin' for trouble now," Barney said as the Black Bullet closed in on the source of the light. "I don't much feel like a swim tonight."

"Quiet," the Griffon hissed, maneuvering down, down, closer and closer. "We have to see just what this—" His voice trailed off in wonderment as the flickering light came into view.

"There's nothing there," Barney exclaimed. "How can that be?"

Indeed, at the point on the surface of the ocean where the light flashed, no ship or even small boat floated along. The light appeared to hover in mid-air, just above the surface.

"Wait—there, you see it?"

The Griffon pointed down, and Barney, squinting, could just make out what his boss was talking about: a slender tube, no more than a few inches thick, extended up from the surface, the light flashing at its tip.

For one horrifying second, Barney found himself at a complete loss, unable to fathom precisely what he was seeing. Then, in an even and unsurprised tone, the Griffon said the words that made it all snap into clear focus for him:

"A U-boat."

O'Dare exhaled slowly, sweat trailing down his face. "Yeah," he muttered. "A U-boat. O'course it is. What else could it be?" But then the tough little Irishman found his dissolving fear replaced by another feeling—one of confusion.

"What in heaven's name is it doin' here?"

"I think I know."

Quickly the Griffon pulled back on the stick and angled the Black Bullet upward, away from the U-boat, gaining altitude and circling around again.

"Yeah, I figured you probably did," Barney snorted. "But—"

His reply was cut off in mid-sentence as he became aware of another unexpected visitor to the area. He patted the Griffon on the shoulder and pointed down, through the clearing night sky, to a larger seaplane cruising along below, a short distance above the sea, headed along the same flight path the Black Bullet had just taken.

"Unless I'm very much mistaken," the airborne avenger observed, peering intently at the new arrival, "that is a Sikorsky 1-S38."

"Aye," Barney replied, nodding slowly, "that she is. And painted up just as black as we are. But where's she goin'?"

As if in reply to O'Dare's query, the signal light in the water snapped off, to be replaced moments later by a bright search beam that speared up, moving about madly from side to side.

"Uh-oh," Barney growled.

The Griffon gripped the stick tightly and curved the monoplane's path around, seeking to avoid the searchlight. Slowly, inexorably, however, it zeroed in on the Black Bullet, tracking their movement across the night sky.

"They know we're up here now, I think it's safe to say," the Griffon growled. Cursing, he dropped the Black Bullet, gathering speed, and angled his plane into a path to intercept the flying boat.

In response the Sikorsky, now obviously aware of their presence as well, dipped down itself, away from the Black Bullet, diving until it nearly skimmed the waves. Quickly it closed the distance between itself and the big spotlight.

"No sense in being stealthy now."

Gripping the controls tightly, and switching off the Skoda mufflers to gain added engine power, the Griffon pursued.

Even as they closed on their fleeing quarry, however, the Griffon and Barney O'Dare witnessed a sight that staggered their imaginations.

The area of the ocean from whence the light originated suddenly boiled.

"Lordy above," Barney gasped. "I must be seein' things!"

Up from the depths came a huge, gray-painted shape, like some vast, mechanical colossus rising out of the sea. The spotlight continued to shine up from its narrow conning tower, upon which was emblazoned a black emblem on red and white—a Nazi swastika.

arney O'Dare openly gawked at the dull-gray monstrosity that had emerged from the North Atlantic, just ahead of them.

"A U-boat, indeed," the Griffon stated flatly. "But such a U-boat! It's tremendous! I've never heard of such a thing."

Even more of the massive vessel continued to break through the surface, water streaming from its flat deck and down the dark gray, riveted sides. Now it loomed dead ahead. The flying boat, meanwhile, hit the rollers hard and came to a stop just short of the submarine's bulky side.

Barney's voice sounded as agitated as Keen had ever heard it. "Time to make ourselves scarce, then, don'cha think, boss?"

Before the Griffon could reply, yet another mind-staggering development transpired. As the two men watched, two great panels on the rear deck of the monstrous U-boat slid open and strange, latticework metal gantries extended upward.

"What do you make of those?" the masked avenger asked, peering down through the darkness.

Barney could think of no answer. He only shook his head. "Oh, I've got a bad feelin' about this," he groaned.

The Griffon didn't reply. Instead he jerked the monoplane's controls hard to the right, sending the jet-black aircraft twisting in a sharp curve, away from the U-boat. The Pratt and Whitney roared as he gunned it, pulling up again and sending the Black Bullet climbing skyward.

Barney glanced back over his shoulder. Two very oddly-shaped objects had emerged from the depths of the vast U-boat and moved up onto the gantries.

"What in th' name of all that's holy are they doin' now?"

Glancing back and down, the Griffon greeted this development with harsh laughter.

Barney gawked at his companion in the front seat with unmitigated surprise. Before he could ask, however, the Griffon made his feelings clear: "Fighter planes," he called back. "They're fighter planes! Now here's an enemy we can deal with."

"Saints preserve us," O'Dare coughed by way of reply. "I never thought I'd see the day we'd be grateful to have two German fighters comin' after us!"

The Griffon's grin spread wide as he pulled back on the stick and climbed high, high up over the frothing ocean. Wind whipped around the Black Bullet, its Pratt and Whitney motor humming splendidly. As if in response, far below on the deck of the U-boat, bright flames flared out in searing gouts to each side of the gantries.

"Rocket-assisted launch," the Griffon observed coldly. "I've heard of such things, but only in theory."

Instantly, he pulled back on the stick and sent the monoplane climbing higher and higher into the dark sky.

Seconds later, first one and then the other of the strange German fighter planes surged up in torrents of fire from the latticework cradles that had held them, hurtling skyward. Rocket engines throttling up, they roared into the nighttime sky over the Atlantic. At a frightening pace they shot upward, closing the distance between themselves and the Black Bullet rapidly.

"Natters!" the Griffon suddenly exclaimed.

Barney fought to keep the O'Doul's Dew he had imbibed earlier down where it belonged, as his employer moved the monoplane through a bewildering variety of convolutions.

"Natters?" the little Irishman cried. "Too right, it's all gone natters!"

"No, no," the Griffon replied, his eyes lighting up at the new challenge he perceived. "The rocket planes—they're called 'Natters.' I believe the translation is 'Vipers.'" He chewed at his lip as his mind worked to dredge up the information he had learned about the odd aircraft, some months earlier, from a munitions contact in Germany. "They're Ba-349s, to be precise. Made by Bachem. Their engines are said to generate nearly four thousand pounds of thrust. I'd heard the SS had them on the drawing board, but I never expected to meet one—let alone two!"

"Well, that's just dandy, then," Barney exclaimed. "Maybe you'd like to get us in even closer, so you can get a good look at 'em!"

"Exactly!"

"Hah?!"

The Griffon wheeled the Black Bullet around and accelerated directly toward the rocketing Natters. The plume of fire from the tail of each German plane stood out, clearly visible now, as the highly caustic mixture of hydrogen peroxide, hydrazine, and methanol combined to push them along at ghastly speeds.

"Do ya really think this is advisable?"

But there was no answer forthcoming to O'Dare's query. For Kerry Keen had remembered one other thing about the Ba-349s: they carried no armaments other than a nosecone full of Henschel Hs 217 Föhn unguided rockets. The German pilots would have no choice but to unleash a full, shotgun-like barrage of the fearsome weapons, all at once.

And that they did, one after the other, the noses of each plane popping off and the rockets blasting away. Twin salvoes of twenty-four missiles each streaked towards the Black Bullet.

"Hang on!"

The Griffon shoved the stick forward violently. Barney wailed in horror. The first fusillade of missiles shot just overhead, their exhausts nearly scorching the two intrepid American pilots.

The second barrage came less than a second later—just time enough for the Griffon to wrestle the stick to the right, fighting the powerful aircraft as if it were a living thing, trying with all his might to shove the plane by sheer strength and force of will out of the way of the buzzing cluster of death that came their way.

As that second salvo from the trailing Natter rushed at them, an excruciatingly long moment arrived for both men—one with gritted teeth, white-knuckled fingers gripping the plane's stick, the other hanging on for dear life. Time itself seemed to stand still, and every heartbeat was separated by a vast eon of time.

The Griffon's display of piloting skills in those brief moments topped anything Barney O'Dare had ever witnessed. Years later, when he would speak of this moment, he would utter carefully chosen words in a deeply reverent, hushed tone. For one tiny instant, all of his bravado was gone, washed away in the wake of Kerry Keen's virtuoso performance.

The long moment passed. The second fusillade swept at, around, and past them. One rocket neatly deflected from the tail section, leaving a dent and a scorch mark but failing to do any lasting damage. The others exploded harmlessly in the Black Bullet's wake.

Barney was bathed in sweat. He crossed himself and forced his eyes open once more.

"How much more of that do we—?"

The Griffon cut him off triumphantly.

"They're done now," he called through a grinning countenance. "Done! In more ways than one, that is."

The two Natters buzzed past the monoplane, their hungry Walter 109-509A rocket motors already almost drained of fuel. The Griffon wheeled the Black Bullet about and swooped down on them as they slowed.

"That was the only way to go," he explained as he lined up behind the two German rocket-planes. "If we'd turned tail and run, they would have closed on us at their own discretion and blown us out of the sky from behind."

"Yeah, I get it," Barney breathed, still mopping his brow. "You charged 'em—forced 'em to fire early, before they were really ready. Gave 'em a smaller target, too."

"Exactly."

"That didn't make it any more fun, though!"

Laughing madly, the Griffon flexed his fingers and squeezed the firing button. His marksmanship was excellent as ever, and each of the Natters in turn received a broadside of fire from the Yakovlev's six Browning machine guns. The resulting meteor-like fireballs tumbled into the sea.

"Two dead snakes," Barney declared, smiling for the first time in a while. "Snakes—that's what you said 'natters' are, right?"

"Indeed," the Griffon replied, his face smiling behind his scarlet mask. "Two dead vipers—but one very live sea serpent."

"So—what're we gonna do about it, then?"

The Griffon's smile didn't waver. By way of reply, he gripped the stick and sent the Black Bullet down in a tight spiral, toward the massive U-boat lying half-submerged, far below.

Now at the controls of the Black Bullet, Barney leveled the aircraft out and held it in a slow circling course, just long enough for the Griffon to dangle and then drop from the cable that extended down from the plane's bottom. The two of them had executed this maneuver a dozen times, if they had done it once, but never before over open water—something that made Barney extra nervous, and extra careful.

As soon as the scarlet-masked vigilante had crossed the short distance and hit the water, Barney followed the instructions he had been given and moved the Black Bullet back out of the range of any weapons that might be trained on it.

"Oh, I hope you know what you're doin', lad," he muttered to himself as he curved back around, peering down through the canopy at the night sky, trying to get a look at what happened next.

In the water below, the Griffon swam steadily and purposefully toward the looming bulk of the U-boat, a hulking black silhouette against the dim moonlight. Anticipating such a situation developing, he had worn his tight, streamlined black wetsuit, complete with slip-on shoes that served as fins. His mask was fastened securely over his face in such a way that he could easily breathe, but still keep his identity concealed.

As he swam through the cold waters, he first heard a low buzzing sound, then looked around and saw the larger seaplane—the Sikorsky. Its ungainly form swooped down, coasted across the water ahead, and moved alongside the submarine, before finally docking against the gargantuan vessel's side.

The Sikorsky's copilot, wearing the bizarre, spherical helmet of the Terror's henchmen, climbed out. Quickly, he used ropes to secure the plane to the broad, gray steel hull. Then the door opened again and two more of the henchmen disembarked from the plane. Between the two of them, Keen recognized the kidnap victim himself, Herr Vogler. The German scientist wore a long, dark coat. Neither of the two henchmen seemed to be making any effort to restrain him.

The Griffon reached the U-boat's dark gray flank, climbed a short distance up, and clung to the metal plating. He shivered in the cold night air, ocean water streaming from his outfit. A moment later, his strength slowly returning, he managed to pull himself up just far enough to continue observing the events occurring on the sub's deck.

The men from the seaplane waited for a few seconds. Then, as Keen had begun to wonder exactly what was happening, a round hatch swung upward from the deck and two uniformed German naval officers clambered out. Their swastika emblems glinted in the faint moonlight; their black boots smacked on the gray panels as they strode arrogantly over to where the new arrivals stood. Immediately they began to speak in hushed but obviously harsh tones.

The Griffon, with his rudimentary understanding of German, strained to hear what the officers were saying, but at first he could not make it out. He climbed further up the side of the U-boat, nearly forced to give away his position in order to overhear.

"…a nuisance, ja," one of the officers barked. "This Griffon—he has proven to be a thorn in our sides before. And now, shooting down our two rocket planes—intolerable!"

A general nodding among the group.

"But we have a way of taking care of him," the officer continued. He gestured toward the broad conning tower of the monstrous sub, and a moment later, a grinding sound emerged from the U-boat's side, a few dozen feet away from the Griffon. Instinctively he slid down, seeking cover.

"There, you see?"

The men on the deck all watched as the grinding sound turned out to herald the opening of a broad hatch built into the side of the submarine, just above sea level. Moments later, a big, gray shape emerged, sliding out into the water with a low splash.

It was another seaplane. A German seaplane. But it was nothing like the bulky, ungainly Sikorsky in which Vogler and the thugs had flown. The Griffon squinted through the dim light at it. It was not a design he recognized immediately.

A general murmur of approval from the deck greeted the plane's emergence.

"Excellent, ja. Wunderbar."

The Griffon continued to stare at the aircraft, his brows narrowing. It looked familiar, somehow, and yet…

"Of course," he breathed softly through his scarlet mask. "It's a Messerschmitt—a Bf 109 W. A Messerschmitt seaplane!" He frowned for a moment, then recalled the full name. "Wasserflugzeug. Yes." He smiled as he stared at it, floating there in the water alongside the U-boat. "A beautiful bird. Beautiful. And deadly as can be."

The sound of booted feet moving across the deck brought the Griffon's attention away from the plane. He saw another German striding across to the group and saluting—this one dressed as a pilot.

"You will destroy the meddling Griffon," one of the Nazi officers barked at the pilot. "Use any means necessary. Blow him out of the sky, and return here as quickly as you can. We must be underway soon."

The other German naval officer, meanwhile, had just handed Vogler a metal briefcase. The erstwhile prisoner smiled flatly at the officer and then moved back a step.

"I thank you for your assistance, gentlemen," Vogler told the Nazis, "and particularly for this." He indicated the briefcase, then handed it over to one of the Terror's henchmen. "However, I am afraid I will not be coming back to the Fatherland. Not tonight—and not with you."

The Germans laughed, as if Vogler had repeated a humorous joke.

"Ah, Herr Vogler, you jest, surely. You know our orders as well as we do, and—"

Vogler reached into a large pocket in his coat and whipped out a mask, pulling it quickly over his head. It took the form of a leering skull!

"You misunderstand me, gentlemen," he cackled, whipping off his long overcoat to reveal a dark gray jumpsuit, mechanical devices set into the metal chestplate. "Herr Vogler simply cannot obey such orders—for there is no Herr Vogler! There is only—the Terror!"

Several things happened very quickly, then.

First, one of the Terror's henchmen noticed the Griffon, where he clung to the side of the U-boat. The man cried out and pointed, but the others were too distracted by Vogler's donning of the mask and his revelation about his identity, and ignored the man.

Second, the Griffon quickly drew two small objects from his

pocket—the same two objects he'd been working on in the hangar earlier—and inserted one of them into each of his ears. Then he scrambled the rest of the way up the side of the submarine, meeting the charging henchman in a diving tackle and sending them both sprawling.

Third, the remaining henchmen drew their pistols and started toward the Griffon.

And finally, the Terror motioned them back with a sharp, "Nein!" He placed one hand over his chest and manipulated a dial set into the gray metal chestplate of his jumpsuit. Instantly a wave of raw, abject horror washed out, clutching at the minds of anyone susceptible to its grasp.

Just as before, the henchmen in their round helmets reacted not at all. The one who had attacked the Griffon regained his feet quickly, there on the slick surface of the U-boat. The lowering moon's dim light dappled garishly off the glassy surface of his helmet as he loomed over the Griffon and struggled to grab him. The scarlet-masked avenger, for his part, shifted his weight at the last moment, dodging to one side, then reached out and grasped the man's ankle. He twisted, and the henchman cried out as he fell, his voice strangely muffled by his odd headgear—headgear that struck the hard surface of the U-boat with tremendous force. Obviously dazed, the henchman stumbled along on hands and knees. The Griffon placed a booted foot on the man's rump and sent him tumbling overboard, wailing, into the cold Atlantic.

Even as the Griffon bested his first foe, the Terror's fear weapon struck deep at the hearts of the three Nazis on the deck. One of the naval officers, his face a mask of utter horror, unleashed a blood-curdling scream and raced for the hatch. He ignored the ladder and leaped down through the opening. The other U-boat officer tumbled through after him a moment later. A hand belonging to one of the men reached back up, grasped for the hatch, seized upon it, banged it closed, and locked it. Meanwhile, the Messerschmitt pilot had simply dashed in horror into the darkness, though he barely made it

**The Griffon placed a foot on the man's rump
and sent him tumbling into the cold Atlantic.**

three steps before tripping on a cable and tumbling overboard.

Having disposed of his first attacker, the Griffon attempted to melt into the shadows again and seek a more favorable avenue of attack. The Terror was aware of him now, however, and could tell that, for whatever reason, his weapon was not working on the scarlet-masked vigilante. With a few harsh commands, the eerie villain directed one of his remaining two henchmen to attack. The Griffon dodged a wildly-swung fist and caught the helmeted man in the gut with his own blow, then reached up and grasped the now-doubled-over man around the neck, wrenching at his headgear. The seal popped and the bulbous contraption snapped free. The henchman staggered, his already pale features draining to near-whiteness. Wild-eyed and cringing, the man screeched, then made an incomprehensible choking sound, and promptly dived over the side of the sub.

The Terror, having watched these events transpire, now seemed to be saying something, though whether the words were directed to his lone remaining assistant or to the Griffon, Keen could not be sure, as he could not hear them—or anything else. The skull-masked villain, some of his bravado now slipping away, took a step back. Seizing the advantage, the Griffon advanced, crouching low.

Reaching up to his chest, the Terror grasped the dial on his chestplate and twisted it again, now turning it apparently as far as it would go. Keen felt a slight chill run through his nerves, and worried for an instant that he had misjudged the strength or the nature of the weapon. At the same moment, however, the other henchman, still holding the silver metal briefcase he had received from the Nazis, stopped dead in his tracks. He whirled around, ignored his master's orders and entreaties, and tossed the metal case aside, then sprinted across the deck toward the Sikorsky.

The Terror turned to shout angrily, his attention divided between his fleeing flunky and the metal case the man had hurled away. In that instant the Griffon struck. Leaping across the short distance that separated the two of them, the scarlet-masked man crashed into his opponent and drove the villain down hard.

The two adversaries tumbled across the deck, each swinging at the other, neither able to gain an advantage. As they rolled over the cold, wet surface, the Griffon managed to get his hand on the Terror's chestplate, feeling the round dial and the components around it. Before he could attempt to sabotage it, however, the Terror wedged a heavy boot against the Griffon's stomach and kicked violently out, shoving him away.

Keen tumbled across the slick surface, nearly tumbling overboard, but caught hold of a cable at the last instant and checked his momentum. He clung to it desperately as the Terror regained his feet and strode over to stare down at him.

"I can't hear a word you're saying, old boy," Keen shouted at the skull-faced villain as the man loomed over him. Then he laughed. "Sorry!"

Neither could the Griffon hear the roar of the Sikorsky's twin Pratt and Whitney engines coming to life—but he did see the big seaplane rushing over the waves and surging up into the slowly-brightening sky. He couldn't resist craning his neck to follow the plane's progress, and in that instant, the Terror rushed forward, hands raised to smash him from the cable he clung to—to send him to a cold, watery grave.

That self-same cold seawater reached the Griffon much sooner than he had expected, however. It came flooding up from below, nearly covering him—and yet he had not moved at all. He still clung to the cable at the edge of the deck.

The Terror, too, was being inundated with water. The villain stopped in his tracks and looked frantically around, now ignoring Keen entirely.

Realization hit them both simultaneously. The U-boat was submerging!

Far above the desperate action on the deck of the U-boat, Barney O'Dare piloted the Black Bullet in a slow, lazy circle, careful to stay out of the range of any guns the big submarine might possess. Occasionally he would bank the plane to the side and peer down at the dark waters, searching for any signs of the Griffon. He hoped the fact that he couldn't see the man meant the Germans couldn't see him, either.

As he brought the powerful monoplane around for another bank, he spied the big Sikorsky seaplane moving away from the U-boat and picking up speed, then rising into the air.

"Oh, ho," he growled low in his throat. "An' just where do you think you're goin', me boyo?"

Moving the stick forward, he directed the Black Bullet down on an intercept course with the ascending seaplane.

Just as he lined up the big Sikorsky in his sights, however, a sick feeling came over him. What if the Griffon were aboard that plane? What if he'd been kidnapped—or had commandeered it?

Frowning in consternation, Barney banked away from the other airship and curved around behind it, then throttled the Black Bullet's engine and pulled up alongside. He squinted through the canopy, trying to see what he could see aboard the other vehicle.

The hail of bullets that came at him then missed the monoplane by mere inches.

Suppressing a wail, Barney shoved the stick forward, diving the Black Bullet beneath the Sikorsky.

"I think it's safe to say they mean me no good will," the little Irishman muttered to himself, before climbing his aircraft back up, high over the other plane, and just behind it.

This time, as he directed the Black Bullet down, he had but one objective in mind. His hand closed over the firing button, and the six Browning half-inchers lit up, their deadly projectiles lashing out into the Sikorsky, tearing the seaplane to shreds, and sending its flaming debris plummeting down, down into the Atlantic.

Barney emitted a single, satisfied snort as he banked again and watched the last few fragments of the plane disappear. Then he directed his attention to the U-boat, and received a shock.

It had nearly submerged. And of the Griffon, there was no sign whatsoever.

T he Griffon saw the debris raining down from above, but he had no time to consider whether the unidentifiable flaming wreckage came from the Sikorsky or his own aircraft. At the moment, he was too busy trying to stay alive.

Fortunately for him, the Terror had given up trying to kill him the moment they had realized the U-boat was submerging. They both knew they had only seconds before the fear-maddened officers, in their horrific reactions to the Terror's weapon, took the sub down into the Atlantic depths.

The only possible answer now, the Griffon realized, was the Messerschmitt. Forgotten by the Germans, it still floated on the waters where it had emerged from the U-boat's hangar. The Terror obviously thought the same thing; before Keen could move, the villain whirled and began to splash his way madly across the flooding deck, racing for the plane.

Thinking quickly, the Griffon scrambled three steps up a ladder attached to the side of the conning tower and leapt out, tackling the Terror from above and behind. Both men hit the water with a splash, and each disappeared beneath it for a moment.

The Griffon came up first, sputtering, his scarlet mask as soaked as the rest of him. A second later, the Terror emerged, choking on the water, obviously disoriented and staggering.

Before the Griffon could assault him again, the Terror grasped the rungs of the ladder attached to the side of the conning tower, and scrambled madly upward. Following him up, the Griffon ran headlong into a boot that lashed out, striking a glancing blow to the side of his head.

Before Vogler could kick out at him again, the Griffon scrambled quickly the rest of the way up the ladder. He lunged at the surprised villain, grasped him about the neck, and in one smooth motion pulled the skull mask up and over the man's head, casting it away.

For almost two full seconds, the now-revealed Ernst Vogler stood stock-still, a growing look of panic—of terror!—covering his face. The machine built into his chestplate, still cranked to full power, radiated its fear-inducing sound directly into his brain, and now nothing protected his ears from the effects. Perhaps one more second passed, as slow as an age of the earth, and then Vogler screamed an unearthly, blood-curdling scream. Flailing madly, he clawed at the Griffon, tearing the vigilante's scarlet mask away. For a brief instant, then, a tiny hint of clarity came to the man's eyes as he gazed at his adversary, and he blinked.

"K—Keen?"

Then, before the Griffon could respond or act in any way, the villain screamed in mindless horror once more and leapt over the side of the tower, plunging into the ocean, gone.

The Griffon watched just long enough to see the man disappear, swallowed by the dark depths of the Atlantic.

"You wanted us to accomplish something memorable together," he whispered. "I think this qualifies."

Water rushed over his feet again as the conning tower sank entirely beneath him, and within moments he was treading water. The cold embrace of the Atlantic cleared his head, and he began to swim. A series of long, powerful strokes carried him the short distance to where the Messerschmitt Bf 109 rocked on the rollers. Halfway there, he noticed something floating in the water just ahead of him, gleaming silver in the moonlight—something he had seen before.

"What have we here?"

He reached out and grasped it, pulling it to himself.

"Well, well."

It was the metal case the panic-stricken henchman had thrown aside. And the Griffon had a pretty good idea as to what it contained.

The vigilante was gasping for breath from the cold and from his exertions by the time he reached the seaplane. With numb fingers he clasped onto one of the big pontoons and pulled himself up. An enormous, overwhelming sense of relief washed over him, despite his physical discomfort.

Seconds later, he was seated in the cockpit, waterlogged and extremely cold, but otherwise intact. Two thoughts occurred to him somewhat simultaneously as he fired up the Wasserflugzeug's Daimler-Benz DB601 engine and sent the amphibious figher plane moving forward: "This aircraft will make a lovely addition to my collection," followed immediately by the worrisome thought, "I certainly hope Barney doesn't shoot me down..."

Realizing the U-boat had submerged entirely beneath the ocean's surface, something akin to panic gripped at Barney O'Dare. Was his boss on board? If so, surely he was being kidnapped by the Nazis! And, perhaps even worse—what if he'd been left, somewhere down there in the water? Could Barney locate him fast enough, if that was the case? How long would he be able to stay afloat in such conditions, having already been in the cold Atlantic waters for some time?

Then he saw the gray German seaplane moving over the waves.

"Time to shoot another one down," he muttered to himself as the Messerschmitt lofted up and zoomed skyward. He squinted at it, puzzled. "An' I don't even recognize the design." He shrugged. "Ah well. They all look pretty much the same when they're on fire, or floatin' in pieces in the water."

He directed the Black Bullet down at a sharp angle toward the rising German craft.

"A shame, though. She's a right fair bird. An' surely dangerous as anythin'."

He moved his fingers over the firing button.

At that moment, even as Barney O'Dare prepared to unleash the six Browning machine guns against his target, the Messerschmitt did something quite unexpected. It banked, turned slightly, and excuted a perfect barrel roll. At one point the plane's wingtip barely missed touching the crest of the waves. Then, just as suddenly, the plane zoomed upward, moving easily into matching formation alongside the Black Bullet.

Had this been the preliminary moves of an attack, Barney knew he would be dead now. He had gawked, eyes wide, unmoving, through the entire performance. His mouth opened and closed once, and then he smacked one hand onto his forehead, rubbed at his bleary eyes, and waved through the cockpit glass to the scarlet-masked Griffon, clearly visible now at the controls of the other plane.

"Yeah, yeah, I see ya there, boss. I see ya."

He thought one last time about how close he had come to turning the Brownings loose on the other craft.

"Sheesh."

He noticed then that his hands were shaking. Inhaling deeply, he breathed out and aimed the Black Bullet for the distant coastline. The other plane duplicated the move.

"The O'Doul's Dew better be nice and cold when we get home. Nice and cold."

Together, the two planes zoomed toward home, the sun rising behind them.

ice and cold, ain't ya?"

It was an hour later, though still very early in the morning, and Kerry Keen sat wrapped in a heavy blanket, leaning back in his favorite leather chair. He and Barney occupied the library room of his penthouse apartment on 55th Street in New York City. His tuxedo, soaking wet, lay in the tub in the bathroom, along with the bundle of towels Keen had needed to dry off.

"Cold, yes—but not as cold as the Terror," Keen replied. "Or should I say, Ernst Vogler."

"So he was the same guy all along." Barney, seated across the room with his feet up on a low stool, sipped at his O'Doul's Dew and shook his head. "Don't that beat all."

"But it's true."

Barney scratched at his chin, still somewhat puzzled. "And those little things you were working on before—"

Keen held them up: two bean-sized objects made of some sort of cloth or foam.

"Earplugs. Very efficient earplugs. They blocked the Terror's fear weapon."

Barney's eyes widened. "I get it, yeah. Sound. His weapon made some kind of sound, an' that's what scared people so much."

Keen nodded.

"Precisely. It must have operated at a frequency that generates a reaction of fear in humans. His thugs wore helmets that must have filtered out the sound, at least at lower levels, while allowing them to hear everything else. Fortunately, my earplugs did the same job on his weapon—or slightly better, at it turned out." He laughed. "Though I couldn't hear a blasted thing, while I had them in."

"But—how did you figure out—?"

Keen shrugged. "It was the lovely Miss Helen Lilley that pointed the way to the solution, albeit indirectly," he replied.

"Lilley? The lady who was—"

"Deaf. Yes." Keen nodded. "She was the only one at the party not to react to the Terror's weapon. I first suspected she was in on it somehow. But the Terror's henchmen were just as susceptible to his weapon as anyone else, once they lost their headgear. The Terror himself, too, as it turned out," he added with a laugh. "Only Miss Lilley proved immune. Now we know why."

Barney took all this in with a look of wonder. "Huh," he said finally. "Huh."

Keen pulled the blanket away and stood, stretching his legs.

"Feeling better now?" Barney inquired.

"A bit, actually," Keen replied. "And it's a good thing, too, because I expect we shall have guests arriving very soon."

"Oh yeah?" Barney downed the last sip of his O'Doul's Dew and frowned. "Who would come a'callin' at this time o' th' mornin?" Then, having considered the question for a second, his face took on a wry expression. "Ohhh. Yeah. Him."

As if in reply, there came a knock at the door.

"Come in," Keen called out. He was clad now in a luxurious smoking jacket and pants; virtually no signs remained of his midnight swim off the East Coast.

Barney had moved to get the door, but it swung open before he could reach it. In walked Detective Drury Lang, dark rings under his eyes, his gray suit appearing somewhat more rumpled and worse for the wear than usual.

Keen's steely eyes peered up at the man intently.

"Hello again, Lang." He smiled a tight smile. "Don't you ever sleep?"

"Do you?" Lang countered, closing the door behind him and standing there awkwardly. "You're up awfully early."

"I suppose you're simply fortunate I'm an early riser." Keen laughed good-naturedly at the detective. "So—what's got you up and around at this time of the day, then? What's the emergency?"

"Somehow, I think you probably know already," Lang replied, his eyes narrow and focused tightly on Keen.

Keen stood and strode casually across the room, standing in front of Lang, arms crossed.

"Unless you're here to investigate a particularly pleasant dream I had last night, I'm afraid I can't help you."

Lang dismissed the comments with an impatient wave of his hand.

"I don't have time to fence with you today, Keen." He walked past the taller man and took the liberty of seating himself in the big leather chair. "There have been some... developments you should know about."

"By all means, make yourself comfortable, then," Keen told him, enduring the man's presence as best he could.

"The Coast Guard found Ernst Vogler's body this morning," the detective said without preamble. "Floating in the waters off the Darkenmoor Estate."

"How tragic," Keen replied evenly.

"Yeah," Lang said, no trace of emotion in his voice. "I suppose the one good thing about it is that the government was just about to drop off the ransom money when they found the body. So, for better or worse, Uncle Sam has been saved a whole lot of money this morning."

Keen said nothing. From across the room, O'Dare muttered a terse, "Great."

After a moment's respectful silence, Keen asked, "Cause of death?"

"Apparently the guy drowned," Lang said, "but with an awful look of horror frozen on his face." The detective frowned, clearly disturbed by that, and ran a hand through his mussed hair.

"Why, Detective Lang, you seem positively beside yourself. Barney! Bring the detective a cup of coffee."

"No, no, save your coffee, Keen," Lang sniped at him. "I won't be staying that long. I just needed to pass that information along, and to request that you come down to the station this morning."

"Why, whatever for?"

"Turns out Vogler had a couple of very interesting firearms on his person, and they'd—we'd—appreciate it if you could take a look at them."

"Firearms? In his possession?" Keen glanced sidelong at Lang. "Very strange, for a kidnapping victim, wouldn't you say?"

"Yeah. I'd say that." Lang paused, then, "He had some other strange equipment on him that you should probably see, too. Mechanical stuff, hidden under his clothes. It looked damaged and pretty much shorted out from the seawater, but still…"

"Of course, yes," Keen replied with a careful smile. "I will be at the station in an hour."

Lang nodded, rose and started for the door. Then he paused and looked back at Keen and O'Dare.

"Oh, one other thing you might like to know. If you don't already, that is. Clutched in Vogler's hand was a piece of red cloth."

Keen gave the detective a puzzled look. "So you're concerned with his taste in handkerchiefs?"

"It was no hanky, Keen. You know exactly what it was. A mask. A mask I've encountered more than once in the past."

"Oh? Is that so?"

Lang summoned himself up to his full height, leaned in toward Keen, raised a pointed finger as if to jab it at the man's chest—and stopped.

Keen waited, anticipating the accusation that always came. Lang had long suspected Keen of being the scarlet-masked Griffon, but the evidence never quite played out the way Lang expected it to— mostly due to careful planning and action on the part of Keen.

Detective Lang stood there a second longer, and then he visibly deflated. He lowered his hand and squeezed his bloodshot eyes closed, then opened them and peered tiredly at Keen.

"You know, I just don't have the energy for this, today. I just don't." He shrugged. "But that situation won't last forever. Give me a few hours of sleep, and maybe we'll talk again."

"I look forward to it, Detective."

"I'm watching you, Keen. Watching you very carefully."

"How wonderful to have top-notch police protection round the clock," Keen replied with a warm smile.

Groaning, Lang turned on his heel and strode out of the apartment, not even bothering to pull the door closed behind him.

ater that afternoon, in the secret hangar at the Graylands estate, Keen busily inspected his new prize, the Messerschmitt Bf 109 W seaplane.

"Not a bad reward for all our efforts," he said as Barney approached, toolbox in hand.

"Yeah, sure, she's a beaut," the little Irishman replied. "Needs one thing, though."

Keen glanced over at the man, puzzled. "And what might that be?"

Barney jerked a thumb at a stack of paint cans resting nearby. Black paint cans.

Keen smiled. "So it's to be the Black Bullet II, then?"

"Maybe so," Barney replied. "I think she needs a—whatchacallit—a more distinctive name, though."

"I'm sure something will occur to us."

"Yeah." He frowned. "What we really need, though, is good ol' cash money. The account's gettin' low again. Too low for my tastes. We're runnin' out of everything." He pointed at the Bf 109. "And nice new German planes don't pay the bills—unless you feel like sellin' it."

"Hardly."

Keen smiled suddenly.

"But if it's money you're concerned about," he said, "I might be able to alleviate your concerns somewhat."

"Oh, yeah?"

Barney watched, puzzled, as Keen climbed up into the cockpit of the Messerschmitt, rummaged around, retrieved something, and climbed down again.

"While our Nazi friends may have escaped in their U-boat—though, given their condition at the time, they might well have steered the thing straight to the bottom of the ocean—they did manage to leave behind something else of value, besides the plane."

He held out a silver metal briefcase, offering it to O'Dare. Cautiously, the other man took it.

"Go ahead. It's not locked."

Barney worked the catches and the lid popped open, spilling the case's contents over the floor of the hangar.

"What in the—well, I'll be!"

His feet were covered, up to his ankles, in bundles of banknotes of some variety.

"You gotta be kiddin' me!"

Bending down, Barney retrieved one of the bundles and studied it.

"German?" He peered at Keen curiously. "German money?"

"Deutschmarks, yes," Keen agreed, nodding. "The money the Nazis were paying Vogler for his work."

"Huh? But I thought—"

"He was using his dual identities to play both sides against one another," Keen explained. "Selling weapons designs to us and the Nazis at the same time."

"You're kiddin' me."

"He would have ended up with the payments from both countries for his work, as well as the American ransom money—for kidnapping himself!" Keen shook his head. "Quite an ingenious scheme."

"Well, he got what he deserved for it," Barney growled. "An' now we're gettin' what we deserve, for dealing with him!"

"You could say that." Keen laughed. "It should be enough, at least, to compensate us for our difficulties. Enough to get the dents taken out of the Dusenberg, and get the seawater stains out of my tuxedo."

Barney, still grinning at their unexpected windfall, bundled the money back into the case and set it reverently on his work table.

"We gotta celebrate!"

He rushed through the side doorway into the storeroom, and Keen heard him clunking around for a few moments. Then, suddenly, he cried out, unleashing a shriek of utter, blood-curdling terror and dismay.

"What is it?" Keen demanded, instantly on his guard, a pistol in his hand and ready.

"We're all out of O'Doul's Dew," came the whimpering voice from the storeroom. "Oh, the humanity!"

Flashback
by Van Allen Plexico

lashback to early 2007: I somewhat unexpectedly found myself becoming a burgeoning pulp writer, though in the broader sense of the term, with superheroes and SF properties. I knew I needed to establish my bona fides in the more traditional vein of pulps: with some of the classic 1930s characters—men who were "mere mortals," but who had guts and brawn to match their particular gimmicks; guns-blazing crime fighters and daring air pilots and the like.

Ron Fortier of Airship 27 introduced me to the Griffon—a character I'd not heard of before—and gave me a shot at writing one of his adventures. I figured, "Sounds interesting. Why not?" Ron tossed me several of the classic Arch Whitehouse stories and away I went.

Approaching one Kerry Keen, the Griffon, required a bit of research on my part. Every bit of that research was a pleasure.

First, I had to know the characters and their relationships to one another. Those supremely entertaining Whitehouse stories gave me a solid feel for who Keen was and what he and his associates were all about. And a lifetime of reading not only the giants like Edgar Rice Burroughs and Robert E. Howard, but also what I would call "near-pulps" (or maybe "neo-pulps") by authors such as Philip Jose Farmer and Roger Zelazny, gave me what I consider to be a good foundation for the writing techniques.

Next came the various aircraft—and in a Griffon story, the planes are just as important as the people! Ron suggested the Sikorsky as the plane for the beginning of the story. Friend and occasional collaborator Bobby Politte suggested using the uber-cool U-boat-launched Natters, as well as a couple of other good ideas for the story. Both the Natters and the Messerschmitt seaplane are real! Hey, I didn't make this stuff up, folks! Well, most of it, anyway...

And finally, what about the overall plot? What nefarious schemes would the Griffon be confronting? I knew I wanted something of a "big" story, with a great big vehicle serving as host to the final hand-to-hand combat at the end. My original idea was to feature a zeppelin, which seemed great until Bobby pointed out that I was somehow channeling the end of "The Rocketeer," a movie I haven't watched in more than two decades. Ah, well. I think the monster submarine turned out even better.

Challenges? Setting the big finale on a submarine meant dealing with the rising water levels at the climax of the story, and that turned into a real headache. I had to get everything wrapped up quickly once the water level started rising! How long do you think it takes a sub to dive, after all? Probably not nearly as long as I made it seem, by necessity.

Surprisingly, at least to me, the other components of this tale—the sound weapon, the earplugs, the deaf woman, the fake kidnapping, the car chase, etc.—sort of fell together naturally, organically, and very quickly as I plotted it all out. That happens rarely enough that a writer has to be excited when it does occur. You can't help but think that maybe the pulp gods are smiling down in approval, and that the story will be an easy one to write and a fun one to read.

Indeed, writing this tale was a lot of fun, but it entailed a lot of work as well. I tried as best I could to absorb and embrace the Arch Whitehouse style, but to do it in my own voice. What resulted is, I think, sort of a combination of the two. I do some things in this story I wouldn't normally do in my writing, in an attempt to evoke even more of a classic pulp narrative feel. Was I successful at all? I have no idea—that's for each of you to decide. But I very much appreciated the opportunity to do it, and to entertain the readers with the best Griffon story I could roll out (or fly out!).

Thanks for reading!

—Van Allen Plexico
Metro St. Louis
June 25, 2009

Author Bio:

A political scientist, historian, writer, and editor, Van Allen Plexico created and edited *Assembled* and *Assembled 2*, works of Avengers-related commentary and criticism that have raised thousands of dollars for charity. He writes various pulp adventures for Airship 27 Productions and the *Sentinels* series of superhero adventure novels for Swarm Press, in addition to writing and editing for his own White Rocket Books line. His pop culture commentary appears occasionally at RevolutionSF.com. He is a member of the Pulp Factory and is a Jarvis Head.

Learn more about him and his various projects at plexico.net, whiterocketbooks.com, and avengersassemble.net.

THE THREE MOSQUITOS

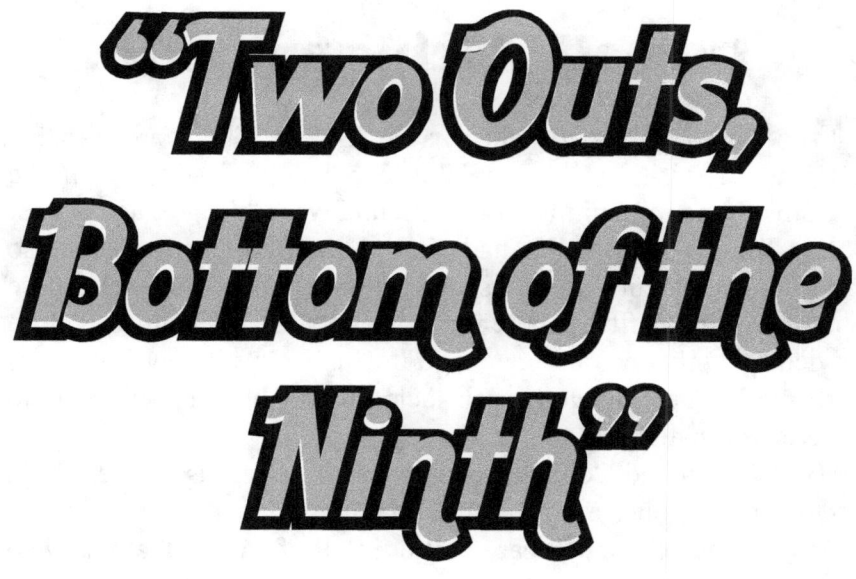

"Two Outs, Bottom of the Ninth"

by
Aaron Smith

Detroit Michigan, 1916:

The crowd at Navin Field was on its feet. The score was 1-0, with the visiting Chicago White Sox holding a slim lead in the bottom of the ninth inning. On the mound was Chicago's ace pitcher, young Tommy Hughes. He had pitched an almost perfect game so far, giving up no hits, no walks, and having only one man reach base on an error in the fifth. There were two outs and his team was close to victory. Only one obstacle stood in Hughes' way now, but it was perhaps the most dangerous obstacle imaginable when it came to America's greatest sport.

Tyrus Raymond Cobb stepped up to the plate, his bat held high and straight. Cobb, a slim, muscular man with a harsh face and keen eyes, was the most feared hitter in all of baseball, a man who consistently led the league in batting. Poor Tommy Hughes would have rather faced anyone but Cobb with the game so close to being won.

The first pitch came in. Cobb stood perfectly still as the ball brushed past him, just touching the edge of the strike zone. "Steee-rike!" cried the umpire.

The second pitch rocketed to the plate. Cobb took a hack and fouled it back. Hughes reached up and wiped the sweat from his brow. He took a deep breath. He had the fearsome Cobb down to his last strike. He began his movement.

The ball flew in; the mighty Cobb swung...and sent it crashing into the outfield fence! Cobb, with blinding speed, rounded first, and then second, sliding into third just as the ball met the infielder's glove. "Safe," shouted the umpire. Cobb stood, brushing the dirt from his pants, tossing a defiant sneer in Hughes' direction, the victor with a triple.

Up next was Sam Crawford. If Cobb was the king of striking fear into opposing pitchers, then Crawford was the prince. He was a hitting machine, often leading the league in runs batted in and holding the all-time record for triples. Crawford was older now and his career would not last much longer, but he could still swing the bat with a power matched by few others of his time. Hughes, somewhat unnerved by Cobb's hit, threw his first pitch to Crawford. It would also be his last. The ball went straight to the deepest part of the outfield, bounced off the wall and ricocheted out of easy reach of the fielder!

Cobb scored easily, tying the game. Crawford, while no longer a youngster, could still turn on the speed that had given him 300 triples. This time, he was determined to turn it up to its maximum. He flew around first and second, shot past third, and went all the way around those bases, a screaming, smoldering inside the park home run! The crowd exploded with emotion. Tommy Hughes sat down on the mound with his head in his hands.

The White Sox took the train back to Chicago that night. Hughes returned to his hometown apartment and opened the mail that awaited him. His hands shook as he tore open an official looking envelope from the Department of War. He knew what it was before he even unfolded the letter. Tommy Hughes had been drafted...and he feared that his ball playing days might be over.

Chaumont Francε, 1918:

The last of the German Fokkers fell from the sky in a spiraling stream of smoke and bits of debris. The American air forces had been victorious once again. Captain Kirby and Lieutenant Travis had no time to celebrate. They turned around in mid-air and looked for a place to land out there in the French countryside. Minutes later, their two khaki Spads had screeched into halted positions in an empty field. Kirby and Travis jumped from their cockpits and ran as fast as they could to the place where another plane of the same design lay smoldering.

"Shorty, Shorty!" shouted Kirby, "Can you hear me?"

"Captain...Captain..." came the weak response.

Travis and Kirby reached the downed Spad and looked inside. The plane was smoking but there were no flames. It did not appear as if there was any danger of combustion. Inside the plane, Lieutenant "Shorty" Carn sat in his seat with a twisted expression of agony etched upon his face.

"I think my leg's busted, Captain. Can you get me out of here?"

Later that day, Kirby and Travis stood at their fallen friend's bedside. Carn was smiling, perhaps slightly inebriated by the pills the base surgeon had given him. His left leg was elevated and in a cast.

"I suppose I won't be up in the clouds with you two for awhile," Carn said, looking disappointed. "The doc says it'll be at least a month...maybe more. At least we sent those Germans straight to Hell!"

"You did well today, Shorty," said Kirby, about to slap the lieutenant on the back, but stopping himself as he remembered his friend's injured state.

The doctor, a bulldog of a major with drooping jowls, kicked Kirby and Travis out in short order, insisting that Carn needed to get some rest. The two uninjured members of the Three Mosquitos exited the medical building and were about to head back to their barracks when a young private approached them, snapping a salute before speaking.

"Captain Kirby? Lieutenant Travis?" the soldier asked, wanting to confirm that he had found the right officers.

"Yeah, kid. What do you want?" asked Travis in his Southern drawl.

"General Saunders wants to see you both ASAP," said the private.

Kirby sighed. "We can't get a moments rest around here, can we Travis? Maybe we should have told the general we had broken legs too!"

Kirby and Travis reported to the command office immediately. Soon, they were standing before the desk of Brigadier General Saunders, commanding officer of the Chaumont Air Base, where the American flying forces had their headquarters in that region of France.

"I know you boys just got back from a dogfight—and good job by the way—but I've got to send you out again," said the stern-faced general. "I could send well rested flyers out, but you three are the best I have, and I need men I can trust to go out on this one."

Captain Kirby, never one to demonstrate too much respect for authority, interrupted the general. "Sir, as you might have noticed, we're down to two Mosquitos at the moment!"

"I'm not an idiot, Kirby!" bellowed Saunders. "I can count! That's why I'm giving you a day to get ready before I send you out on this mission. It can wait long enough for you to get acquainted with Carn's temporary replacement. Lieutenant Hughes, get in here!"

A young officer with close-cropped blonde hair and a serious demeanor entered the office. He extended his hand; Kirby shook it.

"Lieutenant Thomas B. Hughes reporting, sir," said the young newcomer. He remembered military etiquette and turned to salute the general.

"Never mind that, Hughes," said Saunders. "Listen, men. Here's the story. Thirty miles north of here is something going on. One of our scouts thought he saw some German activity in the area. It was getting dark and he was at the end of his patrol, but he swears he saw some ground troops moving around and maybe…just maybe…a small airfield being set up. By this time tomorrow, I want you three ready to take a little trip out there and look around a, if necessary, upset whatever it is that those Germans have going on. Don't waste any time, Kirby. I want you three operating as smoothly as you would if Carn was up and about."

Kirby began to argue. "Sir, Travis, Carn and I have been flying together for over a year now. We can't just break in a replacement overnight. No offense, Lieutenant Hughes, but we have a system of communication and maneuvers that we can't expect a new man to learn right away. Maybe it would be better if Travis and I went out as a duo."

"Nonsense, Captain," said the general. "Three planes are better than two any day. You have your orders. Now get out!"

There was no time for the two healthy Mosquitos, Kirby and Travis, to get acquainted with their new partner, Hughes. A mission awaited them and they had to bring Hughes up to speed on exactly how the Three Mosquitos operated. They headed out to the airfield where Kirby and Travis' khaki Spad planes had been cleaned, repaired and refueled after their ferocious fight against the Germans. Next to the two battle-scarred Spads stood a brand new one, straight from the assembly line, the paint job unblemished, the khaki color fresh and clean and the black mosquito design flawlessly added to the plane's nose. This third plane was to replace the one that Lieutenant Carn had lost, but it would not be Carn who would break it in. Captain Kirby began to explain the Mosquitos' ways to Hughes.

"We usually fly in a V-formation, with me in the lead and Travis and Carn trailing just behind me on either side. In the air, we communicate with hand signals. It's an intricate, detailed system of signs, so it might take some serious effort to get you caught up. Try to have patience with it. Travis, give our new friend a demonstration."

The tall, lanky lieutenant began to make strange motions. He waved one hand in a swimming motion, then the other; he touched his nose, tugged on an earlobe, and scratched the left side of his chest.

"Lieutenant Travis," said Kirby to Hughes, "just informed me that two German planes were heading in from the south, that one looked like it was lagging behind with a weak engine, that he was going to pull off to the right and try to distract the faster of the two German planes, and that Carn would take out the slowpoke while I went on ahead. All that came from those weird movements he made."

Hughes laughed. "You mean these movements?" He imitated Travis' moves, copying each signal perfectly. Kirby was impressed.

"How'd you learn that so quickly, Lieutenant?" said the shocked captain.

"Easy," replied Hughes. "I used to learn signs like that all the time in my civilian job."

Kirby and Travis spent the next hour going over their system of sign language with Hughes. The replacement pilot amazed them with his ability to catch on so quickly. Satisfied that he had the hang of the signals, the next step was for the three of them to take to the skies. The three Spads raced down the runway and took off. Soon the three aviators, Kirby, Travis and Hughes, were soaring in the clear blue air above France, looping and twisting through the skies. Hughes proved to be an able pilot, and a courageous one too. As the sun eventually began to set, the three Spads landed and Kirby complimented Hughes on the skills he had shown that day.

"You did well, Lieutenant. I'm glad to have you aboard. Welcome, for now at least, to the Three Mosquitos!"

That was the end of the day's practice. Kirby, Travis and Hughes walked over to the mess hall, ate dinner, and then retired to the barracks for the night. The morning would bring more flight; not mere practice maneuvers, but a real mission—probably dangerous, possibly deadly. One could only hope it would be deadly for the Germans...and not for the Americans.

Kirby and Travis slept soundly, as both men were used to going into aerial action and knew that rest was vital in the hours before the nerve-wracking jolt to the system that flying headfirst into danger usually involved. Thomas Hughes, on the other hand, had a terrible time falling asleep, tossing and turning for several hours. He finally drifted off to sleep, but awoke after a short time, shaking and sweating from nightmares. It was not the German foes that had haunted his dreams, but an enemy with whom he was much more familiar. Hughes had dreamt of Ty Cobb and the humiliating defeat he had suffered at the great hitter's bat. Even after the draft notice, the weeks in basic training, the months of learning to fly and the eventual commission he had received, the impact of that fateful moment on the field in Detroit had never left the corners of Hughes' mind. It was a moment he would never forget.

Morning arrived quickly enough and the three aviators were up, dressed, and ready to begin their mission. Kirby had decided that the purpose of the morning's flight would be one of scouting, and only scouting. The area which they were to investigate was several miles wide. To make things easier, the threepilots would divide the area into three sections and each would fly over one part; quickly enough to avoid attracting too much attention from whomever might be below them, but slowly enough to get a decent look at any ground activity. The Spads were fueled; they took to the air, and soon the Three Mosquitos were off on their way.

They flew the usual V-formation until they approached the intended area. At Captain Kirby's signal, they separated, with Kirby taking the middle section of the area, Travis veering off to the left, and Hughes taking the portion on the right.

The scouting flight was uneventful as far as action was concerned, as no fighting took place, but quite productive as far as information went, as the three pilots each found something of interest to report. The sights were seen, the three Spads met in the middle of the area, and Captain Kirby led Travis and Hughes back to Chaumont Air Base.

Several hours after the mission had begun, the three young aviators were back in the office of Brigadier General Saunders to report what they had found out there in the wilderness of France.

A large map of the area was pinned to the wall of the general's office. Kirby had told Lieutenant Travis to explain their findings to the commanding officer. Saunders sat silently as Travis walked over to the map. The tall, thin lieutenant took a pencil from behind his ear and circled a large area on the upper half of the map.

"This was the area we were ordered to investigate."

He used the pencil to divide the circle into three parts.

"This is how the area was broken into thirds so that we could each examine one section."

He pointed to each sector in turn.

"I flew over this left portion of the zone…and boy, did I hit the jackpot! The Germans are building an airfield out there! It's not done yet, not even close, but it's beginning to take shape. They've got a runway smoothed out and a few buildings in place, including one that looks like it's got their fueling equipment inside. I only saw a few planes. I counted six, so they haven't got the place ready for operations yet, but if we're going to try to put a stop to their progress, I'd hurry up and get going on that!"

The general nodded. He seemed to agree with Travis' estimation of the situation. Travis continued, pointing to the middle section of the circled part of the map.

"This here is where Captain Kirby flew over. Nestled in a clearing in the middle of this area is a tiny French village. There are a few houses, a little church, and what looks like a schoolhouse. Obviously there are women and children there, so I'd hate to see the Germans put a working airfield so close to those poor folks."

Once again, General Saunders nodded. He gestured for Travis to complete his report. The lieutenant did so without delay.

"This other side of the area, the right side, is where Lieutenant Hughes flew over. This is the scary part, because it shows how the Germans plan to complete their little project. Over there we have a separate encampment of Germans; a whole fleet of trucks, specifically the kind that carry planes and other aviation equipment over the ground. Now it looks as though they've made camp there for today, but I'd bet money that they'll be up and on the move again tomorrow, and the stuff in those trucks is going to let them get that airfield up and running.

"So, general, we've got two things to worry about. First, if they get those planes to that field and ready to fly, they're close enough to us here in Chaumont to launch some pretty convenient aerial raids. Second, the most direct route from that camp to the airfield is to drive those trucks on a path that will send them right through that little French town! Sir, we've got to keep that from happening! Those poor civilians won't know what hit them if the Germans go that way!"

Travis finished talking and stepped away from the map and back beside his two fellow pilots.

"Thank you, Lieutenant," said the general. "I want you three to report back to me in two hours, after I've had a chance to discuss this with my senior officers."

The Three Mosquitos left the command center.

With two hours to spend before returning to see the general, Kirby, Travis, and Hughes wandered around the base. They strolled along, smoking, talking about nothing in particular for the first fifteen minutes. Kirby and Travis were naturally curious about their new partner, so Kirby finally got around to questioning Hughes about something that had been a nagging at the back of the young captain's mind since the previous day. The three had stopped to watch a crew of enlisted men washing one of the base's many planes when the question finally came from Kirby's mouth.

"Hughes, I've been wondering about something. When we went over our mid-air communication systems yesterday, you said it reminded you of your old civilian job. Just what did you do before the war, Lieutenant?" the captain asked.

Hughes fell silent for a moment, seemingly hesitant to answer. Travis, for the moment the quiet observer of the trio, took this to mean that Hughes had regrets, or perhaps that he missed his old life, whatever that may have been. Finally, the newest Mosquito spoke.

"I was a ballplayer," said Hughes.

A look of delight and surprise came across Captain Kirby's face. He slapped his thigh and shouted out as the realization of what he now knew crossed his mind. "Dammit, I knew that name was familiar! Thomas Hughes...or Tommy Hughes! You're the guy that pitched for the White Sox; the kid with the perfect rookie season!"

Hughes corrected Kirby. "Almost perfect year, Captain. Those darned Tigers, Cobb and Crawford, ruined my perfect record with a nasty little rally in the ninth in Detroit. It was the only time I lost in the majors...and the next day I had a draft notice in my hands. But that was a long time ago...and far from France. I'm here now; the past doesn't matter so much to me."

After that, sadness fell across the face of Thomas Hughes, and Travis and Kirby knew that it was best to leave the kid alone and not mention life in the States for awhile. They were both experienced airmen now, and they had seen that look of sadness before, usually on the faces of men who missed their wives or children or sweethearts back home. The three men walked around the base a while longer, until Travis finally looked at his watch and mentioned the time. "We should head back to see Saunders now, Captain. You know how he gets when we're late."

"**C**aptain, Lieutenants, I've made a few decisions," said the general as he motioned for them to sit down in the three chairs that sat opposite his desk. "I've thought over the map and the problem of those three separate areas and here's what I've decided. The best thing to do is to try and wipe out both the airfield project and the fleet of trucks before they can meet and become a whole weapon at the Germans' disposal. That means we've got to hit both sites at the same time. Now, as you know, we've only got a limited number of pilots here, and an even worse shortage of infantry in the area, so we've got to stretch ourselves thin.

"I'm sending the bulk of our planes over to the camp of those transport trucks. With a quick air strike, those boys should be able to knock those trucks out of commission...and maybe even destroy the planes inside them before they can make their way over to that new airfield.

"As for protecting that little village, I don't want to send all my ground troops out there, just in case anything should happen here while all you fly boys are gone. So...I've called up my friend Colonel Rackham of the British Army and he's offered to send part of one of his companies in to defend those French townspeople. Those Limeys move fast when they want to, and they're coming from the opposite direction to get there without German interference, so they should be there by tonight. They won't do anything unless provoked or attacked. Rackham says they're led by a young first lieutenant named Harker, who's one of the best they've got, so the village problem has been taken care of.

"Now, Mosquitos, here's what I need from you three. As I said, I'm devoting the majority of our planes to taking out those trucks. Major Crane will lead that attack. I need the three of you to deal with the airfield. Be forewarned that you might encounter some resistance. If any of the few planes there are up and running, you may have to fight them off. Do what you have to. The main goal, however, is not to win a dogfight, but to make sure they can never finish building that field and all the things that need to go with it. Foul their plans up as much as you can. Blast their fuel supply, wreck the buildings, and do whatever you can. Have you got all that, Kirby?"

"Yes, sir!" said the leader of the Three Mosquitos. Kirby was enthusiastic and looking forward to the possibility of action.

"Good," said General Saunders, waving them out of the room. "You're to leave immediately. Once the three of you have taken off, the main air squadron will be sent out to hit those trucks. Good luck, men."

Kirby, Travis, and Hughes jogged out to their Spads. Captain Kirby gave a quick shout of his usual battle cry, "Let's go!" and the Three Mosquitos jumped into their planes, revved their engines and took off into the skies of what was now early afternoon over France. They flew along at top speed in the direction of the mission upon which they had just been sent by General Saunders.

Fifteen minutes after those first three planes had taken off, twenty-three other American pilots boarded their own planes and the runways at Chaumont roared with engines again. That set of planes took off into the air, much as the Mosquitos had, only this time they set off on a slightly different heading, one that would take them on a mission related to the one on which Kirby, Travis and Hughes had gone.

In a third location, the French villagers of a small town, snugly tucked within the forests, were pleasantly surprised to see a platoon of British troops rush into the midst of their settlement. The platoon's translator assured the people that the British were there to protect them from the nearby German troops. The soldiers were welcomed with open arms. The senior enlisted man, Sergeant Baxter, made his way into the town's little tavern, eager to taste the homemade wines of the region. Baxter's commanding officer, First Lieutenant Harker, liked the village right away, as he caught the eye of a pretty young French girl and flashed a mischievous smile in her direction.

Meanwhile, the first three Spads to leave Chaumont were nearing their destination. They decreased their airspeed slightly as they came closer to the site of the in-progress German airfield. Captain Kirby waved his hands in signals to the two pilots who flanked him, Travis and Hughes. Both lieutenants signaled responses of understanding. The Three Mosquitos assumed their typical V formation on the approach to the airfield. Looking ahead and down, the three American flyers could see the half-finished structures of barracks, a command center, a maintenance building, and the fueling station. There were numerous men on the ground; German soldiers and officers. A small group of planes, Fokkers, sat idly on the dirt surface of the newly grassless runway area. From where they sat among the clouds, the field looked like easy pickings for the Three Mosquitos.

Kirby waved a hand again, this time giving the signal to attack. He hoped that he and his men could move in swiftly and mercilessly, riddling the place with bullets and brutally dismantling the unfinished German base. As they were about to descend upon the Germans, the sudden sound of gunfire came from behind them! The three Americans quickly turned their heads and looked to their rear. Three Fokkers had sneaked up behind them and were raining bullets in their direction, their machine guns rapidly spitting lead into the skies! Kirby gave the counterattack sign.

Travis and Hughes each veered off and away from Kirby's plane. The maneuver's intent was to encourage the three German planes to concentrate their fire on Kirby, who was the most agile when it came to swooping and avoiding incoming shots. While the Germans tried to take Kirby's Spad down, Travis and Hughes would pick the attackers off from the edges of the confrontation.

Kirby turned his speed up a few notches, pushing his Spad as hard as he could. The Germans pursued. On one side, Travis raced up and sent a volley of gunfire into the side panel of one of the Fokkers. The bullets hit accurately and the panel shattered. Travis could see the German pilot slump forward in his seat. The bullets had not fatally damaged the plane, but instead had slain the pilot. With a dead man behind the controls, the German plane spiraled out of control and fell rapidly to the French ground, erupting into a ball of flame upon impact. "One down, two to go," shouted Travis, though no one else could hear him.

With two Germans still on his tail, Kirby swooped and flipped, twisting and turning in mid-air to avoid the deadly machine gun fire. He could keep it up for quite some time, he thought, but hoped he wouldn't have to. Travis had done his job well so far, but Kirby had his doubts about Hughes. He liked the young replacement pilot, but found himself wishing that Shorty Carn were there instead.

Another barrage of bullets buzzed over Kirby's cockpit. It was close, but he had just avoided it. *Hurry up, Hughes, hurry up*, Kirby thought to himself as he dove again, causing the next wave of bullet fire to miss his Spad.

Lieutenant Hughes watched Kirby's maneuvering skill. It was an amazing sight to behold. He could see why Kirby was held in such esteem by his fellow flyers. Putting his awe aside, Hughes began to fly in closer to try to bail his captain out of trouble. There were two Fokkers still chasing Kirby. Hughes picked the one closer to him. He adjusted his altitude to fly up just above the German. Aiming the Spad's Vickers machine guns on an inclining angle, Hughes pulled the trigger. The bullets missed the main body of the Fokker, but managed to tear a jagged hole in one wing. That was enough to make the German pilot lose control just enough to get him away from Kirby. Hughes sent a volley of gunfire at the other nearby

German plane. It missed, but distracted the pilot enough to draw his fire away from Kirby.

While Hughes did his job, Kirby pulled off an incredible mid-air somersault and turned the game completely around on the German with the damaged wing. While he had, moments before, been pursuing the American captain, the Fokker pilot now found himself staring Kirby right in the face. Kirby's daredevil grin was the final sight ever to meet that German flyer's eyes. Kirby blew him away!

Travis, meanwhile, was heading back towards the fray. He flew in next to Hughes to try to finish off the third and last German. As Travis came close to Hughes, he saw Kirby heading in to help them out. Kirby flashed one of the Mosquitos' hand signals. Travis saw that he was telling them to back off the German, get back to trying to shut down the airfield below, and let their captain take out the final Fokker. Travis signaled to Hughes and the two lieutenants did as they had been ordered. Kirby, left alone high above the ground, moved in to face the last of the airborne German aces.

Hughes and Travis sped down towards the airfield. The Germans on the ground ran around like panicked mice, trying to decide where to go, but they had few options. As they approached, Travis and Hughes fired their guns and bullets ripped into the few German planes that sat on the ground.

Up above, Kirby flew straight for the German plane, fingers itching to pull his Vickers guns' triggers and finish the aerial duel. He shifted to the left, then to the right. Finally the German plane was in Kirby's crosshairs. The trigger moved with his gloved finger. Then, in the sort of moment that every aviator-warrior dreads, he heard the terrible "click-click-click" sound that told him that his guns had jammed! A mechanical failure in the midst of an aerial battle could be the death of a flying ace, and Kirby knew it! He saw his life flash before his eyes and waited for the German to unleash his own hot lead in his direction.

The German guns spit fire! Kirby felt his plane shake and shudder as the bullets ripped his wings to shreds! Kirby began to lose control of his plane. He knew that if the next barrage of bullets didn't finish him off, the spiraling crash of his plane would!

Travis, taking a momentary pause in his riddling of the German base with bullets, glanced up at the plane that held his captain. He gasped in horror at what he saw. Kirby was in serious trouble. Travis, loyal to the end, could not stay where he was. He turned his plane around, sped upward, and went to the aid of Captain Kirby, praying he would not be too late.

Hughes saw what was happening, but knew that at least one of them would have to remain closer to the ground, would have to make sure that the mission was completed successfully. He kept his eyes on the targets below.

Travis pushed his Spad to its limits. In a blazing blur of aerial action, he flew up and right between the German plane and Kirby's Spad. His gamble worked, startling the German pilot just enough to delay his firing on Kirby. That was all it took. Travis, as soon as he was close enough to have a sure shot, fired a rapid series of rounds into the Fokker. The German was doomed; his plane erupted into an inferno.

As Travis had been finishing off the German, Kirby had been losing his last battle to regain control of his shatter-winged plane. He was going down fast!

Travis' mind raced. His captain was going down! He thought all his options through rapidly, but there was nothing he could do now. His captain was in the hands of fate. There was one tiny chance in a million for Kirby to save himself from a fiery crashing death. If, and only if, Kirby could manage to touch his landing wheels to the ground, rather than hit the ground nose first, he might be able to make the crash a tough, but not deadly, one.

Kirby pulled up as much as his damaged plane would let him. He could see the ground rushing up at him. At the last possible second, he managed to level off and he felt the wheels touch the ground. It was rough but not disastrous. He bumped along, skidding across the grassy field, but he was moving too fast! He looked up and straight ahead, hoping that there would be enough open space in front of him to gradually skid to a halt...but it was not to be! There were trees up ahead, lined up in a neat little row, like soldiers standing at attention. Kirby knew that his Spad would explode on impact with that unavoidable obstacle. His instincts for survival overwhelmed any thoughts of trying to save his plane. He'd be given a new Spad if he survived…but there was no coming back from the grasp of the Grim Reaper! "To hell with the plane," he whispered to himself. He let the controls slip out of his hands and out of his mind. He took one more glance straight ahead, wincing as he saw that the trees were getting closer, closer. He gathered all his energy and jumped up to a standing position in his seat. He mentally flipped an imaginary coin; *left or right, Kirby?* He leaped out of his seat, to his left, over the wall of the plane's interior, bounced off the wing with a sickening thud, feeling the wind being knocked out of him like he'd never felt before…and landed in a roll on the grassy land of France. He could not believe he had managed to survive the crash! Seconds later came the near-deafening roar of his poor Spad hitting that line of trees and exploding in a blast of sound and fury. His ears rang, his bones ached from impact, but Captain Kirby was alive!

Up in the air, Travis looked down on the tiny figure of Kirby, now struggling to stand, a lone man in a great open space. Travis could not tell, from such a height, how badly Kirby was hurt, but he was overjoyed to see that he was alive.

Lieutenant Hughes had flown higher, pulling up from the airfield to see if he could find out what had become of his two companions. He smiled and let out a wild cry of "Yahoo!" as he saw Captain Kirby standing in that big, empty field, with its grassy covering now torn to green and brown shreds, as his empty Spad skidded on ahead of him, stopping only as it hit a row of tall trees and erupt in a fiery doom! He was amazed!

He saw Travis circling around, presumably, to land and see to the captain, so he turned his thoughts from his relief back to the mission. There was still an airfield to obliterate. "Two out, Tommy," he said to himself, "but you're still in the game! It's the bottom of the ninth for those Germans!"

He began his rapid descent toward the German base again. He

flew in, looking straight ahead at the largest building, the structure in dead center of the area, the one that presumably held the fuel supply and maintenance facilities of the airfield. The target looked easy enough to Hughes. He would fly straight in, strafe the building from front to back with gunfire, and hope to ignite the interior fuel tanks. He began to move in.

Then, as he neared his target building, he saw a terrible sight. The large doors of the building opened. Inside, he could see another German Fokker plane. The ones on the runways were smoldering heaps of rubbish now, but the one inside those doors was in working condition! It was about to roll out that door, straight onto the runway and take off!

Scenarios ran through Hughes' head. If that Fokker took off, he would be the only one left to face it. If it beat him, the mission would fail! Not only would the mission be left incomplete, but the German would be able to easily pick off the two sitting ducks, Kirby and Travis!

"I'm not going to let that happen!" Hughes swore to himself. He could not let that Fokker emerge from that building.

The mind of Thomas Hughes went into a state that he had been in many times before. Suddenly, the situation felt like the pressure cooker of a ballgame! His sportsman's instincts were joining up with his pilot's training…and Hughes knew what he had to do.

"Okay, Tommy," he said out loud in the cockpit, "Two outs, bottom of the ninth, one pitch left! You've got to make this pitch, kid; you've got to make this pitch!"

He increased his speed. The doors of that building were right in his sights, but so was the emerging Fokker! Faster, faster he pushed his engines. He was getting closer now. His finger squeezed the trigger of the Vickers guns. Bullets spat forth. Then he stopped firing. The bullets no longer mattered. Tommy Hughes *was* the bullet. Tommy Hughes *was* the baseball!

"Fastball!" he cried out. His khaki Spad raced toward the doors! He flew into the opening like a ball into a catcher's mitt. Straight into the emerging Fokker he crashed, but not before he turned the plane slightly to the left.

"Now make it curve!" he shouted at the moment of impact. The

"Fastball!" he cried out. His khaki Spad raced toward the doors!

Spad met the Fokker! Metal and wood shattered and splintered! The tangled heap of wreckage, guided by the last willful motion of Tommy Hughes' life, skidded into the large fuel tanks of what would have become a German airfield. The building exploded! Fire grazed the sky!

Out in the distance, Travis managed to land his own Spad on the grassy, somewhat uneven field. Doing so damaged the plane and Travis doubted that he would be able to take off from there again, lacking a proper runway, but he could not simply fly back to base without landing to check on the well being of Kirby. Kirby and Travis had climbed from their planes. They limped and groaned, but both would survive. As the great ball of flame shot up into the sky, they managed to gather enough strength to let out a victorious battle cry. They had won...but from their position they could not tell how high the price of victory had been.

It took several hours for a transport truck to come and collect Kirby and Travis. Eventually, just as night fell on France, the two Mosquitos made it back to Chaumont. They were exhausted, but insisted on getting a full report on the rest of the mission results before even submitting to a medical examination and bed rest.

General Saunders told them that the fleet of German trucks had been finished off by the rest of the squadron of American planes. No trouble had come to the French village—except, perhaps, for the women having to resist the advances of some inebriated British infantrymen.

The next morning, Kirby and Travis woke up in the base infirmary. They had no serious injuries, but General Saunders had insisted on their being kept overnight for observation. They awoke to find Shorty Carn, now able to roam around on crutches, standing there laughing at them.

"Good," said Lieutenant Carn. "Now you two can keep me from getting too bored in here. And from what I hear, we'll all need new Spads now!"

Kirby and Travis dragged themselves out of bed the next day. Travis walked back to the barracks to retrieve some money he had stashed away. Then he walked over to the base stores, hoping they would have a few items that would normally be rather hard to find in France. Once he was done there, he met Kirby and Carn. The Three Mosquitos walked down to the runway to a gray painted hangar where a large panel truck was about to carry a certain cargo to its final resting place. Medical corpsmen with French civilians had retrieved the precious remains from the ruins of the destroyed German hangar. The three aviation officers pulled rank on the poor corporal who was guarding the cargo. They were given five minutes alone in the vehicle's interior. Kirby and Travis climbed in while Carn waited outside. Captain Kirby knelt by the large black bag on the floor. He unzipped the bag. Lieutenant Carn, leaning on a crutch, whispered a prayer in honor of a man he had never met, and Lieutenant Travis placed his recent purchase, a brand new glove and baseball, with the body of Tommy Hughes.

"Your second season was perfect, kid," said Captain Kirby. "Perfect."

Author Bio:

This book marks Aaron Smith's first attempt at writing World War I aviation stories. His work has previously been seen in Airship 27's anthology, *Sherlock Holmes, Consulting Detective*. He is the author of the original novel, *Season of Madness*, which features characters from the worlds of both Sherlock Holmes and Dracula. He has written various other stories for Airship 27, many of which will be available in upcoming books. These include works in many different pulp genres including mysteries, westerns, jungle stories, costumed vigilantes, spy thrillers, horror and science fiction.

✠ Captain Midnight ✠

"The Dawn of Midnight"

by
David Walker

Chapter 1
Flight Into Trouble

Allied Airspace near Le Bourget Field, France WWII

he sun hung warmly and confidently over the sparse clouds. The late morning sky was being protected by America's top secret elite fighters, The S-1 Squadron. The S-1 was patrolling for a squadron of German Messerschmitts that had been attacking the Allied supply lines, keeping much needed equipment, food and medicine from our boys at the front. The S-1's mission was one of search and destroy!

"Hey, Cap, how long we gonna stay out here?" questioned Tut Jones over his radio link.

Lieutenant. Aristotle "Tut" Jones was a tall, lanky light-hearted man and youngest of the team. He was the wingman of Captain James Charles Albright, the leader of the top secret S-1 Squadron.

"Tut, our orders are to guard these supply lines, and that's exactly what we're going to do! Now quit griping!" came Captain Albright's response.

Albright was a natural born leader who demanded perfection from his team but, also knew when to cut up with the gang. He had a friendly, yet stern countenance, with dark hair and steel gray eyes. The features of his rounded face showed the confidence of command.

"But I'm starting to get a crimp in my neck from all this looking for a needle in a haystack," whined Tut.

Albright replied with a chuckle, "Yeah, you're a pain in my neck too."

"Kinda makes you wish you were still pushing a broom at Lexy's ,don't it, Sam?" added Lieutenant Ralph Badger rhetorically.

Ralph was the wingman of Lieutenant Samuel Hedges. They had been friends since before the war and were original members of the S-1. They followed each other everywhere, and were best described as the Abbott and Costello of the air. The third pair of the squadron was newcomer Lieutenant Sandra Shank and the squadron trainer, Lieutenant Donald Carr. Sandra was a blue-eyed blonde with a medium build. The scuttlebutt around the base said there was something going on between her and Albright. Don Carr was the eldest of the group, and was more gruff than the roughest drill sergeant. He never admitted to having a softer side, but was known to care for the occasional stray dog or cat. Tut, Sam and Ralph had a contest going to see who could make him smile first.

"I hate to interrupt you, boys," interjected Sandra "but there is a group of Gerry's comin' in fast out of the sun at ten o'clock!"

"Alright let's go to work!" Albright commanded, partially blinded by the sun.

With nerves of steel, the S-1 Squadron charged to the attack. Albright and Tut broke hard left and barrel-rolled out of the turn to get under the approaching German Messerschmitts. The maneuver would have been difficult for any other pilots, but Albright and Tut were the best dog-fighters in the Army Air Forces and it was a walk in the park for them. Their Mustangs were pushed to their limits as the fiercely driven planes soared under the diving attackers. The other four Mustangs of the S-1 Squadron broke right and went after the incoming enemy's flank.

Captain Albright clearly saw ten German Messerschmitts diving out of the sun at top speed to the attack. Albright and Tut had been building up speed coming out of their dive. The eager pilots nosed their ships into a half loop. They executed a perfect Immelmann turn which brought them into range for the kill. With their guns blazing, Albright and Tut tore into two of the enemy craft from the middle of the pack, then a third, and then a fourth. The German ships death spiraled, trailing smoke and flames to the ground below. The two American air aces banked out of their attack just as the remaining S-1 Squadron separated into two teams. Ralph and Sam went high, while Sandra and Don went for the approaching lower enemy planes. Both teams struck with precision and threw three more enemy planes to their doom.

The remaining Messerschmitts broke off and went after their original prey, which had turned predator. Tracer rounds whizzed past Ralph's cowling as Sam dove in for the kill and lit up the German cockpit. The attacker was sent to the ground in flames. The S-1 regrouped and headed in for more, hopeful that there were still more enemy birds that needed to be downed.

Albright angled his crate toward the rest of the squadron. Tut was lower and followed at a distance. Without warning, flaming red hot tracers screamed within inches of Tut's cockpit! A Messerschmitt had latched onto Tut's tail and the vengeful enemy was hell-bent on Tut's destruction. Tut instinctively side-slipped away, but was too late in his response. Hot lead sank into his left wing.

"Cap, I'm hit!!" Tut yelled.

"Hang on kid, I'm coming!" Albright reassured.

The fearless leader of the team jerked his controls and threw his plane over into a steep power dive to save his wingman from certain death. He pushed his Mustang harder than he had ever pushed before, and the plane groaned with agony as it went beyond its tolerances. Albright banked onto the fiend's tail and let his guns roar with revenge.

The sky was alive with bullets like, bees swarming after a prey. Every enemy bullet came closer and closer to finding a resting place in the already injured Mustang. Tut tried to work miracles to stay away from his attacker, but his damaged plane was sluggish in response. Hot lead and tracers whisked past the busy pilot's head as he tried to wing away from the enemy. He kicked his injured Mustang into gyrations in a final attempt to save himself, and then heard an explosion from behind as a final few rounds found a home in his fuselage.

"We got 'im, kid. You ok?" came Don's relieved voice.

Tut turned and saw that Albright and Don had caught the enemy bird in a cross-fire, and there was nothing left except a burning wing falling to the ground. The German's fuel lines were hit in the attack and the crate's fuel tanks exploded signaling the end of the problem!

Ralph and Sam played cat and mouse with the final enemy as Sandra soared in from above for the kill. She sent the last Luftwaffe crate into a smoky death spiral with her guns.

"Didn't your mother ever tell you not to play with your food?" She questioned.

Sam and Ralph smiled in their cockpits and fell into formation to aid Tut's plight.

By the time they made it to their troubled wingman, black ooze had spewed onto the windshield. Oil was leaking from the engine, throwing off heavy black smoke and soot. Tut was flying blind! Albright and Don were on opposite sides of Tut's badly damaged plane, guiding him back to Le Bourget. He dared not bail out because if the terrain did not get him the German patrols would!

"You three high-tail it back and clear the field!" Albright demanded as he saw the remaining squadron's member's fall into formation. "And make sure they are ready to stretch the net!"

Ralph was the senior ranking pilot and acknowledged the order. He took point and the three Mustangs motored toward home. Albright stayed in constant radio contact with Tut and Don. He kept a steady eye on the injured plane as it limped back to base. The flight took mere minutes, but to Tut it seemed like hours as the toll of the affair was wearing him down.

Finally, Tut heard words that were music to his ears. He was on final approach. The strained warrior took a deep breath and swallowed hard. The only thing visible was the dismal smoke burning from the oil leaking from the engine's battle wounds. Tut watched as Albright and Don stayed on his wingtips every grueling inch of the way.

Suddenly, the engine sputtered and metal parts screeched together as the engine seized and died. The bullet-riddled Mustang was now a glider and was losing altitude fast.

Albright saw Tut's predicament. "Stay with me kid. We're goin' in together. Just watch me and we'll land in one piece."

"But Cap," Don protested, "That runway isn't big enough to set two Mustangs down side by side!"

"I know! That's why I'm going to use the tarmac." Cap responded coolly.

"That tarmac isn't made for landings. It doesn't have the reinforcement that the runway has. You'll fold up like a suitcase! It's suicide Cap!" Don pleaded with his leader.

"I'm Tut's eyes and I'm not going to abandon him and that's it! When we get within four-hundred feet, pull up, Don!" Albright ordered.

Don reluctantly shook his head in agreement, "Good luck to you both."

He watched his altimeter and the landing indicators on the field and pulled away from the other two craft at four-hundred feet.

Terrified, Tut hoped these were not his final words and glanced to his leader, "Cap, I'll fly with you any day."

Albright shook his head with confidence and reassurance for both. "Me too, kid. Here we go. Almost ready for wheels down in five... four...three...two...one..."

Both planes jerked as their front landing gear hit the runway at the same time. Albright's plane only had one wheel on the runway,. The left wheel was on the tarmac, and when it hit the thinner tarmac cement, the pavement buckled. The left landing gear was viciously ripped off the plane, and the craft jerked sideways as it skidded on its metal belly! The aircraft threw off sparks in a violent battle with the ground. Albright braced himself against the inside of the cockpit and rode out the rough landing.

Tut, unable to control his forward momentum, jammed his

controls and held on for dear life. His plane came to a forced stop as it hit the netted barricade strung by the ground crew. At nearly the same time, Albright's skinned and sparking hull slammed into Tut's tail section. Both planes burst into flames in protest of the added insult to injury.

The pilots leapt from their cockpits, and before they hit the pavement the ground crew latched onto them and dragged them far from the burning wrecks. Exhausted from the ordeal and with medical corpsmen poking and prodding them for injuries, the twin heroes finally got a chance to rest. They watched as their planes disappeared in the inferno.

Tut was out of breath and looked appreciatively at his panting leader. "Well they say, any landing you can walk away from..."

Albright laughed as he slugged his troublesome wingman in the arm.

Chapter 2
Orders Into Destiny

The thick humidity of the night was like wading through a slimy, sludge-filled swamp. The air hung ominously heavy and stagnant around the fatigued moon as the insects refused to chirp in the treachery.

The intrepid heroes of the S-1 Squadron worked up a sweat, tossing and turning in their bunks as they tried to sleep in the sauna-like barracks.

Tut struggled awake as he rolled on his sweat-soaked pillow. He lumbered to his feet and tried to dry his face with a towel next to his cot. Failing in the attempt, the sweat-drenched pilot ventured into the night in search of some relief. Tut made his way across the complex and found himself in the kitchen of the chow hall. He opened the large freezer doors and turned a pitcher of lemonade and a plate of leftover fried chicken into a quick snack.

Tut gnawed on a chicken leg as he heard voices and laughing coming from outside the building. As he investigated the noises, Tut found Captain Albright and Sandra walking slowly across the compound with her arms entangled around his one. Sandra gave

Albright a goodnight peck on the cheek and strutted toward her quarters, making sure to swing her hips as she went. Tut watched the scene as he casually leaned against the chow hall doorway. He felt a twinge of déjà vu as he recognized the romantic encounter from last week's Clark Gable movie.

"Ahhh, dinner and a show," goaded Tut, still eating the piece of chicken.

Albright looked over at his wingman and walked his way smiling.

"Care for some lemonade to wash down that kiss?" Tut added teasingly.

Tut expected to hear a juicy story and motioned for Captain Albright to join him. The pair strolled back to the kitchen and Albright found a chair while a glass of cold lemonade was placed in front of him.

Tut picked at the chicken as they sat down to share their refreshment and their evening's activities…

BAWOOM!!!!

A large explosion sounded across the base with repercussions ricocheting off the metal fabricated buildings. Gunfire erupted in the chow hall and the two friends dove for the floor!

"We're under attack!!" Captain Albright exclaimed.

Searching for a weapon to use in defense, Albright latched onto a large chef's knife and slowly crawled his way to the doorway that separated the kitchen from the main eating area. Tut joined him with a chicken leg still in his mouth.

Albright spotted movement, and then red bursts of flame from the muzzles of four attacking automatic rifles. The machine guns sprayed toward the light in the kitchen. Without a chance of survival if spotted by the gunmen, Albright sprang like an attacking tiger onto his prey and sank his knife into the first man's neck. Before the foe could hit the floor, Albright opened fire on the remaining three villains with an automatic rifle acquired from the fallen enemy. Three more dropped and the room went silent save the sound of Albright throwing an automatic to Tut. Captain Albright examined the fallen enemies and found them to be German commandos!

As the pair cautiously crossed the grounds of the military compound, they heard sounds of battle coming from a large, black ,jagged opening that was once the wall of their barracks. They rounded the corner and found their boxer-clad teammates in hand-to-hand with another set of German commandos.

Captain Albright and Tut made a grand entrance with automatics blazing! Albright sprayed hot death into the heart of the German assault and dropped three enemies with the first blast from the procured weapon. Tut joined the fracas and cut down two more enemies. Sam and Ralph were giving three more attackers the business, using nothing but bare-knuckled fists and determination. Don yelled at the final attacker as he held him in one hand and beat him senseless with his other: "I'm not a morning person and I don't like being woken up!"

Albright searched the smoke-filled room for more trouble when he spied Tut slumped on the floor, unconscious while crimson life flowed away from a bullet wound in his back. The worried leader spotted Sandra in the doorway and yelled for her to get a corpsman for their fallen team member.

Several hours later, after a thorough search of the base and the surrounding area was complete, the members of the S-1 Squadron somberly gathered in the briefing room with Major Steel.

The grief of command showed on Major Steel's face as he spoke to the assembled hero's. "Apparently, our operations have been putting a major dent in the Nazi war-making effort, and Hitler has declared war on the S-1! We have interrogated the remaining few Germans you left alive, and they all corroborate the story of being sent to destroy the S-1 Squadron. The Messerschmitts you shot down the other day were also part of this scheme.

"We've found out that the Germans have a doctor who they've employed to make good on their hit list. His name is Ivan Shark, and he is currently working on a project near the Belgian border in a castle the Germans have taken as part of the occupation. We do not know what he is working on, but our contacts in the Belgian underground report that a garrison of SS troops are stationed at this castle along with a heavily guarded air strip. I'm sending the S-1 to airdrop near the castle, find out what Shark's plans are and stop him at any cost. Our underground contacts have made a map of the area and marked the rendezvous point. They will direct you on the best route of approach and assist in the operation. Any questions?"

The Major was greeted with silence and concluded," You leave at sixteen-hundred, dismissed."

"Captain Albright, please stay," the major directed as the rest of the squadron cleared the room.

"The slug the doctors pulled out of Lieutenant Jones was a .45-caliber pistol round, probably fired from a Colt which was different from the eight-millimeter rounds fired from the German automatics. We didn't find any .45-caliber handguns on any of the Germans."

Albright was startled by the news. "Are you saying one of my people fired it?"

"All I'm saying is be careful, captain," replied the major, cautiously.

A knock at the door discontinued any further conversation. The major opened the door and found a tired and worn surgeon who wore gloom on his face.

"How's Tut?" Albright demanded.

The surgeon replied slowly, "We repaired all the damage the best we could. Lieutenant Jones' blood pressure dropped in recovery and he slipped into a coma. We don't know if he'll ever wake up again."

Chapter 3
Death Drop

The afternoon was a sober drudgery. The daily lunch was quiet as the members of the S-1 Squadron just went through the motions of eating food that was tasteless to them. Their minds were fixed upon their fallen team member, Tut.

After the slow meal was finished, the remaining members gathered in the barracks and began the arduous task of packing up Lieutenant Aristotle "Tut" Jones' personal belongings. He was being transferred to a Paris hospital for better care while he was in his comatose state. Captain Albright picked up a photograph of the two friends and stared at it with a remembering smile of a wild night out on the town. After several minutes of studying the bygone time, Albright carefully placed the keepsake in the duffle bag with Tut's clothes and uniforms and fastened it closed.

The C-47, medical transport plane, idled on the tarmac while Tut and his assembled gear were loaded onto the plane. The S-1 Squadron gathered along with Major Steel on the taxiway as the C-47 taxied to its standby position on the runway. Final clearance for takeoff was given, and the medical plane motored up. Major Steel was a top-notch commander and had suffered many losses in battle. The S-1 Commander new the best way to support his troops was to be with them at this most terrible of times, and facing adversity with the brave men and women under his command forged a bond of trust in the chain of command. He called his group to attention and all saluted as the plane rolled down the runway. Not a dry eye was to be found as they watched the plane disappear into the clouds and they bid a sad farewell to their fallen teammate, their friend, their brother.

Major Steel approached Captain Albright after the plane took off and said, "Captain, it's nearly time for your departure. Is your team ready to go?"

"We'll be ready, Major," Captain Albright replied.

Minutes later in the briefing room, Captain Albright met with his team one last time before their mission. He went over their mission objectives to find Ivan Shark and stop his mad machinations. He also reviewed the details of meeting their underground contact, Hans Milner. And finally, they discussed rendezvous points, should anything go wrong.

The young Captain knew that the hardest part of being a soldier was emotionally detaching oneself from a traumatic event like losing Tut. He used this moment to bring closure to the team.

Albright ended the briefing by saying, "I know this is a hard time for all of us. But we are professionals, and we need to keep our minds on our work, or somebody else will be lying right next to Tut. Is everybody clear?"

Sam, Ralph, Don and Sandra all responded in the positive.

"Let's do this one for Tut!" Albright gave the battle cry.

"For Tut!" they all responded.

With renewed resolve, the S-1 walked single file to their transport plane. Their gear was already stowed away. Inside the plane, all were buckled in and waited for their clearance to take off. The plane motored up, rolled down the taxiway and winged its way up into the afternoon blue. The secret operatives were off on another mission to defeat the evil Nazi menace.

The flight went into late evening. All were of good spirits and a single mindedness to complete their task at hand. Captain Albright sat and listened to constant droning of the engines at cruising speed. It was almost a hypnotic suggestion to rest. He took the suggestion and drifted off for a little nap after a very busy night and morning. The sleeping Captain felt comfortable and safe with the steady engine hum.

Albright awoke to a voice from the cockpit: "Captain, your team better saddle up."

"What is it? Some turbulence?" inquired Albright.

"Worse. We picked up a German patrol!" the voice responded.

"Alright, everybody gear up!" Captain Albright ordered.

Adrenaline shot through the awakened leader while he strapped on his parachute. The chute was designed to provide more lift than the standard model since they were to jump from a higher altitude. After attaching the rest of his equipment to his belt and harness, Albright poked his head into the cockpit.

"How far away is our rendezvous point?" He asked.

The co-pilot responded with, "Not far, sir. We are nearly there now."

Albright looked out the co-pilot's window and saw a hail of tracers and hot lead steam over the right wing from the rear. The pilot side-slipped to the left to avoid the hostile fire while Albright watched with approval.

"We are going, right now!" Albright yelled to the busy pilot and co-pilot then made his way to the back of the plane.

Bullets ripped through the fuselage, just missing his outstretched arm. Albright checked the inner wall of the compartment for fire from the hot enemy lead and found the bullets had exited the plane on the opposite wall. Don already had the cargo door open and the evening air was cold as it swirled around the compartment. Captain Albright signaled for the courageous S-1 Squadron to jump. Sandra was the first to comply with the order followed by Ralph, Sam and then Don. Albright waited until his team of expert operators was safely out of the transport before he followed suit and joined them in their freefall into the unknown. Sunlight was still struggling against the dark as the night invaded the day in the late evening sky. The paratrooping S-1 Squadron gathered in a circle with their arms and legs extended and knees bent to catch the air and control their descent. Captain Albright dived out of the plane with his arms flat against his sides and legs together. He sailed like a dart to catch the rest of his team. Falling into position, the steadfast leader outstretched his arms and legs to slow his descent. They pulled their ripcords as a finely honed unit, and the parachutes fluttered out until they filled with air. The secret team lofted toward their destination.

The pilot throttled up the C-47's massive engines and banked her for home while the co-pilot closed the outer door. The German interceptors sent warning rounds after the fleeing plane and then set their sights on the fully deployed S-1 Squadron.

A hail of red-hot tracers rained down upon the expert team of military operators. The S-1 pulled their parachute cables frantically to dodge the enemy assault. Don and Ralph unstrapped their automatic rifles and gave the offending Gerry's some of their own medicine. The undaunted men held their parachute straps in one hand and let loose a barrage of lead with the other. Tracers and hot lead lit up the evening sky like fireflies in the night as the battle raged on. The attackers broke off after they seemingly decided the prey was giving too much resistance. The German planes flew close to the embattled paratroopers and as they did Captain Albright identified them as Focke Wulf 190's as they regrouped and trailed off toward an unseen airstrip. The final German attacker circled for home underneath the S-1 Squadron as they looked on from above.

Captain Albright suddenly felt a loss of lift and jerked his head toward his parachute. It was on fire! He could see holes where tracers had cut a path through the material. His team members looked on with worry and helplessness. Without warning, the damaged parachute ripped and collapsed from the flames! Captain Albright was in a free fall to his doom!

Chapter 4
Flight of Fear

C aptain Albright had one chance at life. There would be no second try. His timing had to be on the money. He watched the last German Focke Wulf approach from below. At precisely the right moment, Albright released his parachute harness and pushed it away. Angling his body with arms straight at his sides and legs together, he shot like a bullet to the approaching German plane. With a flick of the wrist, Albright unsnapped the sheath to his field knife and grabbed it at the hilt. He flew straight at the enemy plane and tackled it like a football linebacker then thrust the blade into the plane's fabric to provide a hand hold. In one fluid motion, Albright swung around on the knife handle until he was standing on the left wing then threw back the cowling and gained a new handhold inside the plane.

Before the pilot could react, Albright pulled himself closer and thrust the knife into the surprised German pilot's chest. Life ended immediately. Captain Albright grabbed the stick and pulled it toward him. The plane started to bank left allowing Albright to unclip the

Albright unsnapped the sheath to his field knife and flew straight at the enemy plane.

safety harness from the dead pilot and drop him out of the plane to the black oblivion below. Albright threw himself into the cockpit and leveled the plane, then pulled the cowling until it clicked into position overhead. The relieved Captain scanned the darkened skies for the other enemy craft and schemed to follow them back to their landing strip. He spotted the trailing ship and opened the throttle to catch up.

The paratrooping S-1 members watched with amazement as their leader single-handedly captured the German fighter plane in mid-air! They now concentrated on their own predicament of landing in the darkened Belgian terrain. The black carpet below them turned into a dark thick forest at three-hundred feet. Each member of the team scanned for a break in the trees to land. They were running out of time as the heavily wooded area quickly approached. The paratroopers each found the thinnest area in the trees and pulled their chute chords to aim for it. Don, Ralph and Sandra made it to the ground safely. Sam's chute became tangled in the towering trees and left him dangling ten feet off the ground. He jerked at his chute chords violently until the chute tore loose and he hit the ground with a thud. Sam stood and checked himself for injuries, then announced he was okay.

Don knelt on the ground and worked steadily at finding their landing spot in relationship to the planned landing zone while the others buried the parachute equipment in hastily scraped ditches. German guard dogs were heard in the distance barking and moving toward their position. The secret operators moved as one through the thick underbrush to avoid the advancing search dogs. The forest foliage made for a thick canopy; little could be seen even with the moon in waning fullness.

The team traveled single-file through the woods. Don took point while Sam worked rear guard. Sandra and Ralph alternated sides and all surveyed their assigned areas to make sure the route was cleared of enemy ambushes and booby traps. The stygian forest opened up into a clearing in a valley with several large pits. The barking of the guard dogs was no longer heard, much to their relief. However, a new threat assaulted their senses. The putrid stench of death prevailed in the fielded valley. Not a single person needed to look in order to know that the pits were filled with the decaying dead.

Off in the distance from the other side of the death pits, a motor sounded along with the grinding of gears, then two bright orbs appeared from the wooded dark. It was a truck moving down what appeared to be a dirt road that led into the clearing. The covert S-1 Squadron took cover in the bushes as the clearly visible truck appeared on the luminated path into the valley. German voices were heard clearly on the still night air coming from the approaching cargo hauler. Don distinctly heard a German voice cursing at the rough operation of the trucks transmission as gears ground in argument while another voice laughed and poked fun at the cursing driver. The truck turned, backed up and stopped at one of the pits.

The two men exited the vehicle, slammed their doors closed, then walked to the rear of the vehicle. They opened the rear gate and tossed four cylinder-shaped, canvas-covered packages into the nearest pit. Little deduction was needed to figure out that these men were tossing dead bodies onto an already rancid heap. The men returned to the cab of the truck and exited the death field using the same dirt road.

The hidden team members regrouped and made their way across the stench-filled valley. They stopped at the same pit where the truck had dumped its death cargo and peered into the mass grave. All had seen death in its various forms, but none were prepared for the ghastly horror they beheld. The white of the moon bathed the hideous remains in an eerie silver light. The bodies were missing patches of teeth and hair. The eyeballs had exploded and oozed down the sides of what used to be faces. The skin was a reddish-gray and jaw bones showed though the taught skin that were once lips and gums. Arms and hands were frozen in place where the victims tried to protect themselves in vain. There were hundreds of bodies in this one pit and all looked like they had been cooked alive!

Bile raised quickly in the throats of the onlookers as they ran from the horrid sight. The vomit-threatened team regrouped just inside the forest's edge. They tried to regain their composure but the sickening stench of death hung onto their uniforms. Don motioned for all to follow him as they continued on their trek toward the rendezvous point with their underground contact and Captain Albright. They reached the ruins of an old burned-out farmhouse with just the foundation, fireplace and chimney remaining. The silent group of professional military operators set up defensive positions around the area. Don started to unpack his land navigation gear when he heard a lubricated metal scraping sound. Looking up, he found himself nose to nose with a leveled German Luger!

The night gained speed as it chased the day away. The blackness below enveloped the earth that was once there. Captain Albright followed his new wingmen to a glow that was not more than two miles away.

This must be the airstrip where the Focke Wulfs were stationed, he pondered.

Albright watched from his new transportation as the gray S-1 parachutes glided to a landing in a dense forest about a half mile north of the airstrip lights. He made a mental note of their final destination and tried to spot the final rendezvous point, should he need to make a hasty retreat when he landed.

The Focke Wul's had fallen into a flight pattern to land. The airfield was clearly visible now, as was a large gray stoned castle that stood sharply on a hill overlooking the airdrome. The castle had a large clock tower for its entrance, and had only a winding dirt road leading up to that entrance. The road followed the contours of the hill and forked toward the runway, while another fork disappeared into the night. Also on the hill was a camouflaged area that looked like an ammo dump and a wooden structure that possibly could have been a makeshift barracks. Albright looked back toward the airstrip and along the northern edge of the runway stood two massive hangars that looked like they were built to house the giants that lived only in nursery rhymes.

Captain Albright banked his aircraft to line up for final approach and reduced his throttle. He gently set the German crate down on the concrete runway and motored toward the other Focke Wulfs parked on the tarmac in front of the east hangar.

The flurry of activity around his plane once he came to a stop was better than he had hoped for. Ground crews and maintenance personnel scurried around the craft while Captain Albright slipped into the east hangar without notice. Inside, he found dozens of Focke Wulf 190's and P-51 Mustangs all without any markings. They were just painted a flat black on the top surfaces and a flat medium gray on the bottom surfaces. All were fully loaded with ammunition and outfitted with mufflers to suppress the sound of the engines. It was obvious these planes were built for the same mission.

The captain of the S-1 Squadron worked his way to the far end of the hangar and found a door that led to the outside. The metal exit door gave with a slight creak from the hinges. He casually strolled to the next hangar which was the larger of the two. He opened another metal door and walked through and was greeted by what was clearly a huge airplane factory. The ceiling had gantry cranes that held empty aircraft shells. Engines, propellers and electronics were found at various stations throughout the massive complex. It was then he saw at the far end of the hangar the strangest ships he had ever seen.They were almost futuristic, like something Flash Gordon flew in the Saturday matinee movie serials. They looked like giant V-shaped wings with a cockpit and landing gear but there was no tail or rudder. Albright examined the underside of the unidentifiable aircraft and found each outfitted with bombing rigs built into the fuselage. Each had the same color scheme as the fighters in the other hangar. Control surfaces extended the full length of the rear of the craft, with vertical stabilizers on each wing tip. The only truly recognizable items of the strange planes were duel propellers at the back to push the birds. Albright examined four of the wild looking bombers. Each showed indications of being flown recently.

These birds are in use, he thought to himself. *This makes more sense now; those fighters are to be the escorts for these bombers. But where are they going?* Albright asked himself.

He was still lost in thought when a challenge in German came from behind. Albright spun and found the muzzle of an automatic rifle leveled at his chest by a German guard. The cautious guard repeated his challenge and walked toward the suspicious man, watching his every move. The courageous captain began to gag and choke, grasping his neck as if he was struggling for breath. In a split second, as the guard moved closer, Albright pushed the rifle barrel away and kicked the German squarely in the chest. The blow knocked the wind out of the enemy soldier. Albright quickly wrapped his arm around the man's neck and squeezed until the German struggled no more. Captain Albright let the body slump to the ground when he was sure the deed was done. Albright hid the body under a cargo tarp, then continued his inspection of the hangar.

Lockers, desks and work areas were examined by the captain of S-1 for clues to the destination of the flying-wing bombers, but he found none. His search was concluded in frustration. The perplexed intruder then found a back entrance to the hangar and slipped unnoticed into the night. Safely inside the thick dark forest, Albright pulled out his map and compass, triangulating his current position in relationship to the rendezvous point, then set off to meet up with his team.

The ominously quiet forest seemed to go on forever. Albright counted his strides as he walked, and knew by their number how far he had traveled. He was careful not to make noise. Even though the trees would dampen it, sound still traveled far in the dark and would give away his position. By Albright's calculations, he was approaching the rendezvous point when he heard noises off to his left and dropped to the ground. Silently, he crawled toward the noise like a cat stalking its prey. Albright peered over a fallen tree from his concealed position and viewed a scorched brick chimney that reached to the sky.

Then he saw it, a man dressed in brown wool pants and a gray jacket was pointing a gun at Don's face. Albright was a professional operator in every sense of the word, and he took up a position just off to the side of the perpetrator. He moved like greased lightning and stuck a chrome Colt .45 to the man's head. The next thing the gunman heard was the cocking of the .45 in his ear and the captain's instructions to drop his weapon.

Chapter 5
Into the Viper's Pit

The gunman slowly bent down and placed the Luger on the ground, then cautiously stood up straight with his hands in the air. He identified himself as Hans Milner, S-1's underground contact. Albright exchanged passwords with the surrendered man and when protocol was satisfied, he released the tension on the hammer and holstered the .45.

The underground spy stood just under six feet tall with short brown hair and brown eyes. He had the appearance that this was not his first mission and life had been hard. His age was difficult to judge, but possibly in his mid-thirties. Milner told the group that he had a place where they could talk and directed everybody to follow him. With Milner at point, the reunited S-1 resumed their combat patrol mode with staggered weapons and single-file movement. The clandestine unit stole silently through the wooded night. Within thirty minutes, they reached the outskirts of a small disserted village. The moon cast an eerie glow on the outlines of abandoned structures, and a strange wind blew hauntingly through the empty town causing doors and shutters to creak. Albright half expected to see a ghost or a dancing skeleton in the stark remains. The team took refuge in a small hut close to the tree line. Captain Albright posted Ralph and Sam as guards on the outside of the lonely enclosure. The other team members began comparing notes on the night's events and findings.

Captain Albright looked at Milner and in a lowered voice questioned, "What do you know about the squadron of unmarked planes at the airstrip?"

"Ivan Shark has developed a radiation bomb. He is going to use his super bombers, as he calls them, to drop the bombs and use the Focke Wulf 190's as the escorts," Milner replied grimly, peering back at Albright.

"Where and when is he going to drop the bombs?" Albright questioned.

"London and Paris; tonight, they leave at midnight," came the response from Milner.

Don chimed in, "We found a bunch of mass graves in a field on our way here."

The contact man looked at Don dourly. "Shark took those people from this village and used them as test subjects for his radiation bomb experiments," he said. "Every man, woman and child was cooked by his radiation."

"Shark has troops garrisoned at the castle. It will take all of us to stop him," Milner added as he pulled out a small map.

"We can get into the castle by a secret entrance; this trail will lead us up the side of the hill unnoticed," he said pointing to the map.

"Once inside we take care of Ivan Shark, then make our way to the ammo dump and blow it. The resulting explosion should destroy the castle and the garrisoned troops. After that, we head back to the airstrip and blow the hangars before those bombers can take off. We have very little time it's already nine-thirty," Milner said glancing at his watch. "So we better get going."

The pathway that led up the hillside was not far away. The night sky had partially cleared, and the trail reflected the gray-stained light from the moon and the stars. The underground contact took point with Albright ten feet behind. The rest of the daring team of experts spaced themselves evenly as they began the treacherous trek up the narrow rocky path.

The hike up the uneven trail was monotonous, but it progressed at a steady pace. Then Milner gave the hand signal to stop. The team instinctively dropped to one knee and scanned their fields of fire for enemies. No sooner had they stopped when a spotlight from a search tower at the airstrip gleamed over them and threw disjointed shadows against the hillside. Had the two German's in the search tower had known the shadows hid the intrepid adventurers, the alarm would have been sounded. The search light continued on its course, and when the probing beam was safely past, the team resumed their travel toward the dreaded castle.

The covert group reached a small outcropping of rocks that hid a steel door near the crest of the hill. From the direction of the door, it led into the castle. The cobwebs that guarded the unused entrance were soon cleared by a wave of a hand. The rusted door took two men to open and gave way with a heavy creaking from the hinges.

The interior was black, swallowing the light from Milner's flashlight. It proved to be a simple corridor that led to the interior of the castle. Moisture had seeped through the mortar of the brick walls and stained the interior. The spider webs were thick and quickly worn by all as the team moved through the dark unknown. The black corridor soon opened up into a large room with stone stairs that led upward and off to the side. There were recesses in the walls for storage that were now barren of any supplies. The only signs of life found in the chamber were the spider webs and a rat carcass laying in one of the recesses. The covert unit cleared the room effortlessly then started up the stone stairway.

The dark stairs spiraled to the left and smelled dank from moisture and mold. The courageous troop of operators rounded the spiral twice before a faint light flickered against the dingy walls. They stopped all forward movement, took up defensive positions along the walls and extinguished their own lights. Captain Albright and Milner moved to opposite sides of the stairway opening and peeked into the newly found light.

The source of the flicker came from torches that were lit around a large room similar to one they had just left. There were no doors or windows—just a hollowed out room in bricks and rock with a darkened hallway at the far end.

The center of the room held Albright's attention. The lifeless form of a badly beaten and obviously tortured man was hanging by his shackled wrists from the ceiling. His feet barely scraped the cold floor of the death chamber. From the look of the blunt wounds, the man had been there for several hours, waiting for death to take him.

Albright gave the hand signal to advance. The complete team moved in and soon centered on the poor soul in chains. Captain Albright checked the dead man's pockets and clothing for a clue to his identity. The S-1 leader then lifted the man's chin to get a good look at his face and reeled in horror. It was Milner's face!

Albright spun on his heels to confront the imposter, but before he could take a step, German soldiers flooded the chamber from the black hallway. The Nazi contingency was well armed with automatic rifles, and had the muzzles trained on the small group in the center. Death was at hand should the American professionals decide to fight.

Seeing their plight was hopeless, the team surrendered as the enemy soldiers gathered the team's weapons. Milner half laughed and half smiled as he began to rip clumps of makeup and rubber from his head, revealing a twisted smirk on a new and decidedly evil face.

"Captain, I believe an introduction is in order," the imposter began. "I am Doctor Ivan Shark. The Nazi high command put me in charge of eliminating the S-1 Squadron once and for all."

Albright and crew scowled with hatred as their deceiver continued to speak. "You are a very hard person to kill. I sent that squadron of Messerschmitts after you, but you killed most of my best pilots in the altercation. Then you defeated my commandoes that infiltrated your camp."

"So you're the one responsible for Tut laying in a coma," Albright spat.

A soft, white female hand rested on his shoulder and whispered into his ear seductively," No Jim, I'm the one who shot Tut in the back."

The temptress then reached up and gave him the kiss of death on his cheek.

Albright immediately recognized the betrayer as his team member and new girlfriend, Sandra! Suddenly repulsed by her touch, Albright went to grab her. Before he could wrap his hands around her beautiful throat, a giant arm grabbed him from behind. He instinctively spun to give fight to his attacker and found himself laying a haymaker on the ugly face of a walking mountain that stood seven feet tall and weighed well over three-hundred pounds.

The giant took offense at the strike and slammed his hand down onto Albright's face, making a smacking sound like a thunder clap. The blow dropped the enraged captain to the floor. Albright thought he had been hit by a sledgehammer, but did not show an ounce of weakness. As he picked himself up off the floor, he wiped a trickle of blood away from his lip with back of his hand and glared at the beautiful spy now standing at Shark's side.

The betrayed S-1 team struggled with the guards to catch the thief who had just stolen their trust and friendship. They were unable to reach her as the guards held them at bay.

"Captain, I almost forgot, let me introduce you to my daughter, Fury Shark," Ivan laughed with delight as he added salt to the jagged wounds Fury made with her deceit.

"I half suspected you when Major Steel gave me the ballistics report saying Tut was shot by a .45," Albright said to Fury with disgust.

"So, Shark, who's your little playmate here?" Albright questioned as he motioned to the walking mountain.

Ivan Shark was savoring every moment of this exchange and responded to the captain's question with a devilish grin. "Captain Albright, meet Igor, my personal body guard. He earns his money don't you think?"

Albright ignored the comment and replied defiantly, "Now that you have us, no matter what you do, you won't get a thing from us!"

Shark smiled fiendishly," My dear dear Captain, you are quite wrong. I will get something from you. I will take great satisfaction when you and your men watch the launching of my super bombers as

"No Jim, I'm thE onE who shot Tut in thE back".

they fly to burn London and Paris to the ground. Your countrymen will look just like those pathetic villagers in the pits your men found. Then at the stroke of midnight, I will take great pleasure in watching you and your illustrious team die!"

Chapter 6
The Dawn of Midnight

Captain Albright took note of the many doors in the darkened hallway as the captured team were being lead to their unknown destination. He thought the corridor seemed to go on forever. He only found one door with any markings along the journey. The placard said, STORAGE. After a quick turn in the man-made stone passageway, the team and their captors entered a lit room that was obviously the old dungeon of the castle.

Rusty chains and manacles rested against the musty wall on the far side of the room like strange tentacles from a brick and mortar monster. Prisoners of old were chained to the wall and left to die in the now empty positions. The other side of the room held barred cells, which were still in use, built into the dank interior of the horror chamber. The first cell held three prisoners, all wearing tattered American pilot uniforms, who watched as the new prisoners were directed into the second cell. The rear of each of the cells had a barred opening in the wall that let in the night air and the ringing of the castle's clock tower.

A solid wood door closed off the corridor behind them and was secured with a chain and padlock. The Nazi troops left the room through a doorway on the far end of the prison room while Ivan Shark, accompanied by Fury and Igor, watched as a guard locked the cage door on the captured S-1 Squadron's holding cell.

Ivan Shark approached the clammy prison chamber and smiled devilishly at Albright as the clock tower chimed in the courtyard outside. "Captain, do you hear the chiming from the clock tower? It's calling you to your destiny. In one hour, the clock will chime twelve midnight. Do you know what happens then? My super bombers will take flight and burn London and Paris to the ground. Then you and your troublesome friends will be disposed of permanently."

"It'll never work, Shark," Albright spat. "I inspected those bombers and they only hold two bombs each. With two bombers going to each city, four bombs will never destroy cities the size of London and Paris."

"My good Captain, you underestimate my abilities," Shark countered. "The bombs have a very high explosive in them— enough to spread the radiation for miles. Four bombs per city will be more than enough to turn your beloved London and Paris to cinders."

Albright lurched toward the cell door trying to grab Ivan Shark by the neck. "You're mad, Shark! What about all the innocent women and children in those cities?"

Shark stepped back instinctively and waved his index finger back and forth. "Shame, shame, Captain. I intend to bring about a quick end to this war with the Fatherland being victorious. Your pitiful attempts to stop me are useless. But nevertheless, do not worry, Captain– Midnight will soon be here!"

Shark quickly turned and left the room with Fury and Igor in tow. The wooden prison door slammed and was locked behind them.

Albright stood silently as Shark left the room, then turned to see Ralph and Don who were testing the strength of the bars, and Sam, who was talking to the captives in the next cell.

Don stood and centered on Albright. "These bars are as strong as the day they were made."

"Cap, this is Lieutenant Mudd, Lieutenant Ramsey and Lieutenant Ryan," Sam said pointing to each prisoner as the introduction was made. "Their entire unit was sent to destroy the airstrip a few days ago. They're all that's left. Everybody else was either shot down by the same Focke Wulfs that nearly got us or were tortured and killed by Shark."

Captain Albright thought for a moment then looked at the captives in the next cell. "You three up to getting out of here?"

The slim-figured Lieutenant Ryan looked up at Albright and in a decidedly female voice said, "We're with you!"

Albright took a double take. "A woman? You're a woman?"

Lieutenant Mudd spoke up, "We've been hiding her features from the Nazi's and they haven't noticed yet. We were afraid what would happen if they found out."

The surprised captain looked at Lieutenant Ryan and found big blue eyes staring back. He found them almost hypnotic, but then quickly recalled the figurative knife in the back from Fury and he regained his senses.

Albright motioned for everybody to gather around him and said, "Alright, everybody, this is what we are going to do..."

A few minutes later the two guards outside the prison chamber were talking softly when they heard yelling from one of the prisoners inside the room. The voice was calling for a doctor.

The jailor of the two Nazi guards worked the key into the lock on the door and then both guards found the triggers to their automatic rifles. The cautious pair entered the room and found one of the newly captured prisoners face-down on the floor inside the cell and not moving. The other prisoners were gathered around him with their leader pleading for help.

The aged gate squeaked as the jailor slowly unlocked it and pulled it open. His partner remained behind to stand watch, just in case the prisoners tried something funny. The over-watch guard then walked into the cell with the jailor taking the over-watch position.

Albright stood to the side and tried to act oblivious to the guard's position. He slowly stepped out of the way of the incoming guard and watched the jailor with his peripheral vision. All attention was on the fallen man as the enemy guard bent down to check his condition. Just then, the body lurched and provided a split second distraction for Albright to spring upon the jailor and throttle him to the ground. At the same moment, Sam and Ralph toppled the kneeling guard and gave him a blow to the head with the butt of his own weapon. Don, who was playing 'possum on the floor, collected the jailor's weapon and assisted his Captain by giving a final blow to Albright's struggling victim.

The plan went off without a hitch, and soon the other prisoners were free. The enemy guards were searched and stripped of two automatic rifles, two Luger handguns, extra ammo for both types of weapons, keys, and several hand grenades. Sam tried to secure the chamber door as best he could since it locked only from the outside. Lieutenant Chuck Ramsey fumbled with the keys until he found one that opened the back door. Not knowing when their escape would be noticed, Captain Albright hastily led the way into the dark corridor and down to the storage room that he had spotted during their arrival.

The lifeless guards were dragged into the room as Albright scavenged through it. The remaining team members and their new partners waited outside mere minutes when a new man emerged from the storage room. It was Captain Albright dressed in black pants, black head gear with the goggles down and a black scarf masked over the bottom portions of his face. The final piece of the outfit was a black leather jacket with only the gold wings insignia of an American pilot attached just above the left pocket in proper award fashion.

The awaiting pilots were surprised by their leader's new garb and Don asked, "What's up, Cap?"

"You take the others down to that airstrip and stop those bombers at any cost," the man in black responded.

"What are you going to do?" asked Chuck Ramsey.

"Ivan Shark wants death at midnight? He's going to get death at Midnight. From now on you boys can call me … *Captain Midnight!!*"

Chapter 7
When Midnight Strikes!

Captain Midnight and his squadron of secret operators ran through the dank storage chambers toward the spider web infested tunnel that led to freedom. They heard shouts from the prison chamber alerting the enemy of their escape. Suddenly, gunfire erupted behind them and bullets sang as they ricocheted off the stone walls. Bringing up the rear, Don gave the pursuing enemy a hand grenade to think about. The concussion from the explosion was deafening as it echoed through the rooms and hallways of the primeval castle. Debris collapsed onto the German assault troops and stopped them for good.

However, the team still quickened their pace as they were being pursued by falling stone, mortar and earth. The explosion had weakened the structure of the ancient castle and the escape tunnel was rapidly being sealed by the fallout. They ran as if the Devil himself were chasing them. Dust and dirt filled the air rendering the flashlights useless as the light was just reflected off of the thick infection in the air. The choking and struggling secret squadron members ran face-first into the steel door and pushed with all their might. They strained their sinews from the lack of air against the girth of the rusted door until the wheezing tunnel finally coughed and spewed them out—along with dust and debris—into the night air just as it went into its death throes.

There was little time to spare. The remaining German Guard contingent would soon be thick in the castle grounds on a deadly hunt for the escapees. Captain Midnight knew the only chance of stopping the bombers before they took off rested with his team, but they were going to need a distraction in order to make it down the hillside. He would be the distraction and, if all worked out, he would lure Ivan Shark into the open and settle the score.

The Gladiator of the Skies gathered the remaining grenades and a fully loaded Luger and then sent his unit down the hillside with Don in the lead. The midnight clad military operator peeked over the embankment near the tunnel door and made a mental note of the positions of several Nazi soldiers. He then scurried over the rock ledge above the doorway and began his one-man war against the evil forces of Ivan Shark. Captain Midnight ran from one target to the next, stabbing hot death into each Nazi he saw. Death laid in his wake.

A gear-grinding and motor noise announced a Kubelwagen, a German transport vehicle shaped like a boxy-looking convertible with the top down. Two German soldiers inside the vehicle seemed determined to run him down. Captain Midnight leapt at the last minute, then rolled onto his side sending two rounds of protest into the back of the driver. The transport rolled to a stop with the driver slumped over the wheel. The passenger quickly turned and fired, but was too late as two more bullets found his chest.

Captain Midnight ran in a low crouch toward the barracks which sat on the far side of the courtyard sheltered by the castle walls. He let loose with a grenade and the makeshift structure, along with all of its occupants, were swept away by a sharp explosion.

The ammo dump was just a stone's throw away from the destroyed barracks, and the one-man wrecking machine dove inside just as German bullets whistled past his head in answer to his assault.

Looking about the ammo storage area, he found a bag and loaded it with bundles of dynamite which were conveniently fused and ready for action.

Back at the doorway, Captain Midnight lit a bundle of dynamite and threw it in the direction of the advancing Nazis. The resulting blast tore away at the wall of the once mighty castle and sent massive pieces of stone and mortar onto the approaching enemy. Their charge ended with shrieks of death. The Champion of Freedom introduced a grenade to the other explosives in the ammo dump and ran with all his might toward the front of the castle. The grenade blast set off cascades of explosions and sparks that lit up the night sky for several minutes.

Lit bundles of dynamite were deposited along the front of the castle parapets and their resulting blasts tore violently into the sides of the ancient stone walls. The powerful concussions stripped the castle structure of integrity as brick and debris were thrown about the blast site. The occupants fled like rats from a sinking ship. Captain Midnight stabbed hot lead at fleeing Nazis until his magazine clicked empty.

Sharp reports from German automatics were heard as enemy bullets flew past Captain Midnight's position from approaching enemy troops. He rolled toward a fallen soldier and picked up an unused automatic rifle. Bent on one knee, he gave the attackers the business end of the automatic and stopped the assault with a hail of bullets.

The final few bundles of dynamite had longer fuses, and Captain Midnight distributed them evenly at the entrance to the castle and at the base of the clock tower. Before he could finish, the clock tower began to slowly strike the midnight hour. Hurriedly, he placed the last charge and ignited the explosive bundles. The damaging blasts and clock tower gongs made a symphony that was heard for miles, and Captain Midnight was the conductor.

The castle was not far from being decimated by the dynamite bundles when two solitary figures emerged from the smoke. Ivan and Fury Shark were trying to escape. Fury looked at Captain Midnight with disgust and leveled an automatic in his direction. She gasped then fell to the ground from a fiery spray of lead. Captain Midnight lowered his smoking barrel and paused as he mourned her death and his betrayed feelings.

Ivan Shark dropped to his daughter's side in grief and held her in his arms then looked at his adversary. "Who are you?!" Shark demanded.

The black-clad aviator pulled down his mask and goggles and revealed Captain Albright's features hidden underneath.

The villainous Shark watched the revelation with hatred in his eyes. "Captain Albright?"

"No... Captain Midnight!" came the steely response.

Just then the final bell stuck midnight and the final dynamite bundle exploded, sending the clock tower debris raining down onto Ivan Shark. When the smoke cleared, the only things visible were rocks and the clockwork gears and springs. Ivan Shark and his traitorous daughter, Fury, had been stopped by the masked aviator, Captain Midnight.

The victory was bittersweet as Captain Midnight heard engine noise and turned to see four flying V-wing bombers and twenty Focke Wulf 190s take to the skies. His team had not been as successful in their mission as he was in his.

Captain Midnight turned back toward the castle to admire his handiwork and to check for any pursuit. All was quiet around the castle ruins while smoke rose from its wounds.

Gunfire from the airstrip interrupted the survey of the castle. Captain Midnight went to the mountain cliffs above the airstrip and found his team pinned down by an enemy pillbox. Midnight ran to the Kubelwagen and ejected it's slumped occupants to the ground outside. Inside the vehicle, he figured out the gear pattern then raced down the winding mountain road that led to the air field and another battle against the evil Nazi menace.

The secret squadron members watched as their leader disappeared over the top of the cliff. Captain Midnight was doing his part and now it was time for them to do theirs.

Don looked toward his new team then asked, "Which of you is the best shot?"

Mudd spoke up, "Chuck, here, won the base sharp-shooting competition last month."

Without hesitation, Don handed Chuck his rifle then looked at Sam, who was holding the other procured weapon. "You two try to take out those guards in the guard tower and then provide cover fire for the rest of us."

"Will do," Sam responded.

Don motioned and the team started their descent down the narrow mountain pass while their sniper teammates took up positions along rock outcropping at the top of the trail. The night provided challenges on the trail that tested the abilities of each member of the descending team. Even though they used the trail earlier, it now seemed totally foreign. The stalwart operators found their way down the treacherous path, then halted when the search light fell on their position. After making sure the light had moved on, the new teammates continued their dangerous trek toward the airstrip. Ralph was bringing up the rear with Lieutenant Ichabod Mudd when he stumbled on several projecting rocks and roots. He was steadied by a helpful hand from Lieutenant Mudd.

"Thanks, Mudd," Ralph offered.

"Call me Icky, short for Ichabod, my first name," Mudd replied.

Ralph nodded in recognition and Icky removed his steadying hand from Ralph's arm. The pair quickened their pace to catch up to the team still moving down the mountainside.

The end of the trail was in sight when the spotlight fell on them for the second time. This was the wrong kind of fame to be in the spotlight for as machine gun fire lit up the dirt and stone around them. The guard tower had spotted their movement and was doing its best to eliminate the intruders. Just then, from further up the pass, two single shots rang out and the machine gun fire stopped. Don looked up and saw his two snipers giving him the high sign as they had performed their assigned task admirably.

The gunfire must have spooked the ground crews as engines were starting all over the airstrip. The secret operators scurried to gain a good firing position on the enemy craft, but they were too late. The Focke Wulfs were taking to the air and were soon followed by the flying-wing bombers. The assault team let off a few rounds, but had no effect on the death squadron in the air.

Their shots gave away their position to an enemy pillbox at the end of the runway. The machine gunners inside the pillbox let the S-1 know their mistake. Enemy slugs peppered the area while the discovered military operators ran for cover. The boys were soon pinned down behind an old building foundation which was rapidly deteriorating from the machine gun blasts.

Almost on cue, a queer looking vehicle driven by their black-clad chief sped toward the pillbox. With unyielding determination, Captain Midnight floored the transport and swerved from side to side to avoid the deadly fire from its guns. The enemy trained their weapons on the vehicle and started turning it to Swiss cheese. Nazi bullets careened through the windshield of the stolen vehicle as Midnight ducked behind the dashboard. Giving it all she had, Captain Midnight rammed the enemy bunker then threw his two remaining hand grenades inside. He dove for cover just as the bunker belched with fire, its guns sounded no more, ending its reign of searing death.

Sam and Chuck ran up to Captain Midnight from the mountain trail. They were soon joined by the rest of the team.

"Did anybody see any P-51's take off?" Midnight questioned.

All responded in the negative. "Then follow me!" He ordered.

Captain Midnight led them to the giant hangers that stored the secret bombers and their escort planes. The massive doors were left open by the Luftwaffe ground crews who were probably on trucks enroute to a safe location.

Inside the massive structures, Captain Midnight and the Secret Squadron found the P-51 Mustang's that Captain Albright discovered

Nazi bullets careened through the windshield of the stolen vehicle as Midnight ducked behind the dash board.

during his first visit to the airstrip. They also found the equipment to fuel the planes and ammo for the guns. Large gas tanks at the rear of the hanger provided the necessary fuel.

Captain Midnight looked at his team and gave his orders: "Alright, everybody, lets get these birds fueled and armed. We have some planes to catch!"

Chapter 8
Race Against Death

The secret squadron of airborne operators found the night air to be alive with the radiant glow of the moon. They kept a tight formation while getting used to their new birds. These rebuilt Mustangs had more power than a standard production model. Their mufflers quieted the engine noise down to a buzz instead of the loud grind the pilots' ears were accustomed too. The formation was so tight that a sudden gust of wind blew Don's ship and forced his wingtip to glance off Joyce's adjacent wingtip.

"Don't get fresh!" She taunted.

"Do I need to separate you two?" Captain Midnight chimed in.

Don turned a bright shade of red as he angled his plane a little further away from his tormentors.

By Captain Midnight's calculations, the enemy planes had left fifteen minutes ahead of his team. Ivan Shark's bombers were fully loaded and not able to fly at top speed. For the sake of thousands of innocent lives, Captain Midnight had to make up for the lost time. He worked the throttle wide open and his Mustang trembled from the horsepower as he poured on the steam; the others followed suit.

The planes settled into a standard formation while charging through the night to stop Shark's evil-doers.

The minutes seemed like hours as the Crusaders of Freedom scanned the skies for their enemy. The task went on tensely for what seemed like days with not a word spoken until suddenly Icky broke radio silence: "Five o'clock!"

As one, the team looked downward onto strange patches of darkness that covered the ground lights. The queer patches could be made out as aircraft and with closer inspection, the four V-wing bombers were at the lead! Luck was with them, the Luftwaffe squadron had not yet separated into two teams, one headed for London and the other for Paris.

Captain Midnight knew the escort Focke Wulfs had to be taken out quickly because dogfights at night were very dangerous especially against an enemy force of superior numbers. The Focke Wulfs were formed in five four-plane wedges which made up a larger wedge formation. The four V-wings flew in a lateral formation in front of the escort fighters.

Upon his command, Captain Midnight's squadron separated into two teams. He led the first team with Don and Joyce on his wing tips. Sam led the second team with Ralph, Chuck and Icky in a perfect wedge formation. The determined leaders started their dives at each of the outer ends of the enemy convoy. They were followed by their team members, except for Joyce and Icky, who stayed in level flight acting as a rear guard should any of the enemy try to outflank the attackers.

The lead Mustangs let loose a maelstrom of hot lead and tracers that tore through the enemy fighters like a hot knife through butter. Captain Midnight sent four enemy crates to the ground in smoking death spirals and then banked hard left to avoid any friendly crossfire. Sam banked hard right after giving his four birds a good dose of lead poisoning.

Don continued the attack on his end of the enemy crates and dropped two more before the Luftwaffe planes broke formation and decided to fight back. Captain Midnight settled in on Don's right and the pair whittled away at the attacking four Focke Wulfs.

The other end of the convoy was no different. Tracers lit up the night sky like fireflies in a pickle jar. Sam went into an Immelmann turn, then barrel rolled to join up with Chuck and Ralph in their fight. It was a pitched battle with the three Mustangs slugging it out with six of the enemy planes. The boys' night vision did not last long when they sent a hail of bullets toward the outer attacking planes. The receiving German pilots tried to save themselves and side-slipped into each other. A propeller imbedded itself into the other's fuselage and set off a huge explosion. The flaming debris caught Midnight's attention at the other side of the battle as it fell through the sky. He turned his attention back just in time as a Gerry pilot was making a suicide run at him. Captain Midnight jerked on his controls and banked hard left. He felt a slight bump when the enemy crate's wing tip grazed the bottom of his fuselage. Midnight continued in a sharp arc while Don emptied a burst of hot death into the offender's canopy.

Captain Midnight watched from his turn as the four V-wings separated into pairs and disappeared into the night at top speed toward their targets. Midnight angled under his remaining attackers and let loose with his guns. His blasts tore away at the life in two more of the enemy planes, and they spiraled to certain doom. A hail of fire ripped past him and stitched its way across his left wing. He looked around for his wingman, but Don was too far away from his last attack to make a difference. Another stream of hot lead and flaming tracers narrowly missed his engine cowling and found a home in his right wing. The plane was getting a little sluggish. He side-slipped and banked away in an attempt to shake his attacker, but nothing worked as more bullets tore through his fuselage.

Just then, duel blasts from directly above him sent his attacker to an early grave and a voice came across his radio: "I got 'em for ya, Midnight!" It was Joyce—and just in the nick of time too.

Sam, Ralph and Chuck were having problems of their own. Chuck Ramsey was being chased by two Messerschmitts. Chuck was a good pilot and had many tricks up his sleeve to dispose of these two troublemakers but they were just hell bent for leather to bring down a yank. He got off several good blasts from his guns and peppered the twin attackers to no avail. The enemy planes continued their desperate onslaught and Chuck thought he was going to buy the farm. Then, out of the night, a lone Mustang power dived with his guns a blazing. It was Icky, to the rescue. The pair of heroes sent a hail of bullets after the Germans and brought down the attackers in dual smoking heaps.

The final two enemy aircraft had broken off and were trying to cut into the left flank of our intrepid pilots. Sam and Ralph were not going to have any of that and banked directly into their paths.

"Hey, Ralph, you think these Gerrys know how to play chicken?" Sam asked.

The Mustangs flew straight into two German Focke Wulfs and all four planes had their guns blazing! They did not waste time with simple controlled bursts. All four pilots held their triggers down, and the sky was alive with red hot death! The smoke from the guns filled the attack run, obscuring the vision of any onlookers. Sam gritted his teeth while Ralph simply smiled as they charged full speed into destiny. The sight would have taken the breath away from any onlookers as the four planes disappeared into a cloud of smoke. Then, after a few tense moments, Sam and Ralp emerged victorious and the enemies of the free world sank to the ground in flames!

Captain Midnight called across his radio, "If you two are done playing tag, we still have some work to do."

Each member of the squadron knew the plan and responded to their chief's voice. Chuck, Icky, Ralph and Sam regrouped, caught their breath and powered up toward London while Captain Midnight, Don and Joyce broke off toward Paris.

Sam's team caught up to the enemy bombers quickly. Sam and Icky went after the trailing bomber while Ralph and Chuck took after the leader. The four pilots let loose with a volley of flaming lead which sank deep into the bombers. The V-wings exploded with a tremendous force that threw shrapnel in every direction! The night sky was lit up for miles around as the burning hulks crashed to the ground. The boys broke formation to avoid being hit by flying debris. The four onlookers marveled at the intensity of the blast as they worked back to a normal formation.

"Wow, I never expected that!" Sam said out loud.

"You said it!" Icky responded as the squad nosed their way home.

Captain Midnight and his wingmen were approaching the other two V-wing bombers when the sky lit up with anti-aircraft bursts! Battery after battery fired throaty explosions into the night sky. The expert pilots maneuvered around the blasts to catch up to the bombers. Joyce was the first to get a shot off at one of the V-wings. Her volley sank into the fuselage and then Don added his two cents worth. His bullets did the trick and the bomber went up in flames. The remaining V-wing angled away from the explosion and poured on the steam. Search lights were now scanning the smoky skies. Don and Joyce were out of range and the task of destroying the last of Ivan Shark's evil plot fell to Captain Midnight.

Midnight sighted up the enemy bomber and let loose with his guns—or so he thought. The guns refused to fire! He tried again and again to blast the bomber with no luck. Don and Joyce were charging to his support when they saw smoke trailing from his wings! "Cap, your wings are on fire!" Don yelled into the radio.

Normally he would have waited for his team members to assist him but by the time they would have made it to his location the bomber would be long gone and Paris would be doomed.

"Why does it always have to be the hard way?" Captain Midnight said out loud as he increased the throttle to full. His injured plane sailed deep into the smoke filled sky. The Guardian of Freedom rolled the damaged plane right and power dived toward the bomber.

"Midnight, NO!" Joyce yelled.

The Mustang hit the V-wing dead center and both planes disappeared into a thunderous fireball! Flames shot through the sky with another explosion that rocked the heavens!

Don and Joyce approached the burning wreckage as it fell to the ground. They circled the crash sight in disbelief. Their courageous leader was dead! Then Don saw it. A pillowy white parachute hung in the smoky night sky and Captain Midnight waved as he floated to the ground.

Chapter 9

Captain Midnight and the Secret Squadron

The buzzer sounded on Major Steel's desk intercom. The senior commander pushed the transmit button then replied, "Yes, Cindy, what is it?"

"Sir, Captain Albright is reporting in from his leave," Major Steel's able bodied assistant responded.

"Good. Send him i,." Steel ordered.

Albright strolled into the office as if he had a song in his heart and gave his commanding officer a leisurely salute.

Major Steel looked up from his paperwork and saw a big broad smile across the face of his second in charge. Steel sat there for a moment, wishing he was in Albright's shoes, and then asked his junior officer, "Well, Captain, how was your thirty days off?"

Albright's smile grew with intensity. "Those French really know how to show appreciation when you save Paris from destruction." He chuckled.

"We'll talk about that later. Right now I have something to show you." Major Steel stood and walked toward the door of his office and motioned for Captain Albright to follow.

"Your antics as Captain Midnight last month," Major Steel continued as the men walked down the hallway toward the Pilot's Briefing Room, "made quite an impression on a lot of people. The German wires are still talking about it, and news even made its way into the White House."

Major Steel opened the door to the new Pilot's Briefing Room and both walked in. Captain Albright looked around at the lavishly furnished room. Maps and charts made up one of the smaller walls, with a fully stocked bar at the end of the room. Soft couches lined the other walls adorned with oak shelving. In the center was a large oak round table with nine chairs. Steel took a seat at the table and Albright sat across from him.

Major Steel continued: "The President has issued orders to reform the S-1 Squadron. You will continue to use the Captain Midnight moniker. The black uniform you created in the field will be your standard dress. I've spent the last four weeks, while you were gone, assembling equipment and completing transfers for your team. The new S-1 team is waiting on us now at Secret Squadron Headquarters."

Albright looked around with confusion on his face. "Secret Squadron Headquarters?" He asked.

"That's right," Steel affirmed, reaching for a statue of Shakespeare sitting on a nearby shelf. He tilted the head back, revealing a hidden switch.

The switch was activated and a portion of the map wall slid away, revealing a secret chamber. Steel motioned for his shocked subordinate to follow. The Guardian of Freedom and his chief walked into the hidden alcove and found a small, box-shaped rail car inside. The major stepped into the hidden train car followed by Albright and both found a seat on the inside. The major tapped a control panel and the strange transport accelerated. The queer rail car glided silently through a cement-reinforced tunnel. As it moved along, lights were automatically turned on in the tunnel and then turned off when the speeding mini trolley passed by.

Captain Albright looked amazed and asked, "What is all this?"

"This is the entrance to your new secret headquarters. It is only accessible by this train car and one other just like it that transports workers to and from the base. The base itself is called Le Bourget Prime, and is located inside a mountain range just to the Northwest of Le Bourget field."

The automated transport rolled to a quiet stop at a platform that opened up into a shallow room that held several empty storage boxes. The other car, Major Steel had mentioned, sat on the opposite side of the platform on a separate track. Both men exited the train car and walked to an elevator at the back of the room. Next to the elevator door was another door that had STAIRWAY printed on a placard.

Inside the elevator, Major Steel pushed the number 1 button and the elevator doors closed. The compartment then slid upward through a stone shaft. The elevator door opened on the first floor, which looked a lot like a hotel hallway carved out of stone. The hall stretched to the left and to the right of the elevator.

Major Steel felt like a tour guide as he showed his subordinate through the mountain headquarters. "The first floor is the recreation area and crew quarters. You have a private room down the hallway to the right next to the other squadron member's rooms. On the left, there is quarter-mile running track, a full-sized gymnasium with every kind of sports gear imaginable, a weight room and a padded exercise room for practicing hand-to-hand combat."

The two men stayed inside the elevator as Steel pressed the number 2 button. Again, the doors closed and the elevator advanced upward through the stone shaft. The doors opened onto the second floor. Voices and the noise from pots and pans being clanged together were heard coming from the left. "That way is the cafeteria." Steel indicated.

"Down on the right is meeting rooms and a science lab." He then pushed number 3. The elevator cascaded effortlessly to the third floor where Major Steel pointed out the medical facility on the right and the weapons storage area to the left.

Major Steel pressed button 4 and proudly proclaimed, "Now, the grand finale of our tour, the flight deck."

The elevator doors opened to a massive structure that was part hangar and part runway. Ground crews were bustling around, unpacking and putting equipment away in various workshops along the sides of the gigantic structure. There were maintenance shops, paint shops, weapons shops and a fuel depot. The flight deck was protected by two huge steel doors at the end of the runway that were currently closed. On the far side of the incredible facility sat several types of aircraft all painted that same paint scheme that Albright had found in the German hangars with the flying wing bombers–black on top and gray on the bottom. Captain Albright was shocked by the number of planes that were apparently at his disposal. With his first glance, he identified two P-38s and two P-61s both with their strange double fuselage designs, two C-47 cargo planes and then more P-51 Mustangs than he could count. All were ready to fly into action at a moment's notice.

Major Steel saw the look of awe on Albright's face. "Impressive, isn't it?"

"Those Mustangs are what we like to call, Super Mustangs. The engines and weapons have all been beefed up. Mufflers have been added for silent flight. They are quite possibly the fastest and deadliest planes in the sky," Steel added.

"This way, Captain." He pointed to the briefing room.

Albright entered and discovered some familiar faces. Don was talking with Joyce while they sat on a couch along the wall. Sam, Ralph, Chuck Ramsey and Icky were all laughing it up in the far corner. Then a voice piped up from the back of the crowd, "Well, it's about time you got here!"

The voice was instantly recognized as two brothers in arms met again triumphantly and began to chatter like kids on a playground. "Tut, I thought you were dead!"

"It takes more than a bullet in the back to keep me down," Tut joked.

Major Steel interjected, "Lieutenant Jones regained consciousness shortly after arriving at the Army Hospital. He made contact with me and requested to come back. How could I refuse?"

Steel raised his hands to quiet the room. "By special Presidential order, the Secret Squadron, code-named S-1 Squadron, is now officially reformed. The roll call is as follows: Lieutenant Aristotle Jones, Lieutenant Ralph Badger, Lieutenant Samuel Hedges, Lieutenant Donald Carr, Lieutenant Charles Ramsey, Lieutenant Ichabod Mudd and Lieutenant Joyce Ryan. The squadron will be led by Captain James Albright, now code-named Captain Midnight."

Without warning, a claxon siren went off indicating incoming enemy aircraft. A crew chief burst into the room. "Major, we just got word that the Luftwaffe is sending an attack squadron to Paris. Spotters at the front count over forty planes."

Without hesitation, Captain Albright said, "Everybody, saddle up. It's time to go to work!"

On a nearby rack, Albright found a pilot's headgear and goggles with a black scarf and a black leather pilot's coat with gold wings on the lapel. As he suited up, he looked out onto the flight deck and saw a P-51 being warmed up for take off. The fighter plane had *Captain Midnight* labeled along the fuselage under the canopy. He glanced at Major Steel. "We have more than enough planes if you want to come along."

Steel smiled. "No, this is a job for Captain Midnight and the Secret Squadron!"

Chapter 10
The Beginning

It had been three days and three nights since the fall of the ancient castle with the clock tower. Smoke was still rising from the rubble and occasionally a brick would fall from a nearly destroyed wall of the remaining structure. The sun was rising on a new day, and a lone solitary giant of a man worked steadily to clear debris. He had been at it since the fall of the aged monument. His hands and fingers were raw meat from digging in the stone and mortar, but that did not matter to him. His master lay buried under the wreckage.

A light rain had come during the night to dampen the dust and powdered stone. As the day wore on, the sun burned away the water ,and what was once a gentle coating of dirt was becoming very aggressive cement. Still, the lumbering giant continued to dig unyielding to pain and oblivious to time as minutes turned to hours and nights turned to days many times over.

The sun drove down on him hard and his skin turned a bright red from over-exposure. The man was using a component from the clockworks as a pry bar when he moved a large slab of stone and found a piece of cloth that went further underneath the rubble. Then it happened. Gravel, rocks and dirt were being forced away by something underneath. It was a hand reaching toward the sky, trying to grasp life.

The worn giant became excited and forced away another slab of debris. Underneath, he found his goal. A man lay contorted and bent in the wreckage, and was near death. The catastrophe had broken nearly every bone in the injured man's body. He could only muster strength to his arm and hand as he reached for his trusted body guard. His eyes, open and alert, burned with rage, yet his face only showed pain and exhaustion from the ordeal.

As the sun-baked digger constructed a makeshift stretcher, the mangled man forgot about his terrible pain and the agonized look on his face changed to a devilish smile. The broken villain was now consumed with hatred. His mind danced with thoughts of revenge. He vowed to himself that one day there would be a reckoning of the titans.

A reckoning unlike any the world had ever seen before!

Captain Midnight and Me
by David Walker

My love of the old movie serials introduced me to a fantastic new character with whom I had not been familiar: Captain Midnight. After watching the serial, I instantly liked the character and tracked down his other incarnations in the 1950s television show and his radio show. I soon became hooked and thought it would be a lot of fun to write a story about Captain Midnight. That fateful day arrived several years ago when I met Ron Fortier for the first time and approached him with the idea. Ron loved it and told me he would work with me to get it finished. The story was started in August 2007 and finished in December 2007.

I wanted to make the story as believable as possible, yet allow for that pulp flare for action and imagination. Topographical maps of France and surrounding counties were used for locations. The mountain range where I built the Secret Squadron Headquarters in the story actually exists! The headquarters bunker concept came from a History Channel special on Super Bunkers of WWII. PBS was also a big help when I saw a program on the Belgian underground movement and how they helped downed pilots behind enemy lines return home. In addition, the PBS show *Warplane* provided information that would later be incorporated into the Captain Midnight story.

My extensive library on WWII airplanes helped me choose which planes would be used. The V-wing bombers from my story were real aircraft, and several different models were actually built by the Germans during the war. However, to the best of my knowledge, they never saw combat. The V-wing plans were used many years later when the Stealth Bomber came into existence and is still being used today.

I like my heroes to be somewhat human. Anybody can write a story about a guy who is invincible, never makes mistakes, and never feels anything because of his higher standards or whatever. To me, that is just not enjoyable. I want to be able to live through them and figure out what would I do in a perilous situation or how I would get out of a mess. Personally, a hero is just a guy doing what he can because he can. He is not out for glory, nor is he trying to save the world, although sometimes that does happen.

The characters from my story were taken from the Captain Midnight serial, the television show, and the radio show. Three original characters were created to be killed off, but they became a vital part of the Secret Squadron. I didn't have the heart to get rid of them. Every character has emotions in the story, and hopefully the reader will feel the full gamut of those emotions as they are expressed. I want the reader to become Captain Midnight and feel how he feels, because that's realistic and relatable.

Lastly, I want to thank everybody who helped me along the way. My brother, Steve, is a gun enthusiast, and he provided the background on all of the weapons and ammunition for the story. My good friend, Cindy Simmons, was my sounding board for new ideas and helped me proofread everything. Thanks to my girlfriend, Stacy Bell, who helped me do a rewrite at the last minute. Special thanks to Ron Fortier for being my mentor on the whole project. The story was really fun to write, and I hope you enjoy reading it as much as I did writing it. Let me know what you think of it. Captain Midnight will return again. I already have eight more stories plotted out, and Captain Midnight number two has been in the works for a while now.

Happy Reading!

Author bio:

DAVID WALKER - was born on February 13, 1968, to John and Pat Walker in Syracuse, a small town that borders two lakes in north central Indiana. The family moved to Fort Wayne, Indiana, in 1979, where David currently resides with his dog, Tango. David enjoys spending time with his daughter, Kim, who also resides in Fort Wayne. David, who is the youngest in his family, has a brother who lives in Michigan and a sister who lives in Fort Wayne.

David has always had strong desire to help others. As a result, he served in the military for several years, including four years of overseas duty, in the Philippines and the Indian Ocean. He is currently self-employed as a property damage appraiser for insurance companies.

David's love of comics often led him to a local comic book shop where the owner came to know David and his interests. The shop owner introduced David to now close friend Wooda Carr, who shares many common interests and hobbies. Through Wooda, David developed a new love, pulps. In fact, David and Wooda can be found at Pulpfest in Columbus, Ohio, each year in July. David's favorite pulps include: *The Shadow, The Spider*, and *G-8 and His Battle Aces*. David can be reached at theshadowreturns@yahoo.com and more information about him and his work can be found on his website at http://mysite.verizon.net/theshadowreturns/captainmidnight.

FLYING ACES
by Ron Fortier

So here we are, at long last, releasing our second Airship 27 Production volume starring the classic Canadian pulp star, *Lance Star: Sky Ranger*. Plenty has happened in the intervening two years since we first launched that book, one of our earliest titles. The rights to the character have passed hands, having been purchased by writer Bobby Nash, one of our four original writers from volume one. Thus, before deciding to produce a second book, we had to sit down with Bobby and not only get his permission, but discuss with him which course these books should take as Bobby has some great plans for this character. He has already launched a one shot *Lance Star: Sky Ranger* comic book and is working on a full-length novel. In the end, we agreed that it would be much more fun to turn the series into a collection of various classic pulp heroes, rather than simply focus on one. I liked that idea a great deal. Bobby would continue to contribute new Lance Star adventures—after all, the book does bear his name—and I would recruit writers to provide us with tales of other famous—some more so than others—aviation heroes; all of them clearly public domain. I'm happy to say that after all that work, we've put together a great collection

A little history is in order on these great characters. Van Allen Plexico had written a Griffon story for another publication which has since folded. It is the first time we've ever reprinted a pulp story, but I felt it deserved a bigger audience and am happy to provide it for you.

THE GRIFFON was created by Arch Whitehouse and appeared in *Flying Aces* beginning with its June 1935 issue. By day, the title character was Kerry Keen, a young, lazy millionaire playboy, but at night he became the Griffon, a costumed crime fighter. Keen put on a red silk and rubber mask and entered the underground hangar on his Long Island estate (Graylands) to fly *The Black Bullet*, his supercharged and heavily armored seaplane, on missions of justice and vengeance. He was assisted by Barney O'Dare and Barbara "Pebbles" Colony, an adventurous beauty who discovered Keen's secret identity during one story and joined the team.

Aaron Smith is another Airship 27 regular whose work has graced many of our titles. When I suggested he tackle *The Three Mosquitos*, he was a bit perplexed, knowing nothing of these aerial musketeers. I quickly provided him with their background data. Next thing I knew, Aaron sent me not one, but two shorts stories starring this high-flying trio.

THE THREE MOSQUITOS were assigned to the 44th Pursuit Squadron and flew khaki Spads. Painted across the fuselage was a black mosquito. They shared a barracks room and were well known on the western front. They were the idols of the entire squadron and set the example of courage and daring for their fellow airmen. Close coordination of the trio and their squadron was maintained with a stern-faced U.S. intelligence chief, Brigadier General Saunders. His main headquarters was at Chaumont, France. Incidentally Chaumont was the selected headquarters of General John J. Pershing, Commander-in-Chief, American Expeditionary Forces.

A reckless, inseparable trio, *The Three Mosquitos* were headed by an impetuous young officer, Captain Kirby. He was a handsome charmer with the ladies but had trouble with figures of authority. He liked to push the envelope and leap into danger. Next was a mild-eyed, little man by the name of Lt.Shorty Carn. He had a reputation of being the "best marksman in the entire Air Service." He was described as quiet, reserved, a classic introvert, a bookworm, only really happy when flying. He was fiercely loyal to his pals. The eldest and wisest was the third member of the squad, lanky Lieutenant Travis, who always spoke with a drawl. A former college professor, he was a world traveler who spoke several languages. He was always attempting to keep Kirby reigned in. Together, the three built up quite a reputation as fighting war-birds, and their familiar war-whoop was always, *"Let's go!"* The trio flew a usual V formation with Kirby leading,and Carn and Travis flanking him on either side.

Finally, writer David Walker, an ex-Air Force veteran, approached me several years ago with a brand new *Captain Midnight* story. His is, by far, the most recognizable hero in this collection, David has done a great job creating a new take on the Captain's origin and that of his Secret Squadron. I really enjoyed this story and think you will too.

CAPTAIN MIDNIGHT was a U.S. radio adventure series broadcast from 1938 to 1949—the creation of writers Wilfred G. Moore and Robert M. Burtt. Captain Jim "Red" Albright was a World War 1 Army pilot. His *Captain Midnight* code name was given to him by a general who sent him on a high-risk mission, christening him when the aviator returned at the stroke of twelve o'clock. He was then recruited to head the Secret Squadron, an aviation-orientated group fighting sabotage and espionage during the period just prior to the United States' entry into World War II.

When the U.S. was attacked at Pearl Harbor, the radio show shifted the Secret Squadron's duties to the more unconventional aspects of the war and introduced such Axis villains as Baron von Karp, Admiral Himakito and von Schrecker. The scripts depicted women who were treated as equals, not just damsels in distress waiting to be rescued. Both Joyce Ryan of the Secret Squadron and Fury Shark, daughter of villain Ivan Shark, pulled their own weight in the stories. Joyce went on commando raids and become involved in aerial dogfights, something her real-life counterparts were never allowed to do. The show ended in December of 1949, but not before the character had been picked up by the comic book industry and brought to the silver screen via a fifteen-chapter Columbia cliffhanger serial starring Dave O'Brian as Captain Midnight and James Craven as Ivan Shark.

And there you have our cast of heroes for this volume. You may have noticed a missing personage—the book's primary hero, Lance Star, Sky Ranger. No, this is not an oversight, merely my not wanting to cover old ground. In volume one, pulp historian Norman Hamilton provided us with a detailed history of the character and his creator, writer, Owen Brown. So if you haven't picked up volume one yet, here's a good excuse. As always, all of our titles are available at a nice discount off the retail price from our online store at (http://www.gopulp.info/).

Thanks for picking up *Lance Star: Sky Ranger, Volume 2*. We've enjoyed bringing you these high-flying action tales, and we hope drop us a line to let us know your thoughts. Are there any other aviation heroes you'd like to see in these pages? Give us a holler and let us know. And as always, thanks for your support.

Ron Fortier
10 Sept. 2009
Somersworth, NH
(www.Airship27.com)
(Airship27@comcast.net)

www.ingramcontent.com/pod-product-compliance
Lightning Source LLC
Chambersburg PA
CBHW071235250626
47163CB00001B/195